THE BIG TILT

THE BIG TILT

DAN FLANIGAN

THE BIG TILT is a work of fiction. All of the characters, organizations, and events portrayed in this novel are either products of the author's imagination or are used fictitiously. Where real-life figures appear, the situations, incidents, and dialogues concerning those persons are entirely fictional and are not intended to change the completely fictional nature of the work.

For information about this title or to order other books and/or electronic media, contact the publisher:

Arjuna Books
600 3rd Avenue, 42nd Floor
New York, New York 10016

ISBN: 978-1-7336103-5-3 (print)
ISBN: 978-1-7336103-6-0 (eBook)

Publisher's Cataloging-In-Publication Data
(Prepared by The Donohue Group, Inc.)

Names: Flanigan, Daniel J., 1947- author.

Title: The big tilt / Dan Flanigan.

Description: New York, New York : Arjuna Books, [2020] | Series: A Peter O'Keefe novel

Identifiers: ISBN 9781733610353 (print) | ISBN 9781733610360 (ebook)

Subjects: LCSH: Private investigators—United States—Fiction. | Mafia—United States—Fiction. | Murder—Investigation—United States—Fiction. | LCGFT: Thrillers (Fiction)

Classification: LCC PS3606.L3587 B54 2020 (print) | LCC PS3606.L3587 (ebook) | DDC 813/.6--dc23

Cover Design by www.milagraphicartist.com
Book Interior Design by Amit Dey

Printed in the United States of America

Thank you again to my daughter Meghan—who has once again served the cause in every useful capacity from muse, to research assistant, to literary scullery maid—who responded to almost every crazy request (or were those demands?) with only occasional constructive complaint and never cavil.

Thanks to all the others who helped shepherdess this book along, especially Ericka McIntyre and Keri-Rae Barnum.

Thanks to my colleague Brian McEvoy for sharing his deep knowledge of federal criminal law and procedure with me (though he cannot be held responsible if I still didn't get everything right) and also to my colleague Tom Isaacson for helping me resolve a critical circa-1987 "technology" issue.

And, again, as always, most of all, to that One No Longer Here—to whom I tender this futile, this impossible, this hopeless dream—

Vague memories, nothing but memories,
But in the grave all, all, shall be renewed.
The certainty that I shall see that lady
Leaning or standing or walking
In the first loveliness of womanhood,
And with the fervour of my youthful eyes,
Has set me muttering like a fool.

"Broken Dreams"
William Butler Yeats

"Sire, what ails thee?"
Perceval to the Grail King

CHAPTER ▶ 1

THEY MADE NOTHING, absolutely nothing, that could match this near-new 1986 Lincoln Town Car. Black with black-tinted windows. Big and heavy but still sleek. Perfect shocks, a ride as smooth as a steak knife cutting through soft butter. Easy handling and maneuverability despite its size. Plush, comfortable seats—he preferred the fabric to the sweaty-ass leather his colleagues always suckered for. Supreme conjunction of power and comfort. They bought them one year old with low mileage after the idiot prior owners had purchased them new and suffered a big price ding the moment they drove off the lot, and even more idiotic, traded them in for the newest model the following year. They could take all those Mercedes and BMWs and other Yuppie-mobiles and ship them back across the sea where they belonged.

Could Robert, in the passenger seat sleeping off a Friday night of carousing, be called a Yuppie since he drove a Mercedes SL convertible, an indulgence Robert's father-in-law had inexplicably allowed him? *Let's see.* Young? Yes, mid-30s. Upwardly-Mobile? That would depend on events—he had come a long way already, but he might have advanced in the world as far as he ever would. Still, close enough. Professional? Not the kind the name implies, but, arguably, yes; in his way, in their way.

The phrase "better be lucky than good" occurred to him. Robert had been endowed with ample portions of both. Lucky enough to be born handsome, thin and refined, one of those old sculptures come to life. Smart too. A real mastery of the numbers, which so far had compensated for his seeming aversion to necessary violence. Lucky and good enough to have attracted Snow White herself, Rose Jagoda, compared to whom all the young boys in her world seemed like mere dwarfs.

He, Paul Marcone, the Town Car's appreciative driver, not so bad looking himself, had been one of those dwarfs—Bashful, perhaps—in silent, distant longing to be of service to her, ready to leap to her command if she ever deigned to issue it. He was a year younger than Robert and Rose. Too late. That cursed one-year gap might as well have been a Berlin Wall separating them as children and adolescents. By the time they embarked on their adult lives—when a one-year age difference really made no difference—too late.

He turned on the wipers slow-speed to fend off light raindrops hitting the windshield. He kept the cruise control just under the speed limit both to reduce the risk of a skid and to make sure not to bring the cops down on them, with who knows what consequences, but, at a minimum, making them late for the appointment and, thus, at risk of losing the visiting "privilege," as the prison authorities called it. He could not let that happen. It was too close to the end, and it had been made clear to him that this appointment was as essential to his life as the inhalation of his next breath.

They drove through what seemed like a punishment of wheat and alfalfa fields, crappy little farm houses, and decaying barns until, all of a sudden, a campus of imposing brick colonial-style buildings sprouted up from the landscape like ol' Jack's beanstalk. *It looks like a college for Christ's sake.* Well, yes, except for that electrified fence surrounding it and those looming towers that weren't for housing church bells.

"Robert, we're here."

No response.

He reached over and shoved gently. Robert woke with a start and squinted to take in his surroundings.

"Jesus," Robert said, "I feel like shit."

Paul eased the Lincoln up to the gate and the guard emerged from his station, clipboard in hand, to greet them.

"Paul Marcone and Robert Sciorra" he said. "I'm Paul, he's Robert."

Since neither of them had a felony on his record, the Feds had pre-cleared them for the visit, as if they were doing them a big favor. *The pricks.* They should have just released the now-harmless old man to his family so he could die at home. No, they said, they would have to provide twenty-four security to protect the public, and the federal budget contained no item labeled "Coddling Dying Mobsters."

Inside it looked just like a regular hospital but with extra security. The two visitors were treated, it seemed, just like regular people, although, like regular people visiting a prison, they were searched and allowed to carry only "a small clear plastic purse, no larger than 8" x 8" to be utilized to carry only these items into the institution:

1 handkerchief

1 comb

Coins or $40 of currency per adult visitor

Female hygiene items

An identification card.

But they didn't need, and so did not carry in their little prison-provided plastic purses, anything other than the prison-provided identification cards.

A federal cop escorted them to the room. The chart in a clear plastic pouch next to the door of the room said "Carmine Jagoda." It was even a "private" room, though surely bugged. But what to say anyway? No business to do. The Boss had been mostly comatose for days. But he was awake now and even seemed alert.

Robert went straight to the Boss, while Paul held slightly back, in respect, at the foot of the bed, simply nodding toward the Boss in salutation. Robert did not try to hug or embrace the old man, did not even try to grip his arm or hand, just laid his own hand lightly on the old man's arm.

"Hello, Carmine," he said.

Carmine said, "I'm almost done. Outta here. And I don't mean this jailhouse."

"What do you need? What can we do?"

"First, be strong. Like the son I never had. Second, honor my daughter. Third, quick-like, bend down like you're kissing me on the cheek."

Robert bent down as instructed. Paul could see that the old man was whispering something. He looked around the walls of the room and up at the ceiling and wondered who might be watching and suddenly burst in.

Robert raised up, looking solemn. Resolute or fearful? The Boss gestured to Paul to come forward to the bed. Robert moved out of the way to make room. "Bend down like you're kissing me on the cheek," the Boss whispered to Paul just as he had to Robert. After the Boss finished whispering, Paul rose up, now understanding that strange look on Robert's face after the old man had whispered to him. He stepped aside, providing room for Robert to move back closer to the bed.

"Go on now," Carmine said. "I might as well spend some time prayin' for my soul. Can't hurt anything."

Robert impulsively bent down, kissed the old man on the forehead, and said, "Goodbye, Carmine," brushed past Paul, and headed toward the door. Paul tried to say goodbye to the Boss with his eyes, but the old man had closed his, so there was nothing for him to do but give the wrinkled and spotted old hand a quick squeeze and follow Robert out of the room.

In the parking lot they stopped next to the car. "Let's compare notes out here," Paul said. "They may have bugged the damn car while we were in there."

"Okay," Robert said, "what'd he say?"

"He told me not to tell you."

Robert's look went hard. A look Paul had not believed Robert capable of. A look he had to respect.

"Well, *I'm* telling *you* to tell *me*."

Shit, a dilemma. His future, the quality of it for sure, even its very existence, might be on the line right now. The old man seemed near dead, but what if he survived? *I could lie. But what to say?*

"You can either obey a dying man or one who's gonna live a long time," Robert said, bouncing slightly with impatience.

The King is dead, long live the King. "Okay. I'm your man. I hope you protect me if the Boss ever finds out I told you. What he said was, 'Here's what I told Robert, and you make sure he does it. That fucking private detective O'Keefe. He killed our people, that's enough right there, but that's not even it. He caused a thousand spotlights and searchlights to shine right on us…right in our faces. Everything went to shit after he showed up. He's bad luck. It's like he put a curse on us. Lift the curse. Kill the motherfucker. No ifs, no ands, no buts. And don't fuck it up like they did last time.'"

"Yeah," Robert said, "that's what he told me too. And I might do that, or I might not. I'll do what *I* think's right when and how *I* choose.

I assume this is the first and last time we'll discuss this and you'll do your best to forget about it."

"Exactly, Boss." The first time he had ever called Robert that. And he was glad he left out the last of what Carmine had said: "I'm not so sure Robert has the stomach for it. So your job is to help him along."

As they pulled out of the prison hospital gate, Robert said, "I guess he didn't trust me."

"Nah, that's not it," Paul said. "I'm like an insurance policy or something. Like Ronnie Reagan says about the Russkies—'trust but verify.'"

CHAPTER ▶ 2

JUST AS DUSK was fading into night on a Saturday, the phone had rung.

That must be her. Picking up the phone, O'Keefe said, "You?"

"Yeah, me," Sara Slade said in a low voice, just above a whisper. "And they just took her in. I think the house is full of them, just waiting for it."

"On my way." O'Keefe said.

"I don't think you can get here in time."

"Twenty minutes max."

"No telling what'll happen by then. How about Morrison?"

"Stay put. I'm already out the door."

Well, not quite out the door, but Sara needed to believe that. But in less than five minutes he had climbed into Sara's car, switched on the portable phone he had temporarily installed in it, and called the direct line to the Missing Persons Division. He hoped, first, that someone would answer; second, that someone would recognize him; and third, that someone would actually pay attention and recognize the emergency.

After five rings, someone answered.

"This is Peter O'Keefe. Who's this?"

"Sergeant Briggs."

"Maybe you know my name. I'm a private investigator. I've been working with Morrison on a lost girl. She's in immediate danger of gang rape or worse. I need the police at 648 Patterson Street right now."

"Morrison ain't here."

"But you are."

"I don't know..."

"Please. I guarantee you won't regret it if you get going now. A lot of us might regret it if you don't."

"Who says?"

A long pause. O'Keefe waited to hear something hopeful, but all he got from Briggs was "I'll try to find Morrison."

"It'll be over by then. Now! Don't fuck this up!"

But it seemed too likely that Briggs would indeed fuck it up. So he called George. No answer. No surprise. His operative George Novak would consider it a sacrilege to be available for anything but party time on a Saturday night. He hung up and drove as fast as he dared, breaking what traffic laws he thought he could without getting pulled over—that would be disaster—better late than too late.

~

THEY HAD BEEN IN THE HOUSE for over ten minutes now. Sara wondered how much time remained, if any. Maybe they wouldn't go right to it, maybe play around with the girl some, maybe get the girl higher than she already seemed to be, so she might even go along with the program, be some fun, not just a slab of meat. But then maybe they were already at it. She would never forgive herself if she just sat there and let something horrible happen, something that might scar the girl for life, if what the girl had so far endured had not already done irrevocable harm. So close now after all this effort and hope.

The pimp had snagged the girl at the bus station where she had planned to escape to some far off and better—or just other—place. He made use of her for a few days, decided she was inferior goods, then sold her to these men, a well-known, semi-organized gang of thugs.

O'Keefe, get your ass here.

Sara cursed O'Keefe's van as she drove it past the house. It might be super stuffed with a state-of-the-art car phone, the best surveillance equipment he could afford, and weapons in a hidden panel, but it might as well be the Goodyear Blimp, especially conspicuous in this neighborhood. There were bad neighborhoods, and then there was this neighborhood. The worst. She had managed to avoid detection as she followed them in the Blimp from a decrepit abandoned-looking garage in yet another grubby part of town. There, crouched behind a rust-mobile, nothing left of the wheels but bare iron rims, she had watched them from a block away as they escorted the docile, wacked-out girl from the garage to the beaten up, dented, and bruised Grand Wagoneer, shoved her into the back seat, flanked her on each side with a nasty looking gentleman, then took off. Sara hustled back to the van, which she had parked out of sight. They had disappeared by the time she sped by the garage, and she would likely never have found them if she had not correctly suspected that they would head to the house that she knew served them as a drug house and a sort of headquarters. Following that course, she picked them up. *Luck. Keep on holding, please.* But she couldn't rely on that now, she had to *do* something.

The Grand Wagoneer and a pickup truck stood in front of the house. Four of them in the Grand Wagoneer, probably no more than two in the Truck. That meant at least six, maybe even more, in the house. And her out here. *O'Keefe, get your ass here.* She moved the van down the block so it couldn't be directly observed from the house. She knew how to open the panel that hid O'Keefe's M-16 and pistols, but she lacked confidence in her proficiency in using them, even though she had been practicing lately. The Glock in her jacket pocket would have to be enough. But something other than the feeble quotient of violence she could muster up on her own would be needed against these men, who were likely drunk or drugged up or both—sociopaths even when sober, murderously maniacal on their sanest day.

She scooted out of the van and headed to the house. A short way down the block she remembered that she hadn't locked the van. There might be nothing left of it when she or O'Keefe returned for it. There was a reason this particular house thrived in this particular neighborhood. But she did not believe she had time to go back now. It might already be too late—in there.

She wore all black, long pants and a boyish shirt, deliberately chosen to give the impression on first sight of a police uniform. She had tucked her hair under a baseball cap so she would not be too quickly recognized as a female. She only had to create a diversion that would keep them off the girl for the few minutes until O'Keefe or the cops showed up. In the gathering dark she could not see a rock or brick or anything else she could hurl through the window. She clenched her chest to force back down the gorge of fear trying to rise up to her throat and make her vomit, then ran the rest of the way to the front door and banged on it with the side of her fist and kicked it a few times as well.

From the other side of the door a voice: "What?"

"Gas company! There's a leak. Get out now! The place is gonna blow any second!"

"What the fuck?" the voice said as the door opened.

The man was massive, a three-hundred-pounder for sure, with long, dirty, stringy hair and a beard that reached to his chest.

"Gas company!" she screamed. "Get everybody out!"

"What the fuck!" he said. "I don't smell no..."

"Now, goddamn it, it's gonna blow!" she yelled and turned and ran for the street as if the blast would occur any second. The Hulk reacted as she had hoped he would, jumping out onto the porch on the assumption that things must be imminently dire if the gas company woman was herself running for cover. He yelled back through the open door, "Get the fuck out! Gas leak! It's gonna blow up!"

They came bounding and leaping out of the house, stumbling over each other, a couple of them falling on the ground, then scrambling up and heading for the street. *Like clowns out of a VW Bug at the circus*, she thought. She counted six including the Hulk. No girl though. She saw headlights coming at her fast down the street, brights on. She had to gamble that it was O'Keefe. She ran for the house. "What the fuck," the Hulk mumbled as she passed the stupefied men. She stopped at the front door and turned to them.

"Is it clear? Anyone still in there?"

They looked at each other. Finally, one of them said, "No. All out."

Liar.

"What the fuck's she doin'?" she heard one of them say as she opened the front door and entered the house.

In the tiny vestibule she pulled the pistol out of her pocket and headed into the interior. The place looked like someone had strewn the contents of a couple of trash cans around. On one wall a Confederate flag, on another a Skull & Crossbones. She picked her way through the living room to a short hallway to her right and to a bedroom with only a bed in it. Tied to the bedpost was a girl, seemingly in a state of shock or just a drug-induced stupor, her chin lolling against her upper chest. Sara fumbled with the rope, wishing she carried a knife strapped to her calf like O'Keefe did. *Next time.*

She couldn't budge the knots. When would those animals figure things out and come in after her? She ran back through the hallway and into the kitchen, rummaged through the drawers and found nothing better than an old steak knife. She ran back to the bedroom and started sawing away at the rope, wondering whether the knife handle or the rope would give way first. The girl came awake for a moment, muttered something, then passed out again.

Sara kept sawing, making little progress, emitting several small cries of panic, near weeping in frustration, then heard someone burst noisily through the front door. What a bad idea this had been. She switched the knife to her left hand, pulled the pistol out of her pocket with her right, and whirled to face the door. A tall man's silhouette filled the door frame. She pulled the trigger. Nothing. *Forgot to turn the safety off!*

"Sara," the silhouette said, moving toward her, not noticing that she had just tried to shoot him.

"O'Keefe! Goddamn. Where are they?"

"Hauled ass. How did you get them outta here?"

"Later. Help me with this damn rope," she said, almost out of breath. "I can't loosen it or cut through it either."

"This is our girl, huh?" he said as he reached for his calf, pulled up his pant leg, and extracted the knife from its sheath.

She didn't answer. She might have killed him but for the safety being on, one mistake miraculously correcting another.

O'Keefe crouched down, bent the girl forward, draped the upper half of her body over his shoulder, lifted her up, and carried her out of the room, through the living room, kicking trash out of his way, and outside to the front lawn though no grass had grown there for years. The commotion had roused some neighbors who could be just as dangerous as the drug house crowd. He had left her car running with the headlights still on. They jogged to it, she opened the back door, and, though he tried to be gentle, he banged the girl's head a bit against the roof of the car as he stuffed her into the back seat.

"You drive," she said, "I'll take care of her back here." Neither of them mentally noted then, though they would both separately do so later, how quickly, easily, and naturally she had assumed the leadership.

They drove down the street toward the van.

"Better get the van," he said.

"Nothing is rousing her. She's maybe overdosed. Better get her to the hospital ASAP or we might lose her."

He floored it. Looking in his rearview mirror toward the van, he said, "I hope there's something left of it when we get back."

She decided not to mention that she had mistakenly left it unlocked—or that her mistake with the safety had saved her from having to drive both the girl and O'Keefe to the emergency room for treatment that night.

As it turned out, the girl was in the throes of overdose and not far from death, but the emergency room staff saved her. Sara called the parents. O'Keefe called the police, though not Briggs. He would speak harshly to Morrison on Monday about his shitbird duty sergeant. He explained to the officers who came to the hospital that he had been working with Morrison on the case, that he had tried to obtain police assistance, and that his operative had no alternative but to take emergency action.

They called in another car that drove him back to the house where they had to roust out some of the neighbors who had invaded the dump looking for buried treasure. The van remained pretty much intact except that someone had ripped out his expensive radio and CD player and left a sort of payment in the form of a considerable mound of human dung on the passenger seat. Which greatly amused the cops. “Make sure that’s in the report,” the senior patrolman said to the junior, both laughing so hard that O’Keefe had to laugh as well.

When he returned to the hospital, the girl still slept, and the sad but grateful parents were fulsomely expressing their gratitude to Sara. This had been Sara’s case, her first one. O'Keefe had hired her as his secretary, but he had promised her more real work almost a year ago, then kept holding back and making excuses. But when these parents contacted her through a friend, she persuaded him to let her work it, really work it.

“I hope they’re still that grateful when they get the bill,” O’Keefe said as they watched the parents holding hands and walking down the hospital hallway toward their daughter’s room.

“Come on!” she said. “Consider what we just did. We saved the girl from who knows what. That’s why you should love this work.”

She continued to watch the parents walk down the hall. “Just think what they have to deal with now,” she said, “whatever caused her to run away and end up in that house.”

He gave her a “what’s next” look.

“I’m hungry as hell,” she said. “Let’s get barbecue.”

THAT NIGHT, O’KEEFE would turn over in his mind again and again—as he was doing right now while sitting in his office studying his accounts receivable list—her statement: “That’s why you should love this work.” Maybe so, but this list might be why you wouldn’t love this work so much, at least the business part. The grateful parents still had not paid him in full, even though he had given them a big discount. And now their daughter had run away again, and made it out of town this time. They came back to him, but he did not feel he could throw good money after bad. Sara agreed. A good sign. She had a crusader in her but also a practical side.

He had kept a vow, made almost a year ago, to give up certain kinds of work he considered either morally questionable or psychologically or spiritually draining. It had cost him. Back then he had also come to believe that he had been mistaken in taking on too much work, loading himself up, hiring additional full-time and part-time employees and still having to subcontract frequently with mixed results. But he had now learned the hard way that he had lurched too far in that direction. You had to run this like a business, not like some knight errant *sans* portfolio. Adventures did not come free of charge. He figured out the trick was to find a way not to depend on a client just walking through the door. He needed a new approach, a way to create pipelines of work that could be profitable even if he personally did not spend anything other than supervisory time on them. He had watched his friend Mike Harrigan build a dynamic and profitable law practice in exactly that way, which O'Keefe realized could be adapted to his own profession. Most of all, he needed to act against his basic nature and seek help, which was why he had humbly summoned George and Sara to a meeting, these good employees and friends, both of whom he had almost lost last year when they separately concluded they could no longer endure his self-destructive ways. Their separate refusals had helped him come at least somewhere near the vicinity of his senses.

She came in first, always eager but self-composed and steady. She had large brown eyes and brown hair, free of hairspray or anything else artificial—a longish bob that fell to the top of her back and slightly over her shoulders. It was long enough for her to do several things with it, including bangs, a side wave, a pony tail, or a chignon, allowing her to present herself in different ways and looks, which would be an advantage to her in her lately chosen line of work. She had two freckles on each side of her nose. Braided silver hoops hung from her ears. She was neither overweight nor too thin. Unless on assignment, she dressed upscale, today in a long tight black skirt and a purple blouse. She had begun her career in banking but found that way too dull. She answered O'Keefe's ad searching for a secretary, but got him to agree that he would teach her to become a private detective. She had just turned thirty-one and seemed to have come from nowhere. Whatever her past might be, she had no interest in sharing it and made that clear to anyone who tried to probe.

"Big summit meeting, huh?" she said, "Even got George to come to the office."

A little later George Novak shambled in, affecting nonchalance whether he felt it or not. He might sometimes be as eager as Sara, but would do everything he could to keep from showing it. George, O'Keefe, and Harrigan had grown up together. George was the largest, toughest, and least "drama queen" of the three. An All-City pulling guard in high school, he proved too small to play college football and too adverse to studying to finish college. He managed to achieve an associate's degree in law enforcement from the local junior college, then joined the police force but stayed only two months, unable to tolerate either the martinet discipline imposed on street cops or the demands of the too often undeserving citizenry that he was supposed to serve and protect. He was a skirt-chaser, in both word and deed, but seemed unable or just did not want to create a real relationship, and remained in confirmed bachelorhood at age thirty-four.

"Well," George said, "I see that someone here is as beautiful as ever, and that someone is not Peter O'Keefe."

"And you're a liar, a seducer, and a general blackguard," she said.

"Nice. Can I put those on my business card, Boss?"—the "Boss" part being sardonic, as he respected O'Keefe but would never show it, especially in company.

"I know you get hives when you spend too much time in the office," O'Keefe said, "so let's get going."

He first explained that the changes he had made a year ago were well-intended mistakes. They needed to pursue a different course. "George, I think we could develop a helluva security business, and not just a bunch of six-dollar-an-hour guys trudging around warehouses at night either—something we can build into a really sophisticated operation including high-level executive security and other bodyguard work. But you'll need to reach beyond yourself."

"I ain't so dumb, Boss."

"You're plenty smart, much as you try to hide it. But you're gonna have to do more than gumshoe. You'll need to sell and manage...persuade, lead, inspire."

O'Keefe turned to Sara. "I need a nerd. Two of them actually. One, a computer nerd. That's the future, and we need to get in front of it. They're developing databases all over the place. Searching for and surveilling people will be a whole different thing, and sooner than later. And there'll be way more than that...stuff I can't even begin to envision. Second, I need a bean-counter nerd. Forensics. Financial skullduggery. We already have the foothold there with the banks and the lawyers."

"I thought you didn't want to work for bankers anymore."

"I was wrong about that. Some kind of knee-jerk 1960s counterculture snobbery or something. There's some pricks and predators in that business, but there's some good people too. My business needs to be to know one from the other. *Our* business, I mean. I'll work the lawyers. I want you to work the bankers. That's if you want to."

"That's okay, but what if I want to do what you and George do? I'd like some adventure, not just snuggling up to bankers who'll be more interested in getting in my pants than onto their vendor lists."

"I won't tell you it won't be hard for me. It scared me to death that night when I pulled up and realized you were in that house with who knows who. But I mean it. It's your call."

"Thank you," she said, her tone somewhere between gratitude and entitlement.

"But you'd better understand something. There's damn little adventure. It's mostly tedious as hell."

"I make my own adventure."

He laughed. "You sure do."

"And I like to get out on the street."

"Town's hot and humid in the summer and freezing-ass cold in the winter."

"Give me a pen, I'm ready to sign up."

"Just one condition. You've gotta make us money. We can do some do-gooding, but we've got to make a living."

"Deal."

"We'll get you off that reception desk soon. Help me find a replacement. But mostly find me those nerds. I see not long from now us presiding over a stable of computer geeks and bean-counters and having adventures too."

They looked neither disappointed nor daunted that the "O'Keefe Detective Agency *Lite*" had not worked out so well and they would be embarking together on a new quest.

"Guys, I want to say that from now on this is gonna be a partnership, but right now that would be the biggest disservice I could do you. You'd be buying into a losing enterprise."

"You can have all the money I've got," George said, smiling and making a zero with his thumb and index finger.

"Same here," said Sara.

"That's not my point though. You'll be working damn hard. You'll be creating something. You'll deserve a decent living for that. What I'm saying...if this works, I'll pay you well."

"No qualms about that, Boss," George said, "you're a good guy."

"And if you don't think it's enough, or you think you want some ownership...if it's ever worth owning it anyway...speak right up. I'll do what makes sense."

"What if it doesn't work?" Sara asked.

"Something will. Columbus didn't sail out to discover America. The point is to go sailing."

"Right on, my Captain," she said, giving a mock salute.

George got up and sauntered out, and Sara followed, her happiness expressed in the lilt of her gait. O'Keefe was happy to have made her happy. But happiness was too tame a word for the mixture of admiration and affection he felt—yes, also another emotion, a desire not of the platonic sort. Not good. Complications galore. And pain he didn't need. She gave no sign of inviting any romance. That, much more than their employer-employee relationship, held him back. He knew he would go to bed with her in an instant and worry about the complications later if she gave the slightest signal. But since she did not tender that invitation, he kept himself firmly in check, not wanting to risk ruining the good thing they did have. But it wasn't easy. There were times, when thinking about her, he felt like jumping out of his skin.

CHAPTER ▶ 3

"DOES THE NAME Peter O'Keefe mean anything to you?" Robert asked.

"Sure. Local PI your daddy-in-law made famous a while back."

"Unfortunately, you're right. Know what he's up to?"

"Not much. Doesn't seem like he even tried to milk that publicity. No book. No interviews with the press. Just faded back into the woodwork. Probably smart of him, huh?"

"He can't be smart enough to save himself. He owes us a life… Carmine's specific instructions."

He said nothing, waiting to see where this might be going. He did not have to wait long.

"And you owe us a favor," Robert said. "Maybe a couple of favors."

"Why drag me into it?"

"We've got to keep it way away from us. I'm not gonna make the same mistake Carmine did."

"Puts me on a helluva spot."

"You're already on that spot."

He decided to take a risk. "Would this get me off of that spot? All the way out? I didn't like to hear you saying 'maybe *a couple* of favors.' Seems like it oughtta be worth a whole truckload of favors. And some credit beyond that."

"Maybe we could do something extra. But don't get greedy."

"What assurance can I get that I'm off the spot?"

Robert snorted, his face rippling into a mask of disgust. "What? You want me to draw up a contract?"

Robert sounded vaguely like Carmine, his father-in-law, but could not pull it off. A deficiency of nerve, of resolve, or both? He thought it better not to say what he thought—*What if you're not around, Robert?*

"So the spot will be gone," Robert said, "and you'll get something extra. Think about what that extra oughtta be, and I'll do the same."

Time to leave, and Robert said to his departing back: "I mean it. Don't get greedy. Would be bad for both of us."

~

"I'LL BE A LITTLE LATE, but I'm on my way," O'Keefe said as he mentally twitched, a leftover from what used to be an actual physical flinch when not so long ago Annie would seize such a moment to sock him with a sharp vocal punch. But not anymore. Not since those people had almost killed him in the desert last year. After that, she had found a way to make peace with their divorce, and, it seemed, even with him. At that he felt a complicated mixture of relief and regret. It seemed that a certain amount of love must have drained away with her overflowing anger—the proverbial "baby out with the bathwater" deal. He knew he did not deserve that love at all, but it still made him sad to see it disappear, and it made him feel not just lonelier—lonely was just fine with him—but more alone.

Less than a minute later the car phone rang, her calling back. "Say, if you don't mind, come in. I'd like to talk for a minute." He hung up, doubting this meant good news.

Soon he pulled up in front of the house, smaller than the one he, Annie, and Kelly had lived in together, this one little more than a cottage but exquisitely decorated and kept. After the divorce, out of which he voluntarily emerged with nothing other than both alimony and child support obligations, she had overcome the debilitating pain of her grief and smartly mustered the piddling amount of assets they had accumulated. She sold the house in a good market and used all the available cash to move her and Kelly into this smaller but adequate space with a mortgage that seemed right-sized to match her modest earnings as supplemented by his alimony and childcare payments.

She set a cup of coffee down in front of him and one in front of her. Her hair was thick and brown with streaks of auburn. She had a finely sculpted nose, thin lips, a narrow, pointed chin, all of it in suitable proportion. Her dark brown eyes seemed to take you in. He kept his eyes on her face. He knew her body too well and had enjoyed it too much. Their minds had separated them, not their bodies.

"I know you're not exactly raking in the cash, but can you pay me some more money for a while?"

He said nothing, but his look was a question.

"I've been just scraping by for a long time. I know the alimony and child support is 'generous' as far as the court's concerned, but it isn't enough. I'm even having trouble paying the mortgage."

She stopped, fighting back tears, and he had a sudden impulse to hold her, at least grab her hand, touch her, physically reassure her somehow, but he thought that would be a mistake, would lead into unmapped territory he was reluctant to explore.

She went on, "To say nothing about saving anything. How about college? Might seem a long way off, but will we be able to help her with college when we can barely make it ourselves? This crappy retail clerk job of mine doesn't pay enough, and its prospects are dim to nonexistent. I have to figure out a way to make more money. The only thing I can think of that a woman who partied too much, dropped out of college, and has developed no marketable skills can do with a good upside is real estate sales. I've been taking classes and I'm ready to take the test for the license. I'm sure I'll pass. But then I'll have to take the leap and start out working for nothing until I can earn some commissions. But people tell me I'd be good at that..." She broke off, having blurted out what seemed like a carefully researched speech that had suddenly sped up and galloped away from her and left her not knowing where to go next.

"You would be," he said, coming to her rescue. She had taste as good as her looks and a mind far superior than her college grades would indicate, far superior to his when she set her mind to a particular thing, and she had a knack for salesmanship when she wanted to turn it on.

"So if you can't..." She hesitated there as if wondering whether to say the next two words, "or won't," but decided against it—her hesitation nevertheless accomplished her purpose anyway. He heard the two unsaid words.

"Jesus," he said, "I feel terrible. Why didn't you tell me you were having trouble?"

"Pride, I guess. I hoped you'd figure it out for yourself and volunteer."

No, I was probably too busy thinking of myself. "I'll pay extra. Your current paycheck amount plus some more. I'll do all I can. I've got nothing else to spend it on...if it's there."

"I'll pay you back."

"Come on! I don't expect that."

She cocked her head back slightly, thinking about it. "Okay. Truth is, I think I'm pretty much entitled. You did just abandon us to this."

She said it with no anger, no recrimination, just a deadpan, implacable statement of fact, and he could summon no suitable response to that except silence.

"I'll get Kelly," she said and left the kitchen to retrieve her.

He felt uncomfortable sitting at her kitchen table as if he still belonged there, so he stood up and moved through the charming little house toward the front door near the staircase where Kelly would descend to meet him, which she soon did, with a small overnight bag in one hand and a basketball crooked in the other arm. It was still summer, but basketball season, treasured by both of them, was not all that far away.

"We're gonna play some, right?" she said.

"Sure thing."

He opened the door for her. Annie did not come down to say goodbye.

~

HE PARKED ACROSS the street from St. Jude's, Kelly's school. Neither he nor Annie still believed the Catechism, the Apostle's Creed, or pretty much any of the rest of it, but they still thought of themselves as "Catholic" in a tribal, ethnic sort of way. They valued the education they each had received, so they sent Kelly there despite their discomfort with the religion part, especially when she came home imperiously preaching the dogma taught to her. The complex—the typical Catholic trio of the church, grade school, and playground—covered an entire block. Six basketball hoops lined up along the asphalt, three on each side, opposite each other so that full-court games could be played. The playground was empty except for a few boys playing a "shirts vs skins" half-court game at one end, and he thought of himself long ago playing there in the same kind of contest.

Kelly jumped out of the van and began dribbling as she crossed the street to the playground, being careful to watch for cars. A low stone wall separated the sidewalk from the playground. She bounded up the three stairs of the stone staircase, headed for the nearest hoop, and began shooting. When O'Keefe joined her, she passed the ball to him. He quickly tossed up a shot that did not even make it to the rim. Shaking his head in disgust, he gestured to her to pass the ball back to him. This time he concentrated better and took a short hitch of a jump shot off the back of the rim. Close enough for a second try after a long period of shooting atrophy.

She had been playing now for several years. She and her teammates had come a long way from the "dribble to the corner and all converge" beginner-girls'-basketball style of play. In her personal game she had progressed slowly but well. She had a slight tendency toward awkwardness and was a bit too tall to be a "drive to the basket" type. He did not try to make her something she wasn't. He had tried to focus her on good defense, precision passing, and shooting, and taught her a shot somewhere between an old-fashioned set shot and a one-handed jump shot with only a slight jump to it, just enough to help put some extra force on the ball and ascend slightly above the opponent's outstretched hand. She had become a good shooter from what constituted long-range in young girls' basketball and was usually among the highest scorers on her team. He still tried to emphasize in practice the things she needed to work on—footwork, driving to the basket, positioning herself for rebounds.

They often finished their practice sessions with a game of "Around the World." He told her when they first started playing, "I'm never gonna let you win. I want you to know that, so when you do beat me, which you will eventually, you'll know that you really did win." And he adhered to that over the years, never deliberately missing a shot, but sometimes just throwing it up there casually, without concentration, when he thought she might be getting discouraged. And as time went on, she did end up legitimately winning her share.

"Hey," she said. "Got an idea."

"I'll bet it involves pizza."

"No. But it does involve popcorn."

"Anything for you, my dear."

In the car on the way to the movie she gave him a cautious sideways glance. "What were you two talking about?"

He wondered whether to be honest. "Big people stuff. Money… you."

"I caught her crying in her bedroom the other day."

He shook his head sadly. "Well, I'll do what I can to make it better."

"Really?"

"Well, I mean whatever can be done with money."

"You know she has a boyfriend, don't you?"

Why did that sting him? He had no right to react that way.

"You know what I heard her say to one of her friends on the phone the other day?"

He was pretty sure he did not want to hear it.

"What she said was, 'I really think I could get married again one of these days. Despite everything.'"

He thought he heard something far off, something like a dying fall.

Kelly's faced squinched up. She was trying to keep from crying. But she couldn't manage. "Dad, before long it's gonna be too late."

He had no idea what to say.

CHAPTER ▶ 4

"GUESS WHO'S ON the phone," Sara said.

"Your favorite lawyer?" he said.

"The very one. But he *is* growing on me…slowly though."

He picked up the phone. "Hey, it's been a while," he said.

"Too long," Michael Harrigan said. "I wish I had more to send you. You know I'd commit a crime myself if it'd make some work for you."

"No need to go quite that far."

"The new O'Keefe *Lite* kind of rough, is it?"

"To tell the truth, it *is*. But I've got a plan."

"If it works, sell it to me."

"You need a much bolder and bigger plan than I could ever devise."

Harrigan moved on. This had probably exceeded his quota of small talk for the entire day.

"Well, I may have something for you," he said.

"Yeah?" O'Keefe said, making no effort to disguise the hopeful eagerness in his voice.

"Can you be here at 9 a.m. on Monday?"

"I can hardly wait. What is it?"

"It's a surprise."

"Come on! You know I can't stand suspense. I'm a detective. And that's *your* fault."

"Nope. You're just gonna have to put up with it."

"All right, but that I'm putting up with it only shows how desperate I am. Let's get good retainers. I can't afford to get stiffed on this one."

"No chance of that."

"Of the retainer or getting stiffed? How about a hint?"

"Okay, here it is, and don't ask for anymore, not a word. 'Should old acquaintance be forgot?' That's it. Goodbye."

Harrigan hung up the phone before O'Keefe could sputter even one word. But he smiled. Things might be looking up.

Sara arrived at the door of his office moments after he hung up.

"Well?" she said, as eager as O'Keefe was to hear some good news.

"He's got something."

"Not another mink farm, I hope," she said, referring to the mink farm Ponzi scheme case the year before that had gone tragically awry.

O'Keefe winced, tried to stifle the frown that automatically came with the remembrance of how badly that case had gone, and said, "He won't tell me what it is until we meet on Monday."

"What a prick."

"But he says it'll pay well."

"But a useful prick...sometimes."

Harrigan was O'Keefe's blood brother. At eight years old they had sealed the bond by jabbing the tips of their fingers and pressing them together. Then Harrigan had read a book on King Arthur's Round Table, which he forced O'Keefe to read, and they began to conceive of themselves as "Grail Knights"—not the perfect Sir Galahad or Perceval, those "goody two shoes" types, but sinful strivers like Sirs Hector, Gawain (the "ladies' knight"), and Lancelot. It was one of those kidding things that was not entirely kidding—earnest sincerity with an overlaid disguise of irony to deflect ridicule. They hoped to achieve something wonderful, something transcendent one day. They just were not sure what that thing might be.

Their paths had diverged radically in the late 1960s. Harrigan finished college and managed to enlist in a Marine Corps reserve program that required six months of active duty, including the dreaded Boot Camp as well as Advanced Infantry Training, plus five tortuous years of weekends once per month and two-week stints in the summertime, but no immediate multi-year interruption to his civilian progress. O'Keefe drifted into booze and drugs, dropped out of college, received a low draft lottery number, was drafted into the Marine Corps (which needed men so badly then it had to abandon its previous, proudly proclaimed all-volunteer stance), and found himself plunged into the darkness of Vietnam. He survived, barely, and came out lost, a CPTSD-tormented cocaine addict careening in a rollicking, high-speed bumper car toward a jail term. Harrigan had pulled him out of that hell and made him into his "semi-slave private detective," as Harrigan described it, until O'Keefe could establish himself on his own.

Harrigan had always been a somewhat unlikely out-of-nowhere shooting star across the city's legal and business firmament, but lately he had been outdoing himself. He had developed a stable of bank clients who considered him a perfect combination of wizard and warrior, and looked to him to document their trickiest loans, work out their thorniest troubled deals, and chase down their biggest defaulting borrowers, of which there were more and more as the go-go 1980s hurtled along toward a fearsome reckoning that few saw coming.

His largest and most prominent client was not, technically, a bank, though often called that anyway, but a "savings and loan association," an "S&L." It was owned by Morris Manning and Mark Marcus, the "Double M&M's" they called themselves. The two young mavericks had acquire an up-to-then small and sleepy S&L known as

"Home Savings," re-named it "Vanguard" in accord with their ambitions, and set about building it into a powerhouse, meanwhile thumbing their noses at the snooty old-guard, self-anointed banker elite of the city who made loans only to those who didn't need them. The Double M&Ms, young, dynamic, and risk-taking, supported entrepreneurs like themselves, especially real estate developers, and they even became business partners with their customers to the limit—and sometimes beyond the limit—of what the banking laws and regulations allowed. Their ambitions initially squared with the intent of the United States Congress, which several years before had passed legislation "deregulating" savings and loan associations, freeing them to make much riskier loans than previously, unleashing the animal spirits of the nation's hustling entrepreneurs, creating forests full of trees sprouting a multitude of precarious limbs to crawl out on—everything from real estate deals to casinos. The results by 1987 were a cascading series of S&L failures across the land, hundreds of them, and billions of dollars of losses, with more sure to come, a result of reckless lending at best or outright fraud and corruption at worst.

And Harrigan himself was becoming something more than a lawyer. He had gotten tight with one client in particular, Eddie Tremaine, who had landed in town from the Far West in his own plane, not a jet but a damn nice prop. In his briefcase he carried a lively financial statement with asset values estimated high and liabilities low (and sometimes conveniently forgotten about entirely). He had descended upon them from the bright blue sky to rescue a local bank from a bad deal by acquiring the troubled borrower company and substituting his own shell company as the borrower with a letter of credit from a Nevada S&L, a "credit enhancement" that allowed the bank to keep the loan from the prying eyes of the regulators. At the same time, the bank lowered the interest rate and the loan payments and stretched out the loan term so Tremaine would have a chance to pull off a turnaround before the deal started circling the drain again.

Harrigan appeared on the other side of the table on Tremaine's first deal in the city. Tremaine was impressed and retained Harrigan on all his future deals, in the city and elsewhere. Harrigan returned the favor by introducing Tremaine to other local high-cash-flow deals that Tremaine needed to keep his lifestyle boat afloat—deals in which the anxious sellers were desperate for a buyer who could convince a lender to loan the buyer enough to pay the high purchase price the sellers desperately needed to relieve themselves of a mountain of debt. That lender often turned out to be Vanguard Savings, and the team of Harrigan, Tremaine, and Vanguard and the Double M&Ms started flipping deals like flapjacks.

Tremaine, in his late fifties, quickly became somewhat of a father figure to Harrigan, substituting for the actual father that had abandoned Harrigan and his mother when the boy was only four years old. Eddie took to giving Harrigan small pieces of deals as a sort of "tip" for Harrigan's expertise, connections, and, above all, his fierce dedication to his clients' interests. "My clients know I'm not a blood *sucker*," Harrigan once said to O'Keefe, "they know I'm a blood *donor*."

Harrigan had occasionally tried to involve O'Keefe in the group and its proceedings as a sort of mascot figure, an exotic and colorful private-eye flower to enliven the blander money-green merchant plants. O'Keefe made excuses and ducked every invitation because he had dedicated himself to quitting drinking and avoiding the temptation to do so in every way he reasonably could, and that group and their doings seemed like nothing more than a shiny-bright wagon built for him to fall off of.

Yes, it was a wagon those guys were driving, careening wildly along beyond its inebriated drivers' ability to control. The Double M&Ms

were earnest and well-meaning but naïve, deluded, and too willing to take risks and cut corners. Eddie Tremaine was clearly a polecat barely covering his stink with high-priced cologne paid for with borrowed money. O'Keefe could only guess that Harrigan's usually unerring bullshit detector had malfunctioned, unable to penetrate the haze of alcohol-fueled deal frenzy. It was never the money for Harrigan. It was being needed, wanted, and called upon to perform on the biggest stage he could climb onto. It gave him the worth that his childhood hadn't. But now the local newspapers published articles on troubled loans resulting from questionable lending practices all over the city (and beyond—across the entire nation) with frequent mention of institutions such as Vanguard Savings and the Nevada S&L that had provided Eddie Tremaine that letter of credit that had greased his original entry into their town of ambitious but callow provincials.

AT 9:00 MONDAY MORNING O'Keefe walked the familiar halls back to Harrigan's office, saying hello to the secretaries he knew well, nodding to those with whom he was not so well-acquainted, and waving to the lawyers who had left their doors open and were looking out at the hallway instead of the view outside their windows. When he arrived at Harrigan's office, the biggest and best corner on the top floor of the building, assigned to the founder and leader of the firm, he found Harrigan standing at one of the floor-to-ceiling windows, staring, it seemed, with a certain longing, beyond the densely built downtown, out toward the distant, rich bottom-land farm fields on the other side of the big river that split the town in two.

Harrigan turned around in greeting and tried to smile but looked not only hungover, even worse—harrowed—as if something terrifying were chasing him and quickly catching up. O'Keefe thought of

Francis Thompson's "Hound of Heaven": "I fled Him down the nights, I fled Him down the days, I fled Him down the labyrinthine ways…"

"Hey, man," Harrigan said, feebly grappling for a joyful tone. He moved to O'Keefe and, with uncharacteristic physical intimacy, hugged him. The smell of last night's whiskey oozing from Harrigan's pores made O'Keefe anxious and sad for his friend, and guiltily grateful, in the way of a survivor, for his own fragile sobriety.

"Okay," O'Keefe said, "no more fucking around, what's the surprise?"

"Not yet, my friend. Our guest will be here at 9:30, and your thirsty curiosity will be slaked."

"Someone from our past, I assume, based on the 'Auld Lang Syne' thing."

"Brilliant, my friend, Peter. Great detective work. You should do it for a living."

"I wish I *was* making a living at it."

"Damn, Pete. What happens if you have to fold up shop?"

"Hope not, but, you know, I've been thinking about a way to *really* help people. If I could skip the patrol officer part somehow and go right to detective, I'd become a cop."

"That's *really* desperate. Immediate rescue required. Luckily, I don't think you can make that jump. Got to do the 'flatfoot' thing first. Instead we'll work on getting you more business."

"I've worked out a business plan. I'll show it to you."

"Do that. I can probably help."

"But I'll need a loan to make it work. And Annie and Kelly aren't doing so well on what I give them. I need to come up with more there too. How about a good word for me with the M&Ms?"

"I can get you some help somewhere, but the Double Doubles aren't the place to go right now."

O'Keefe cocked his head and summoned a quizzical look, asking the question without words—"What's wrong?"

"You must not have read the paper this morning. The regulators shut them down yesterday. I own some of the stock. Goodbye to that. And they owe me a load of legal fees. Sayonara to those too. On top of that, one of the main areas of interest to the regulators are the loans of a certain Mr. Edward Tremaine, and I'm the one who introduced the bastard to them. And here's the real fun—the U.S. Attorney's office has formed a special financial crimes task force—its primary focus: local financial institutions and especially their ties to real estate developers."

"So Tremaine's a 'bastard'? That's a turnaround. I thought he was your new blood brother."

"That's fucking mean, Pete. He's a bastard and also a scumbag, liar, and a crook. His only purpose in acquiring properties and businesses is to skim every dollar to support his big-time lifestyle...and pay just enough on his ocean of debt to keep his nose just above the water level."

"Really?" O'Keefe said with a half-hearted attempt at putting surprise into his voice. But he was surprised only that Harrigan had fallen for the guy and his story even for a moment.

"I missed all the signals," Harrigan said, "and now I'm afraid it's gonna cost me. He's one of those guys our mothers warned us to stay away from."

The phone buzzed on Harrigan's desk. He hit the speaker button. The receptionist said, "Your guest is here."

"What's his name?" O'Keefe said to the phone, but she had abruptly hung up. "God, is she in on your scheme too?"

"'Auld Lang Syne.' You haven't guessed yet?"

"Someone from our past, that's the hint?" O'Keefe said, as they both left their chairs and headed for the hallway and toward the big conference room. "That narrows it down to what—a thousand people or so?"

"Just don't act too shocked when you see who it is."

CHAPTER ▶ 5

THE GUEST SAT at the far end of the conference table, but O'Keefe did not have to squint to recognize the handsome face of Jerry Jensen, their high school classmate—All-City in four sports, smart as hell too—successful businessman, recently announced mayoral candidate, considered a shoo-in for a job that would surely be a mere stepping-stone to much bigger political things. He did not stand up to greet them. They approached him in a ceremony of long-established, unspoken, unconscious obeisance between theoretical equals but one of them far more equal than the others. He extended his right hand as if there were a ring there to kiss, but it was only the firmest of handshakes that each of them had to reciprocate.

"The Siamese Twins," he said. "Some things never change."

"I couldn't resist," Harrigan said. "Just thought it would be fun to bring Pete along for old-time's sake."

"No problem," Jensen said, acknowledging and visibly basking in Harrigan's implied acknowledgment of his celebrity status. "Actually, I think we'll probably need his services on this. He'll be perfect for this job."

Jensen looked around the room and out through the windows at the display of clouds and skyscrapers. "Pretty nice, Mike. Congratulations. Sorry I haven't hired you before. But the old man put me with Fielding Lemon early on, and there's been no escaping their clutches."

"Well, we'll see if we can liberate you from those clutches," Harrigan said, moving to the credenza where a silver coffee urn, crystal pitcher of water, and breakfast pastries were spread in attractive array. "And from those astronomical legal bills...Coffee?"

"No thanks. Had my first cup at 5 a.m., and I need to spend some time somewhere other than the john."

Harrigan sat down and, with a subtle gesture, signaled to O'Keefe he should do the same. O'Keefe sat down across the table from Harrigan, with Jensen bracketed between them.

"So what could possibly pry you away from the hallowed halls of Fielding Lemon?" Harrigan asked.

"Is Pete covered by the privilege"?

"Yes. He's my agent. Attorney-client privilege, just like me. But I should probably be making sure there isn't any conflict. Who's the adverse party?"

"I can assure you that you aren't representing this particular adverse party."

"Who is it?"

"Our old friend, Beverly. Beverly Raymond Bronson."

"Really?" Harrigan blurted.

O'Keefe remained silent. Had Harrigan been as infatuated with Beverly Raymond as O'Keefe had been, as about every boy in the school had been? O'Keefe had even been vouchsafed the privilege of a few dates with her. The first was a blind date, and, to O'Keefe's shock, she initiated an intense backseat make-out session at a drive-in movie. They went at it so hard that Bev ended up with her chewing gum tangled in her hair. Something similarly intense happened on every date with her, too few though they were, whether in a car ("parking," they called it) or the couch in the living room of her parents' house. Even these days she would occasionally flash across his mind—how soft she was, how compliant, at least up to the furthest point he himself would go, as he was quite "moral" back then, puritanical even, and not because the Church called it a mortal sin. Other things held him back. Not the fear of going to hell, but a fear of going one step too far and offending the girl so deeply she would hate him. And the dread of getting her "knocked up," as they called an unwanted pregnancy back then. But, most of all, a feeling akin to reverence for the imagined ultimate experience. He had sensed, not entirely consciously, that this surpassing consummation should be reserved, not necessarily for marriage, but for a special commitment of some kind, at least a special feeling or bond.

"She called me," Jensen was continuing. "What a cunt."

O'Keefe winced at that, inwardly and probably even outwardly, and he hoped Jensen hadn't noticed. Which did not turn out to be a problem because Jensen was entirely focused on his own anger. "After all this fucking time, the cunt says that kid of hers is mine and wants big money for it. The damn kid isn't even a minor now. Seventeen or just turned eighteen and in the Marines. Not the best kid either. I understand it was the Marines or a jail cell."

"And what's she up to these days?" Harrigan asked.

"You haven't heard?" Jensen said. O'Keefe winced inwardly again. He had heard things he didn't want to believe.

Harrigan shook his head. "Not a thing. Missed all the reunions."

"Rock bottom. Junkie. A heroin whore to boot."

"No way," Harrigan said softly. He looked like the wind had been knocked out of him.

"A junkie too. Off'd *himself* a few weeks ago. Blew his brains out. Not that he was worth much to her, but he was all she had. No or damn little life insurance, I expect. It's not exactly a portfolio item for junkies."

O'Keefe slightly averted his head to keep Jensen from seeing his face, the look of disgust that passed over it.

"All this time passed," Harrigan said. "And her history. Nobody'll believe her."

"Here's the problem. If they do a paternity test, he might just turn up mine."

Even she had succumbed to him, like so many others, unable to resist him. But why hadn't it been locker room news, at least until it turned into a pregnancy? Jerry always broadcasted his conquests far and wide.

"Even so," Harrigan said, "there's the statute of limitations, laches, estoppel, waiver." O'Keefe wondered if this was just Harrigan's poker face. Was he really as unfazed as he seemed to be by the tragic fall Jensen had just described?

"It could still ruin me all the same," Jensen replied.

Harrigan nodded his head slowly and thoughtfully and said, "What can we do for you?"

"The problem is that even if I pay her, how does that stop her? How do I keep her from sucking my blood forever?"

After a pause, while Harrigan's eyes lowered to the desk surface in concentration, he said, "I'll need to think on that a bit. Maybe something like an escrow. Escalating payments every couple or three years. Large enough to be a big loss if she doesn't keep her end."

"Not a bad idea, but what if she goes off the junkie deep end and stops caring about the money...just wants to hurt me?"

"Yeah," Harrigan nodded again. "Problem."

"Here's what I'd like to do first, and that's why I came here. I want you to go talk to her. Better someone she knows than some anonymous, intimidating guy in a suit. It might even be better if Pete does it. You dated her some, didn't you, Pete?"

Again the inward recoil, the wound opening. Why did he interpret that question as an insidious, snarky dig?

"Yeah, I did, but it doesn't sound like that could possibly mean much to her anymore...if it ever did."

"It's worth a shot. I have to think she'd be more comfortable with you, more likely to tell the truth. The wall won't be up the same way with you as with some other guy, even Mike."

"I'd have to tell her I'm working for you."

"Why?"

"Ethics."

"I didn't know PIs had those."

O'Keefe did not respond. He had long ago passed from idolizing Jerry Jensen to mostly disliking him, which was now rapidly turning into hatred.

"'Fraid so. Not many, but some."

"Well, I'll have to trust that you're good enough to get past that."

Someone knocked on the conference room door. Harrigan, irritated by the interruption, said "Yeah."

The door opened, a secretary appeared, and said, "There's an emergency call for Mr. Jensen. Should I put it through?"

"Please," Jensen said. He looked around the room for a phone.

"On the credenza there," Harrigan said as a button on the phone lit up and buzzed. Jensen covered the distance to the credenza in a couple of the long strides that had made him famous on the gridiron, picked up on the phone, listened for a moment, asked the other party to hold on, and turned to Harrigan and O'Keefe with a an apologetic "I have to be alone" look.

"Need some privacy?" Harrigan said.

"Sorry, but yeah. This running for office is something else. They try to dig up everything they can on you, and they'll pretty much make it up if the facts aren't juicy enough. My secretary'll call you right away to work out the payment details."

Harrigan and O'Keefe repaired to Harrigan's office. Each lit up a Marlboro and blew the smoke in the other's direction.

"Well, what do you think about that?" Harrigan said.

"Sad about Bev. What a descent. And Timmy. I never cared for him, but how sad."

"I remember you and her, what there was of it anyway."

"Not enough. 'Unrequited,' as they say."

"You think she's telling the truth?"

O'Keefe shook his head. "Can't say. Who knows what happens to people? But it sure makes me wonder why she blamed Tim for it when she could have pointed the shotgun at Jensen instead."

"You strong enough to go see her? You don't want to end up in another 'Tag Parker' situation."

Anger rose and flashed red in O'Keefe's face, but he quickly caught himself and held his tongue and relaxed his hand, which had involuntarily clenched into a fist. Harrigan, Sara, George, they all seemed to want to keep reminding him about the mink farm debacle. But he knew he should not confuse Harrigan with Jerry Jensen. Harrigan was the opposite—not snarky or malicious, but genuinely concerned, protective of his friend, who had only a year before, with Tag Parker, fallen too hard for a beautiful woman in distress.

"Well," O'Keefe said, "I would say the 'heroin whore' thing was enough to blow off pretty much all the bloom left on that rose."

"Wonder if that's true or just locker room talk?"

"I hope it's not true, but it probably is. Does every damn illusion have to explode and every damn dream have to die?"

"So you'll go see her?"

"I need some time...a few hours anyway...to think. The real problem is that people like Jerry Jensen are exactly the types I vowed last year to stop working for."

"Whoa! Where did that come from? I always thought he was okay...that he handled the ego thing pretty well."

"I can't quite explain it. It's just that one night a long time ago, I thought I saw something that seemed really ugly hiding behind that shining surface. A predator beneath the mask. And isn't it enough to hear him call her a 'cunt,' and then in the next breath say he probably fathered her child, while obviously not giving a shit about her or the kid?"

"Well, how about this? Maybe you can help her. We don't have to be brutes about it."

"Unless our client wants us to?"

"We only go as far as we're willing to go."

"He'll be hard to resist. Big business. Big politics. Still in his thirties and sure to be the next mayor."

"Seems like you'll be plenty moral compass for me on this one."

"Seems like at best a load of pain."

"What were you telling me a few minutes ago about Annie being strapped for cash and Kelly's future? Like our friend Dylan says, 'You gotta serve somebody.' Hell, there might be a trifecta here—Annie, Kelly, and even Bev—and throw in her kid if Jerry's really the father. What's four of them? Is that a quadrafecta, or maybe a quadfecta?"

O'Keefe rose to leave. "I'm sure I'll do it. I just need to clear my head a bit. Call me once you know for sure we're getting paid. I sure as hell don't want to do this and then get stiffed by the Wonder Boy."

"And I'll talk to the bank about that loan. I'm sure they'll do it. Don't sweat that. Just sweat how to pay it back. Don't ruin my good name...such as it is."

~

THE LAST TIME he had seen her he had visited her at her house after learning she had left school. He had called her from a pay phone a couple of blocks away. He did not want to surprise her, intrude on some awkward situation.

"Hey, it's Pete. I'm close to your house. I heard the news. Can you talk?"

She hesitated. For a moment he thought she would refuse. Then, uncertainly, "Sure, Pete. I'll come out."

They sat on a small weather-beaten wooden swing hooked to the ceiling of the porch. "I don't know what to say," he said, "except is there anything I can do...anything I can help with?"

"I wish," she said. "Too late."

"What are you gonna do now?"

"They want to send me away to have the baby and then give it up..." She looked furtively toward the front window as if her parents might be listening. "But Tim and I are gonna elope if we can. I want this baby. I'll be a good mother, I know it. I won't let this ruin my life."

He contemplated the choice she now faced. He felt badly that he could muster no wisdom to offer. Too young. Neither of them had lived long enough to know how to deal with what she faced now. She lowered her head, chin on her chest, in shame. Her shiny, still mostly blonde hair fell to her shoulders. She wore faded jeans and a white peasant blouse that gathered underneath and emphasized her breasts, which were on the small side like the rest of her but ample enough. She was in her stocking feet, white athletic socks, and a small hole in one of the socks exposed part of one of her toes. That little hole, seeming to somehow symbolize her plight, made him sadder than anything else, and the image of it had remained stark in his mind all these intervening years.

She again looked furtively toward the house. "I've got to go back in," she said. "They're watching me like hawks."

They stood up.

"A hug?" he said.

She looked nervous but allowed it, and when she came into his arms, she showed no hesitation. She felt the way she had felt every time he had embraced her in the past—pliant, going with it all the way, the essence of softness. But he had learned from previous times that this apparent surrender was all provisional, for the moment, no promise of a future, and there was certainly no future for them now.

Tears formed a film across her eyes. "Goodbye, Pete."

"Hey, Bev. Everything'll be all right."

What a lie.

He walked to his car and looked back just before opening the car door. She was gone. That was the last time he had seen her.

CHAPTER ▶ 6

THE BACKGROUND WORK on her, piecing together the existential arc—all sadly downward since age seventeen—that had brought her to this place had been painful but easy enough given their shared past and old mutual friends. He started right in his own shop, with George, the very pulling guard that had so often cleared out the opposing linebacker for Jerry to zoom by and, a few yards later, stiff-arm the overmatched cornerback on his gallop to the end zone. George had kept more in touch with the old crowd than O'Keefe and quickly asked around.

"Hey, Pete. First, can I ask? What's the goal here? Surely you're not trying to rekindle an old flame."

"Not at all. But it's a long, weird story."

"You're not keeping secrets from me again, are you? That didn't work out so well last time."

Arizona again. The mink farm. Tag Parker. All these reminders. But I deserve them all.

"No way, George. Just trust me, whether I deserve it or not. It's too long and complicated to tell right now. And I need some things to fall into place before I even know what's going on."

"Well, she got knocked up of course—one of that slew of homecoming queens in town that bit the dust that year. Ran off with Timmy and got married. Both sets of parents, especially his...remember... they had more money than the rest of us, dragged them back and tried to force them apart. They just ran off again. To Denver this time. Up there for several years. And I don't know what happened up there, but when they came back to town, they were junkies. They disguised it pretty well for a while but finally couldn't anymore. They both got to be bad, bad into that stuff. In and out of rehab and all that. Even some jail time for Timmy. Their kid got in some trouble too. He's in the Marines now. That or jail, I understand."

"Is the 'heroin whore' thing true?"

"Don't know. My guess is yes. Hard to take that one, huh?"

"Real hard."

"Finally, I guess Timmy couldn't take it anymore. Blew his brains out a few months ago."

"Don't know how I missed that one."

"Well, it didn't exactly make the headlines. Who cared by then?"

"And her?"

"She went into rehab again right after he killed himself. Hasn't been out long. I have an address and a phone number."

~

HE CALLED THE NUMBER several times before she answered. Was his impression correct that her once-silken voice was now harsh, cracked?

"Bev. A voice from your past here. It's Pete."

A pause. Just as he was about to say his last name, she said it—"O'Keefe?"

"Yes."

She remained silent.

She's waiting for me to explain myself.

"I do private detective work these days."

She continued to be silent. He could almost feel her wariness through the phone.

"You remember Mike Harrigan, I'm sure."

"Yes" she said. "Big lawyer now, right?"

"Yeah. And I work with him quite a bit."

"Still blood brothers, huh?"

"I guess."

"And?"

"Jerry Jensen came to see us."

She exploded: "That motherfucker. Sending Harrigan, and *you*, of all people, after me. Like I'll wilt like a little flower just because an old friend shows up to put me through the third degree. Well, fuck him, and fuck you and Harrigan too."

"That's not what's going on. All I want is to hear your story. I don't intend to talk you into or out of anything. I might even be able to help."

"But you're on his payroll?"

"Yes."

"How am I supposed to trust that?"

"You're not. Don't trust it. But better to deal with an old good friend than somebody else."

"Well, I guess if there's anyone that has 'nothin' left to lose,' it's me. Can you come see me soon? Now?"

"I can get there in an hour or two."

"Okay. But don't be carrying any tender images in your head. Snow White's the Witch now. And this place is a war zone. You'll be lucky if all they do is steal your hubcaps. Hell, they'll steal the tires too...maybe even the car."

He arrived early for the meeting, while it was still light, so he could scope out the entire surroundings—the gestalt; not just the parts, the whole; the forest, not just the trees. He did not drive the van, it would be too conspicuous, would draw the wrong kind of attention, to say nothing of her comment about stealing the hubcaps. He quickly made a couple of calls and borrowed a beat up old car more appropriate to the place she had described.

It turned out to be a trailer park, not that far from where they had grown up, in a spot of rough country that urban development had bypassed, the expanding city metaphorically closing its eyes and holding its nose, preferring not to see or smell this place or even acknowledge its existence. During all these years nobody had wanted to pay the owner's price to buy it and obliterate it to build something better. O'Keefe drove slowly along the road next to the park. "Park." What a misnomer. On the other side of the road a freight train pulled up beside him, metal wheels screeching on metal track. He couldn't say that the park was on the wrong side of the tracks because in this neighborhood both sides were wrong. The few houses around were tiny and looked to be the homesteads of the original pioneers, seemingly one strong wind gust away from collapse. The park itself looked like it had been thrown from a speeding car, the trailers strewn around as if they had just remained in the random spots where they had happened to bounce. The oldest area of the park sat at the bottom of a hill, and the owner had built new sites upward; thus, the newer, larger trailers stood on higher ground. The bottom was just that, in every sense, and that's where Bev and Tim had ended up.

He could not believe that beautiful girl had come to such a pass as to live in such a place. She and O'Keefe, and Harrigan, and George, and most of the rest of their classmates were children of blue collar parents who lived, for the most part, from paycheck to paycheck, but none of them had lived like this or could even imagine the possibility of growing up to live like this. The dented, rusty trailers had not been painted in decades if ever. The little stairs, some wooden, some metal, that led up to the trailer doors slouched in various states of disrepair—at best splintered, at worst outright busted, one or two missing a step altogether. He noticed a trailer covered with bird shit, although someone was living there as evidenced by what looked like a barely drivable car parked in front. In a couple of places junk cars without wheels were perched on cinder blocks. There were almost as many motorcycles as cars parked throughout the area.

As he drove slowly up the gravel driveway that separated the two rows of trailers in this section of the park, he craned his neck in search of her address, or any other address that might give him a clue to which one might be hers. He wondered if anyone was watching, if they could even see him through the grime on their tiny windows. He suspected hers was the one at the end of the road, backed up against a tangled, impenetrable-looking jungle of small trees, vines, bushes, and weeds. One of her windows was cracked and held together with tape. He thought it best to maneuver the car to park it facing back out toward the entrance to the park.

Once he got out of the car, he hesitated. No telling what might be on the other side of that door. But she must have been watching for him. The trailer door opened, and there she stood. "Smart move," she said, indicating his parked car. "Ready for a quick escape...if you have any wheels left anyway."

As he stepped into the trailer, she stepped back and swept her right arm backward to indicate he should walk in front of her toward a linoleum-covered metal table in the tiny kitchen. "Welcome to the Promised Land," she said. To their right was a few square feet of a living room, a built-in couch below built-in shelves containing a few paperbacks, an old TV dwarfed by its rabbit ears that seemed made for a much larger set, and two framed photos of a child who O'Keefe guessed must be her son. Even from that distance the resemblance to Jerry Jensen was obvious, though maybe it wouldn't have been if he didn't know what he now knew. Two other photos lay face down on the shelf, and he wondered if those were of Tim, or her and Tim. Beyond the kitchen he could see a short hallway, off of which he guessed was a bathroom on one side and a closet on the other, and beyond that likely a bedroom hardly large enough to contain the smallest possible double bed and a built-in, fold-down bedside table—only one because there was not space enough to fit one on each side—no room for lamps, overhead lights only. He heard the labored chugging of a window air-conditioner and felt the cool and was grateful for that. *These tin cans must be hell on earth in the summer without air conditioning.*

"I can't offer you anything but a stale cup of coffee," she said.

"I like it that way," he said, forcing a smile at her, hoping its insincerity was not too apparent. She gave him a quick smile back that seemed no more genuine than his own. He stood awkwardly, not able to bring her into full focus in the low light. Although cleaner than might be expected, it was a Spartan lair, all hard surfaces, nothing comfortable, nothing soft like the girl she had once been. And she was no longer soft. This soft girl had become as hard as a petrified stick. He avoided more than fleeting glances at her, fearful his face would register a shock that could be mistaken for disgust. He wondered if her beauty had disappeared forever or had just temporarily burnt out, like a forest after a fire ready to spring back to something like new life. Her face had the hollowed-out gauntness of the heroin addict. Big dark circles under her brown eyes. Once shiny hair now dull and unwashed. She wore a long-sleeved blouse. To hide needle marks on her arms? Her fingernail polish had partly worn off. Her feet were bare, and her toenail polish, like her fingernail polish, had not entirely worn off, a reminder that not so long ago there had at least been a gesture toward a more decorative existence. He remembered that tiny hole in her sock from that day on her porch. She wore cotton shorts. Her legs, always delightful, were still smooth, even inviting. But he did not feel even a flicker of desire. "Heroin whore." The words kept bouncing around his mind. His compassion could not overcome those words, at least for now.

She indicated he should sit down, poured a cup of coffee, and pushed it toward him. In front of herself she set a pack of Marlboros and an ashtray already almost overflowing with old, foul-smelling butts and ashes. He wondered if his whole generation smoked Marlboros. The Marlboro Man. He pulled out his own pack, and she pushed the ashtray between them. She lit a cigarette with a Zippo, then slid the lighter over to him so he could light up himself. She took her first drag, inhaled, parted her lips slightly, and directed a thin line of smoke up toward the ceiling to avoid directing it at his face, a delicate, courteous gesture that seemed incongruous somehow.

"You look good," she said. "Wish I could say the same for myself."

He started to offer a feeble contradiction. "Don't," she said. "No lies today. In fact let's see how honest we can be. What exactly did he hire you and Harrigan to do?"

He hesitated, thinking about what he would say, making sure he would tell her the exact and entire truth, hoping she would not think his hesitation was actually for the opposite purpose—to perfect a lie. "To talk to you. Find out what you want. Figure out how to keep you from holding this over his head forever."

"Did he admit it?"

"What?"

"That he's the father."

"Don't make me answer that."

"That means he did."

"He said it was possible."

"Did he admit he raped me?"

Again, he wondered if his flinch had been visible. His eyes narrowed in concentration. *No, Jerry hadn't admitted that. Why does it make me feel better that she was raped, not seduced? What a jerk.*

"No, he didn't."

"Well, that's what he did."

"So why didn't you call him out?"

"Oh yeah. Call out the big star. Who would they've believed? And I did let him get close enough that he didn't have to do much to complete the act. What would they have made of that?"

"But you could've at least named him as the father."

"When I couldn't deny anymore that I was pregnant, I went to him, and he said 'You whore. I'll not only not marry you. You'll have to prove I'm the one, and not all those other guys you fucked. Half the football team at least, and I'll get them to say so. Even if you prove I'm the daddy, you'll get nothing, just go down in flames while I go to college.' So I panicked. Blamed it on Tim. And it could've been Tim. We had done it once. Too many times we got too close until he finally got to slip it in. I kept saying, 'Don't come, Tim. Don't make me pregnant.' What a joke, trying to stop that. But I knew better. I knew it wasn't Tim. But it seemed like Tim was a better bet back then than the rapist football hero. And I'll burn in hell for that. Already burnt in hell on this earth for that."

"Did Tim ever find out?"

"No. Not even when it was obvious the kid didn't look a thing like him. He was too busy fucking off and nodding off. He repaid my sin against him big time. He hooked me and worse. He turned out to be just a weak, nasty punk. Took the easy way out. Left me holding both of our bags. Didn't even care enough about the kid to stick around and try to help him in life."

He was that all along, Bev. You fell for his boyish good looks and hot car. "You didn't say a word all these years. Why now?"

"Part of it was Tim. I couldn't bear to have him know that. Not that he deserved it, the pimp. But now what I feel, what I know, is that the world got knocked off its axis back then, and now it has to be set right. It started with a crime. Jerry Jensen's. It got compounded with a lie. Beverly Raymond's. And it's produced nothing but tragedy. I came out of this last rehab with a vow to tell the truth. I don't think I can stay straight without it."

He purposely gentled his voice, hoping not to push her over the edge, and said, "And make some money out of it too."

She got it, looked guilty and regretful for just a moment but moved quickly past it. "Damn right. I've done nothing but suffer, and caused others to suffer, for his crime. And he's done nothing but prosper. But I don't want any of it for me anyway. Maybe just enough to not have to fuck the ugly-ass owner of this shit-can to pay the rent. But I want my son, his son too, goddamn it, to have something. And here's the bottom line. I want to stay clean, and I have zero chance of that unless I tell the truth."

"But no truth's coming out if he pays you."

Her face dropped in recognition of the imperfection of her rationale. Her eyelids closed for a moment, then she said, "I might as well make some money for my son. Someone ought to get a reparation. And a few people will know. You, Harrigan…"

"Jerry will deny it."

"The paternity test will blow him away."

"But nobody'll believe the rape. The story will be, like he said, about a girl who was supposedly screwing everyone in sight."

"Well, you of all people know that's not true."

"The truth doesn't matter. It was just a lottery which one of them fathered the kid. It may not be true, but they'll believe it's true. They'll say 'she didn't even tell him it might be his.' You've got no proof you told him, right? And the story will be 'the girl went right on her whoring ways...became a hopeless junkie heroin whore. Now she's looking to ruin a man for a youthful indiscretion because he won't pay her off.'"

She looked stricken. "'The truth doesn't matter?' Is that the kind of shit you and Harrigan do...the kind of stories you tell? Seems like a long way from the 'Grail Knights.'"

That one stung, since it was not all that far from what he had been feeling for years about himself and where and how he had ended up.

"You remember that, huh?"

"How could I not? The rest of us thought you were crazy with that 'Grail' stuff, but it's occurred to me a few times later on that you were the only ones who had it right."

"You ask, 'is that the kind of shit we do?' The answer is maybe. Sometimes. Hopefully not often. But if we don't, someone else will do it to you...tell that story. That's my point."

"I have to bet he won't take the chance. It might kill his political career. What about his business partners...his family?"

"It might just be like the tree falling in the forest when nobody's there. No sound."

He could not recall ever seeing pain as stark and sharp as the pain in her eyes. It beamed at him, stabbed him. But he kept on. "Another problem. How does he ever know he's done with you? That you won't be back again time after time with your hand out and palm open?"

"I don't know. You and Harrigan think of something. Don't they pay you for that?"

"We'll try. Believe me, I would like to see you get paid."

"Really? Does that mean you believe me? Junkie whore or not?"

"I do."

"Why?"

"Because I may not know who you are now, what you've become, but I know what you were back then. And I know what he was. And still is."

When he left, she followed him outside. "I can't believe you drive such a crappy car," she said.

"It's not mine."

"Oh, you're a smart one, aren't you?"

"I listen…Ya know, I've had some of the same problems you've had."

"Which? Knocked up, drugged up, or just totally fucked up?"

"Drugs and alcohol."

"Heroin?"

He shook his head. "Luckily, no."

"Heroin's a whole different ball game, Pete." Her face softened, and she tucked in her chin and looked down at the ground. He stood staring at her and visualized her not as she was now but as she once had been. Somehow this tiny once-beautiful creature, devastated, and standing now here in the midst of this desolation, had fallen into hell. More proof, one of so many proofs, that the world was inexplicably unjust and life unfair. He felt like he should embrace her again, like he had done that day on her front porch.

As he turned from her toward the car, she said, "And Pete, if he wants to take me on, I know something a lot worse about him than what he did to me."

He turned back. "And what am I supposed to do with that? What is it?"

"Just know it. I know something a lot worse about him than what he did to me."

He started to argue further with her, but it seemed useless to try. He accepted her decree and headed toward the car, relieved to be able to escape from this.

He again proceeded slowly along the gravel driveway from her trailer and through the park. He did not turn on his headlights until he was out of the driveway and on the pavement of the road when he stomped on the gas pedal hard and his tires squealed as he sped away. He felt tears trickling down his face. Some detective. Hard boiled he surely was not.

~

FROM A CONCEALED spot in the jungle-like growth at the rear of her trailer, he watched O'Keefe drive away and continued to observe Bev as she stared after O'Keefe's car until it disappeared, embraced herself as if feeling a chill, then turned and climbed the little rotting-wood staircase back into her trailer. *What the hell was O'Keefe doing in a place like this?* He would find out who this woman was. Was she involved in some case of O'Keefe's? Or could O'Keefe be slumming here, *really* slumming, for an occasional piece of ass? If so, O'Keefe must be damn desperate. But that might furnish the perfect opportunity. It was hard enough to kill any man, and especially to kill him in a way that left not a trace of evidence of foul play. But this was not just any man. This was an ex-Marine; tall, lithe, a private detective who should naturally be alert to danger, especially after what had happened to him only last year, and what he must be afraid might happen again, notwithstanding Carmine Jagoda's recent incarceration and impending final demise. And this was a man who had surprised, overpowered, and hogtied an adept killer,

Karl "Dry Ice" Manzotti, who had been trying to do the same thing to this Marine as the watcher in the jungle had now been instructed to do and intended to do. If only O'Keefe would come back here for more. They would find him with his guilty dick in his guilty hand, he and his trailer trash whore, with their throats slit, maybe by a jealous boyfriend or husband. Or the gas stove might just explode and quickly burn them up in that little tin-can love nest. This shitty job had been forced on him. He had no stomach for it. But it had to be done. And it had to be perfect—no clue left, not even a speck.

CHAPTER ▶ 7

HARRIGAN AND JENSEN had already installed themselves in Harrigan's conference room when O'Keefe arrived. Harrigan looked eager and Jensen looked anxious. Nobody showed interest in small talk today so he launched right in. Unusually for him, he had carefully practiced the delivery of this speech.

"Here's how it is. She seems to be clean at the moment. She is just out of rehab and feeling extremely righteous. Tim killing himself seems to have freed her from a big restraint. She didn't want Tim to know the kid wasn't his—"

Jensen interrupted. "We still don't know it wasn't his."

"—She has no doubt. And if you saw the photos I saw, I don't think you or anybody else would have any doubt either."

"Shit," Jensen said.

"She says she wants nothing for herself. As she put it, she would just want enough to keep from fucking her ugly-ass landlord for the trailer rent."

"Trailer?" said Harrigan.

"Yes. The trailer park from hell. Actually, *in* hell."

"Jesus," Harrigan said, in anguished surprise.

Jensen emitted a snort of disgust. "How'd she look?"

"Bad. Hollowed out. The old Bev is long gone."

"Jesus," whispered Harrigan. "How sad."

"Hold the tears, Mike," Jensen said, "she's extorting me, remember?"

Harrigan's eyes closed into slits. He looked away from Jensen toward O'Keefe. His look said "Pete, you might be right about him."

"Yeah," O'Keefe said, "she says she wants it all for the kid. *Your* kid."

"What horseshit," Jensen said.

"And for the truth. She seems to think that her cover-up of the alleged rape and the lie to Tim was sort of the Original Sin that poisoned the world...hers anyway."

Feeling an almost physical twinge of guilt knowing he would too much enjoy saying what he was about to say, he went on. "She says you raped her."

"No surprise she would claim that."

He seemed so ready for that, he knew it was coming. Why did he not at least fake some outrage?

Jensen continued, "So what does she want?"

"Money."

"So much for the truth," Harrigan said.

"I pointed that out to her."

"What'd she say?" Jensen asked.

"Shrugged it off."

"How much?"

"She didn't say, and I didn't ask. I thought it might look weak. I emphasized what an uphill battle it will be for her even if you're proved to be the father. All the years, all the miles, all the bad road."

"And what did she say to that?"

"She didn't seem to care."

"Nothing to lose. Cornered rat. Most dangerous kind. How do I keep her from having her hand in my pocket forever?"

"Hard," said Harrigan. "Maybe impossible. The best I can think of, like I said before, is hook her on the payments. Make her think hard about getting greedy and screwing it up. Just like stock options for an executive...make the big payoff come way down the road."

"There's no road long enough," Jensen said. "Pete, does the kid know?"

"Surely not," O'Keefe said. But he was embarrassed. He hadn't asked her that. Not such good detective work.

"Seems pretty basic, Pete. We've got to know that. She could've decided to come clean with him after Tim killed himself."

"Agree," said Harrigan.

O'Keefe knew he had to tell Jensen one more thing. A part of him would enjoy it. Another part of him wanted to hold back. She had seemed to regret saying that last thing. What could it have been? But Jensen was the client. He guessed he owed the client a duty on that.

"One more thing. Right as I was leaving, it was like she felt she needed to up the ante. She said, 'I know something a lot worse about him than what he did to me.'"

He watched Jensen carefully. For just a moment the pupils of his eyes registered something that seemed like confusion, close to panic, but his recovery was immediate, and majestic. "You know what, Pete," he said, "that's the best piece of information you brought in here with you today. That shows weakness. That shows she doesn't think the paternity, even the so-called rape, is enough. Maybe it got to her what you told her about how hard it will be for her if I fight."

"Could be."

"But we've got to know if the kid knows. That's vital. You've got to find that out."

"She could just lie about it," Harrigan said.

"Well, if Pete here is a good PI, then he must be a good lie detector. Figure it out, Pete. We've got to know. We might not be sure, but we've got to make a judgment. Just like which way to break at the line of scrimmage, or what to offer the guy across the negotiating table in a business deal—instincts based on experience, information, and smarts."

Okay, you patronizing fuck.

~

O'KEEFE THOUGHT about just calling her and asking her straight out. He didn't really want to see her again. Too depressing. But he could not assess, evaluate, make a judgment based on a voice over a telephone line. He would have to see her again, but he wanted to avoid another visit to that trailer park. He called and proposed they meet at a well-known diner in the area.

"I passed on the information," he said.

"Is this a stall?"

"Not at all. In utmost good faith."

"Bullshit," she said. "Jerry Jensen doesn't have a good faith bone in his body. But maybe you do. But why can't you come here?"

"You ought to get out some. Let me buy you a meal. How about an AA or an NA meeting? Do you go to meetings?"

"I guess one trip to Paradise was all you could stand, huh?"

"Maybe."

"That's honest. Maybe I really can trust you. But I have a problem. This'll sound ridiculous, but I need gas money. I might have enough in the tank to make it there, but I won't be able to get back."

"I'll fill your tank."

~

HE MADE SURE to arrive at Ernie's All-Day Diner before she did. He sat, sipping at his coffee in a booth by the window where he could see her drive up and be in a position to signal his presence to her. He did not want her to be uncertain or uncomfortable in any way. Ernie's had been around forever as far as he knew, at least since long before his time. Successive teenage generations, including O'Keefe's, had adopted it as a late night after-party-and-before-curfew place to hang out. He supposed that tradition had faded away by now in the wake of the death of one world and the birth of another that had been in process since the 1950s.

O'Keefe had a weakness for Ernie's famous blueberry pancakes, but he intended to avoid those today, both because he was trying to keep the weight off and reduce his sugar intake, but also because it just did not seem right to be slurping pancakes and syrup when engaging in the particular conversation he needed to have with her. It was more of a scrambled egg and toast sort of conversation, or, really, nothing at all—a fasting sort of conversation. He would eat only if she did, and then only to be polite.

She arrived on time and walked toward the diner in what he interpreted to be a weary and resigned sort of way. But when she saw him sitting at the booth by the window, she waved, and he swore he could detect a lilt enlivening her step. Tears nearly came again. How had he become such a crybaby all of a sudden? He would have to control himself in this meeting, not let himself get anywhere near the weeping point. Or maybe not. Maybe that would be what she needed to fully trust him?

"God," she said, as she maneuvered herself into the booth across from him and dropped her keys, cigarettes, and the big silver Zippo lighter on the table, "I haven't been in this place since I was seventeen."

The harsh daylight only made her look worse, and she seemed to know it, avoiding his eyes when he looked directly at her, which he was trying to do as much as possible. He wanted to practice looking at this new bombed-out version of Beverly Raymond Bronson, so he would not unintentionally shame and humiliate her by registering some combination of shock, sadness, regret, panic, or disgust every time he looked at her and remembered who and what she once had been.

She ordered a big breakfast and proceeded to consume it heartily. Just to be polite he ordered two soft scrambled eggs and near-burnt toast.

"I've been famished lately," she said. "Hope that's a good sign. This recovery stuff is, to be blunt, a real motherfucker."

"What can I do?...Do you go to meetings?"

"I do," she said as she generously buttered a piece of toast. "I don't overdo it, but I do it. And there are special aftercare sessions at the hospital. I think I've got a chance of making it this time. At least I want to this time. But what a bitch it is."

She chewed the toast, swallowed it, and pushed the plate away from her toward him, signaling she was finished eating.

"So I forgot to ask you an important question," he said.

"What's that?"

"Who else knows about you and Jerry?"

"You mean who else knows that Jerry raped me and knocked me up and then refused to take responsibility for any of it? You mean that? Let's call a spade a spade, Pete, no sugar-coating, no polite language."

"Okay, yeah, that."

"Not a soul."

"Not even your son?"

"He's the last one I'd want to know...now anyway...later, yes."

"Why?"

"First, I'd have to tell him the *whole* truth then, including that I lied to him and to his dad, or who he thought was his dad, meaning Tim, which is gonna be damned hard and I'm not quite ready for that. I'd like to give him some good news with it. Second, who knows what he'd do? Something violent and stupid probably...that seems to have become his way...he wasn't raised all that well, you know. He certainly couldn't do anything constructive."

"Okay. That's really important. If we can't believe you about that..."

"Who's 'we'? I could care less what Jerry Jensen believes."

"But to make this work he has to believe that the odds are that only you know."

"Do you believe me?"

"I do."

"About everything?"

"Everything. And the believing starts with me. If I believe you, Harrigan will likely accept that, and then Jerry might come around."

She looked relieved. "How did I get so lucky that the prick hired you and Harrigan?" Two tears wended down her face. She took a finger and rubbed them away before they could reach her lips. He was overcome with pity for her—and something else—not desire, for she was not desirable to him now, but an absurd wish that somehow her shattered life could be restored, that what had broken in her could be somehow repaired. He looked at her hand resting on the table. She had cleaned up her nails and painted them a soft pink. It seemed like it might be the start of something.

"I believe you, and you need to believe me. I want you to come out of this with everything you can reasonably squeeze out of him."

She put her left hand over his. "You were always the good knight. Always stopped before things got out of hand, no pun intended. Meanwhile, I went after the prettiest face and the hottest car. What an idiot."

"I didn't turn out so great either. Like I said, I've had my own problems, and caused plenty of pain too."

"I don't see a wedding ring or even a mark showing it was there."

"Divorced."

"Stupid lady."

"No, it was me."

"Stupid you then. Kids?"

"A daughter. Eleven years old."

"Uh-oh. Things are about to get out of hand. You two get along?"

"Yeah, but she could have done better for a father. But I keep at it. It gives me a reason to go on when I don't want to anymore, and I hope I get a little better all the time..."

"That's what I'm hoping for too. But a long way to go."

"Back to the 'believing' thing. For you to accomplish what you want, Jerry has to believe that there's a much better than even chance that you'll live up to whatever deal is made. And Harrigan's a lawyer. Even if he doesn't much care for his client, he has a duty to look out for the client's legitimate interests, so you might be asked to do things you'd rather not."

She went rigid and her eyes hardened. "What might that be?"

"I don't know. But don't be either too greedy or too...you know the word 'punctilious?'"

"I didn't do that well in English class."

"You might want to look it up."

~

HE WALKED HER to her car and gave her enough cash for several tanks of gas. She took it without resistance, just a "thank you," then said, "How long will it be? I'm not letting him get through that mayor race without having to deal with this."

"I'll stress the urgency."

"And that other thing I said...as you were leaving my place the other day, about there being something worse...did you tell him that?"

He hesitated, considering for a moment whether the truth was the right thing to provide here. "I did. Not only was it my duty to tell him, I thought you wanted me to. I thought that was your point. To raise the stakes."

"Well, I wish you wouldn't have, and I wish I wouldn't have said it to you."

"What is it?"

"Nothing. Just me trying too hard."

"I'm guessing you're saving something for a last round of negotiations."

She shook her head vigorously and desperately. "That's not it, I swear."

"Whatever you say. It's your game to play."

"Just please tell him you probed, and…"

"But I didn't…probe, that is."

She shook her head at him, irritated by his own "punctiliousness." "Then just tell him I denied it, that I admitted I was just bluffing."

"Okay. I can do that."

"Good. I'll be waiting by the phone for your call. Just like a high school girl on a Friday night. Is that sound I hear a tree falling in the forest?"

~

O'KEEFE WASTED no time in reporting to Harrigan, who immediately passed the word to Jensen, who asked them to meet him at his office on the following Saturday.

"What was his reaction?" O'Keefe asked Harrigan.

"Nothing. Very clipped. Very abrupt. He just said, 'Let's meet, and if you've got a plan, Mike, it'll be time to hear it.'"

"Saturday? That's a long time away for someone who ought to be really impatient."

"And at his office. Maybe because no one's around then. Maybe because we're his little secret from the rest of the world."

CHAPTER ▶ 8

THE BUILDING THAT housed JJ Enterprises was owned by one of Jerry Jensen's many companies, each of which owned only a single asset in order to shield each one from the others' liabilities and potential failure. Nothing spectacular about the place, located in a fading suburb—drab, entirely utilitarian, purely functional, no personality at all—until they reached the third floor, the top floor, which housed the inner sanctum of the JJ empire. Understated elegance, portrayed subtly by the plushness of the carpet, the black walnut furniture, the shiny brass accessories. Jerry had greeted them at the front door of the building and escorted them upstairs. There didn't seem to be anyone else in the building. He seemed light-hearted, considering the circumstances. He was dressed for the golf course.

"Thanks for coming, guys. I appreciate that I didn't have to go clear downtown. I'll have to put up with that too damn much when I'm mayor."

As they followed him from the elevator into his personal office, he said, "It's not quite as fancy as your place, Mike, but this has been JJ Enterprises since my dad started it, and he pounded it through my head never to show off."

Jerry was a "clean desk" man all the way, the only items on it a decorative lamp, an ivory-handled letter opener, a sleek multi-line telephone, and a small stack of papers held fast by a brass paperweight that looked as if they never had been and never would actually be read or otherwise disturbed in any way. With a gesture, Jerry directed them toward a shiny round conference table with room for only four chairs, suggesting intimacy. One of the chairs, to O'Keefe's surprise, was already occupied by the thinnest of men, with a rooster's comb of blond hair standing straight up from his scalp and a smile more sinister than welcoming.

"You guys know David Bowman?"

O'Keefe, and apparently Harrigan too, were both at a momentary loss for spoken words because David Bowman was plenty well-known in the part of town that O'Keefe and Harrigan had grown up in. Mercifully, neither had actually suffered the displeasure of any intimate dealings with him, although he had menaced them and countless other weaklings on various occasions in various venues, if not up close and personal, then at a distance, by his very presence. The first words that came to O'Keefe's mind were "by notoriety damn sure," but that didn't seem like the right thing to say. Harrigan rescued them both from a stupefied, embarrassed silence with a "No, we've never met," which contained an implied acknowledgment, without having to come right out and say so, that Harrigan did indeed know Bowman "by reputation."

The guy had seemingly emerged from the womb a vicious hoodlum. He was shaking down kids on the playground by third grade and brandished a steak knife at his fourth grade teacher, Sister Josephine, when she tried to mete out minor punishment for one of the multitude of infractions he unfailingly committed every day. Then he flunked the fifth grade and was held back a year. The final straw, as far as St. Jude's was concerned, occurred in the winter of that repeated fifth grade year when he was banished to the cloak room for some offense and expressed his protest at such treatment by throwing some of the girls' coats on the floor and pissing on them.

When St. Jude's threw him out, the public school had to take him. He soon graduated to switchblades and brass knuckles. Although he served one stint in reform school, he later managed to dodge recondite punishment for his long list of offenses because his family enjoyed local political and law enforcement connections that protected him most of the time. Right now he just sat there, hostile and arrogant, fully aware that Harrigan and O'Keefe knew exactly who he was. He knew that when they were kids, he had likely at least threatened, if not physically attacked them, at one time or another. And now he would have yet another opportunity to instill fear in their excessively palpitating hearts.

"David is doing some security work for me," Jerry said.

At that one, O'Keefe was just glad he did not have a mouthful of coffee because it would have exploded out of him and sprayed all over his table companions. If David Bowman was involved, nothing was secure other than Bowman himself.

After the introduction, Jensen revealed no interest in one word of small talk. Addressing O'Keefe, he said, "Mike tells me—"

Harrigan interrupted. "Before this goes any further, Jerry, you need to know that nothing said in here, including by me or to me or to Pete, in front of Mr. Bowman is likely to be privileged."

"I'm not worried about it," Jensen said. "He's my employee. Right, David? As of now."

"I have a notoriously bad memory anyway," Bowman said. "Near premature fucking senility actually."

"So, Pete," Jensen said, "you believe that no one but her knows?"

"I do."

"Well, I don't," Jensen responded. "I think something, maybe old romantic twinges, like a phantom limb or something, are zapping out your lie detector signal."

O'Keefe, taken aback, thought it best not to respond. He wondered if the conversation had just ended as soon as it had begun.

"What do you think, David?" Jensen asked his security advisor.

"No way she hasn't told someone," Bowman said, staring contemptuously at O'Keefe.

A CPTSD flashback seized O'Keefe. He was again in the helicopter above the jungle, his finger on the trigger of his machine gun. But he kept his temper under control, with difficulty. This wasn't the playground anymore. Bowman probably didn't know he was talking to a guy with a knife strapped to his lower leg.

"Why are you so sure?" O'Keefe said evenly, as if he was actually interested in the answer to his question.

"Because I know human nature."

"Well, this human is a little different," O'Keefe said. "She's fresh out of about her fifth rehab, hasn't even begun to recover from her husband's recent suicide, feels like she committed even a worse crime than Jerry did..."

"'Jerry' did no crime, Pete," Jerry said.

"Sorry...alleged crime...She feels like she committed an even worse crime than the one she alleges Jerry did...and she's, through and through, about as down and out as a person could possibly be. I'm not sure regular human nature is at work there."

"Hey, Jerry," Bowman said, "you hear what I hear? I think it's that phantom limb talking."

Jensen interrupted, "All those rehabs. All that group therapy shit. They confess every damn thing in those."

"All I can say is that I disagree," O'Keefe said.

"That's issue number one," Jerry went on. "Second issue: Mike, how do I keep her from milking me the rest of my life?"

"As I said before—difficult. As I also said before, hook her with periodic payments at the beginning but put the big money at the back of the deal, out in the future. Plus, obviously get her to sign a full release...but more than that, an affidavit that says she lied about the rape, that it never happened, and that she has no other negative information about you."

"How about saying she never told me she was pregnant, just blamed it on Tim and went on weaving her web around him?"

"I can't do that, Jerry, because that would be suborning perjury since you admitted to me she did confront you with it," Harrigan said.

Bowman emitted a snort of contempt, apparently at the idea that perjury or the subornation thereof was any kind of problem.

Harrigan continued. "There's another piece of bad news here. What I'm suggesting will never hold up unless she has a lawyer. We can get her one that won't be overly fussy, but there's a risk to that, obviously."

"I would say that's the understatement of the century so far," said Jensen. "Another person to worry about not keeping his mouth shut? Is that it, guys? That's all you've got for me?"

Harrigan did not try to explain or save the situation. He just looked hard at Jensen and said with steel in his voice, "That's all there is. Nothing else."

"Guys, please excuse us for a minute. David, let's talk."

After Jensen and Bowman left the room, Harrigan said in disgust, "Can you believe this shit? David Fucking Bowman!"

O'Keefe, though pleased with Harrigan's reaction, quickly shushed him and gestured toward the ceiling and around the room, pointing to his ears and making a zipping motion across his lips and indicating to Harrigan to do the same. They kept silent after that for the few minutes until the two men returned.

Jensen sat back down at the conference table while Bowman irritatingly remained standing with his hands gripping and his body leaning on the chair he had been sitting in, effectively announcing that "this meeting is over already."

"So here it is, guys," Jensen said. "We're calling the cunt's bluff. Once she realizes what she's up against, she'll back off, just like she did seventeen years ago. And even if she does try to make a stink, nobody'll listen. And even if it turns out that somebody'll listen, I can get past an ancient tale from a junkie whore who admits she lied to her son and her husband for seventeen years. If she lied to her husband and son, for Christ's sake, about something that important, sacred even, how can you believe her about anything else?"

"Who's gonna tell her this?" O'Keefe asked.

"Well, not you, for sure," Bowman said. "That phantom limb might get in the way of proper delivery of the message."

"If you mention that appendage one more time, you might just experience my phantom limb squeezing your actual fucking voice box."

O'Keefe waited for Bowman to come at him, but Jensen quickly intervened. "Okay, guys, let's cool it. I started that, Pete, and I'm sorry. I was probably right to hire you to do what you've done, take advantage of the 'old friends' thing, make a soft approach to get the most out of her, but now it's a different sort of task. David will handle it from here."

Recalling Sara's comment that night of the girl's rescue about why he should "love this work," he thought, *And this, Sara, is why I don't love this work.*

In master politico persona Jensen continued, "I've got no quarrel with what you guys did. You did as well as could be expected. You obtained valuable information. I'm happy to pay you. Take it out of the retainer and send me a check if there's any left."

"When do you intend to tell her?" O'Keefe asked.

Bowman responded. "That's not your concern. We'll decide that."

"If she doesn't hear soon, she might call me. What do I tell her?"

Bowman, who seemed to have taken control, answered. "Avoid her as long as you can. If you have to talk to her, tell her you gave your report and that Mr. Jensen is considering what to do."

"Well then, I guess that's all you need from me," O'Keefe said, abruptly standing up to go.

"Thanks, guys," Jensen rushed to say, trying to straighten something that seemed to have gone too far sideways. "You did a good job. It'll work out in the end, I promise. You'll be working for the next mayor before long."

Harrigan and O'Keefe took a grim silent ride down in the elevator, O'Keefe looking around for any tell-tale signs of an eavesdropping device. Once they achieved the privacy of the parking lot, Harrigan said, "I guess that explains the Saturday meeting with not another soul around. What the fuck just happened in there? What a shit-show. Has he lost his mind, bringing Bowman, of all people, in on this?"

"Actually, I think they're two peas in a pod. Jerry's found his soul mate...I don't know what to do now."

"There's nothing to do now."

"I don't know how she'll take this. She's a damn fragile woman. She may go off the deep end."

"That's her business now...and theirs. We tried to help. It didn't work. We're done."

"I'm not so sure."

"Shit, be careful, man. He is, or was, a client. You owe him some duties."

CHAPTER ▸ 9

OVER THE NEXT few days O'Keefe squirmed on the horns of the dilemma that had been forced on him. He supposed he owed a professional duty to his client to follow instructions that did not violate the law, especially something as simple as an instruction not to further communicate with the target of an investigation. Their suspicion that he might not be the best one to deliver the brutal "fuck you" message they had decided on was more than justified, and he could not blame them for that. It was also their perfect right to deliver the message in the manner they preferred.

But then there was the rape, a crime his client had committed. "Allegedly." Only her word on that. His belief in her by no means constituted evidence. And the statute of limitations had long since passed. Jensen could not even be prosecuted now. But did O'Keefe owe an overriding human duty to Beverly Raymond Bronson, especially since he believed every word of her story? Not really, he concluded. Would he have even felt this moral impulse if he had never known her, never seen how beautiful she once was, never kissed her, held her long hair in his hands, laid himself down gently on her softness, spent that last morning with her on her porch with the hole in her sock?

He decided the dilemma was artificial, self-created. She had "made her own bed" (he cringed inwardly at the unintentional irony of that phrase applied here) with the cover-up, the toxic lie, and her subsequent descent. He had crossed ethical and legal lines before, with tragic consequences. So he did nothing—and remained uneasy about that decision. But after only a few days the call came to him on his car phone as he headed in the van to the bank to sign the papers for the loan that Harrigan had arranged for him.

"O'Keefe?"

He could not quite recognize the voice and wondered how this person had obtained his car phone number.

"Bowman here."

He could tell from the slight echo that Bowman had called him on a speaker phone, Jensen probably sitting there listening.

"The message has been delivered. We thought you'd want to know."

"Thank you," O'Keefe blurted, surprised at Bowman's courtesy. But he had foolishly mistaken courtesy for something else. "She may contact you. If she does, we expect you to say nothing and report to us exactly what she says to you."

"I understand. May I ask how she took it?"

"Hysterically."

O'Keefe waited for more, hoping Bowman would volunteer, that he would not have to pry the conversation out of him. Thankfully, Bowman obliged. "First, she asked why you weren't the one calling her. I told her that Jerry felt you had done your job and that your services were no longer required once Jerry had made his decision. Then the bitch screamed at me: 'You tell that motherfucker Jensen I'll ruin him. And if I can't get that done, I'll hound him forever. I'll follow him everywhere. I'll personally tell his wife and kids and the whole rest of the world exactly who and what he is. And if none of that works, I'll sneak into his bedroom at night and cut his fucking vampire heart out with a sharp fucking stick.'"

Jensen's voice now: "Fortunately, we recorded that conversation, which might come in handy someday, in a court of law or the court of public opinion or whatever, especially the death threat."

O'Keefe managed to control himself, stifle the words that wanted to come rushing out of him, but he could not help making some small gesture to register his disapproval and contempt. The best he could do was to abruptly hang up the phone.

~

THE BANK OFFICER'S secretary placed him in a small conference room containing only a laminated table, a standard-issue multi-line phone, four hard plastic chairs, and a carpet so thin it might as well have been a bare concrete floor. Soon the officer arrived with a brown folder stuffed with papers, plopped the folder on the table, and held out his hand to O'Keefe, who rose halfway out of his chair to shake the man's hand.

"I'm Gordon Mason," the officer said.

"Peter O'Keefe. Nice to meet you."

"So you're a friend of Mr. Harrigan's."

"Yes. Long time."

"We very much value Mr. Harrigan's opinions around here. He's saved us a lot of money. Helping us not make mistakes, and when we inevitably do, helping us minimize our losses."

"That seems to be his mission in life."

"Well, he's doing an excellent job so far."

Mason flipped the well-stuffed folder open and a clutch of papers slipped partly out of the folder onto the table. "Everything is ready to sign, and we can start advancing as early as tomorrow. But I do have one question."

"Glad to answer."

"Your financial statement shows a significant decline in revenue and profitability in the last year or so. What's that about?"

O'Keefe had anticipated such a question, although he thought it would have been asked before now and over the phone rather than in person and at the signing. Luckily, he had rehearsed the answer repeatedly and hoped he had found the right words to put the best face on a complicated situation. For the last year he had turned down a lot of the business he had previously taken but had not yet been able to fully replace it. He had terminated one employee but kept George and Sara on and paid them the same amount plus a small cost of living increase though he really did not have the cash flow to support that. But they were too valuable, now and for the future, to risk losing, again.

"It occurred to me that the whole business world is changing. Like it or not, technology is transforming everything, and the private investigation business won't be immune. So I decided to phase out certain types of business that can't be done efficiently and that don't have the effect of creating a pipeline...a continuous flow of new or recurring work. That transformation has just begun, and I need some additional capital to get me over the hump."

"So exactly what do you see as the new, more promising lines of business?"

"As a start, and this is more of a *way* of doing business than a *line* of business—more technology, which really just means more use of computers. It'll probably revolutionize everything, like it or not. As far as lines of business—forensics, starting with forensic accounting...to detect, for example, financial fraud..."

"Interesting," Mason said. "So, for example, there might be sophisticated techniques to smoke out certain borrowers who might be manipulating their financial statements to defraud us?"

"Exactly."

Mason was waiting for more so he obliged. "And then, though this isn't a new line in the PI business, but will be new for me—security—everything from old-fashioned security guards to high-level personal security, sort of a Secret Service for celebrities and other people vulnerable to everything from kidnapping, to stalking, to just being bothered more than they like."

"That's interesting too. But not many celebrities in this town."

"Got to start somewhere."

"And these loan proceeds are to invest in these new lines?"

This could be a dangerous question, and O'Keefe realized it needed a careful answer, especially after Mason's expressed concern about borrowers misrepresenting themselves and defrauding his institution. He and Harrigan had both defended—and on the other hand, pursued and put people in jail for—false financial statements containing relatively minor puffery and omissions. The federal criminal laws were terrifyingly broad and vague, plenty of room in the language to prosecute anyone who strayed even slightly over the line. As Harrigan said, "If you don't take a lunchbox to work, there's a good chance you've committed some kind of financial crime if they want to pin it on you."

"Yes," O'Keefe answered the banker, not wanting to hesitate too long, then added what he hoped would be the saving grace someday if accused of misusing loan proceeds, "and working capital to keep me going during the transition." *And to put food in the mouths of my kid and former wife,* he thought, and wondered if someday someone would say he was himself committing fraud by not disclosing that. He would make sure that no loan proceeds went directly for that purpose.

"Well, good luck," Mason said as he gathered up the papers O'Keefe had signed. "Seems like you've got a good business head on your shoulders."

Well, that was one compliment he never expected to hear directed at him. A businessman now, for Christ's sake. George Babbitt O'Keefe. But it really was time, way past time, to grow up.

Climbing into his van in the bank's parking lot, O'Keefe had that uncomfortable physical sensation, he had felt many times, when a cocktail of hope and fear surged within him, stirring up a chemical brew—half bane, half balm—which rendered him excited but unsatisfied, somewhat of a high, but like a sugar high, always on the verge of crashing—something achieved (the money he had just borrowed) against the challenge of performance (to pay it back) and the related fear of ignominious failure. And overlaying all that like an impending doom was the tragedy, or maybe it was only a soap opera, of Beverly Raymond Bronson. He had to restrain himself from calling her until he could think it through. What duty did he owe Jerry Jensen now? Not much, he concluded, except to keep his secrets other than criminal behavior and protect Jerry's strategy for escaping the fate he deserved. Was there any reason he shouldn't seek to comfort an old friend and fellow addict as she struggled to survive? By the time he arrived at his apartment, he had decided to call her—well, *provisionally* he had so decided since his nature was to keep his options open until the last possible moment for useful decisive action.

Opening the front door of his apartment, which took up the lower floor of an early twentieth-century Victorian house in an older but gentrifying neighborhood, he disengaged the alarm, which he had installed in his place—and an even more elaborate one in in Annie and Kelly's place—after the violence of Halloween night last year and the ensuing days of gunfire and death in the Arizona desert. He wondered if he needed it now that Carmine Jagoda was dying of lung cancer in the prison hospital down state. Entering his apartment, his eyes went automatically to where they always went—to the answering machine and the light that blinked red when someone had called and left a message. He dropped his copies of the loan papers on a chair as he passed it on his way to the phone. The display indicated that only one message waited for him. He punched the "listen" button and heard Kelly describing some things going on at school.

In the middle of her message the phone itself rang. That voice that had become dry, harsh, and cracked. "Well, I got the word—'Get fucked, Bev.' Again. Over and over again. If you're not really careful, Pete, this world can become a permanent shithole."

"I don't know what to say."

"Say nothing, just listen. What I said about him doing something a lot worse than what he did to me. You remember Mary Jane Donovan?"

He remembered. The name, even almost twenty years later, still drained the spirit out of him, and surely it had the same effect on many others who had been around at the time, leaving them with a chill of horror and then a pall of sadness—for Mary Jane herself, but also for a world that her murder seemed to have brought to an irrevocable conclusion. Mary Jane Donovan was one of those sacrificial human portals through which a new manifestation of evil announced its presence in their world. After Mary Jane, the world seemed far less safe than before, and humanity far less human.

She was a schoolmate, two years younger than Pete, Harrigan, Bev, and Jerry. Pretty, rumored to be on the wild side. She sneaked out her window late one night. Nobody knew exactly why. They found her several days later in a ravine near one of the renowned make-out "parking" spots in town—beaten with fists and finished off with either a log, a board, or some other wooden item that her attacker had apparently carried away from the scene. Although the cops rousted every weirdo in town, trying desperately to pin it on someone, they never found the killer.

Bev continued. "It happened to Mary Jane on a Thursday night. I had my fateful date with Jerry on Friday, the next night. And here's the thing... the knuckles of his right hand were bruised and cut. I said, 'What happened?' He said that he got angry at something the coach said to him in practice that day... that it kept eating on him, and, like an idiot, he slammed his fist into a concrete wall. That was the night he raped me. I call it rape. I think it was, but someone might say it was more complicated than that. I did resist. Some. At first anyway. Until he grabbed me by the throat. That was all he did. He didn't say a word. He didn't have to. There was something terrifying in those eyes looking down at me. I let him in then.

"But I was crazy about him anyway, and, for all I know, I unconsciously welcomed the excuse. I had already done it with Tim. There went my virginity, which turned out to be not so much the prize they all told us it was. Later, when they found Mary Jane, and I read she had been beaten that way, and when they couldn't find the person who did it, and remembering those banged up knuckles, and experiencing what he did to me and how he treated me afterward, I started wondering if maybe Mary Jane didn't give in to the hand around her throat and paid a horrible price for it."

"But you never reported any of it to the police?"

"Not to the police or anyone else. I wasn't brave enough to try to do anything then. And the newspapers said *that she wasn't raped.* Which confused the hell out of me. What if I went to the police and they didn't believe me, or it wasn't enough to make a case? What would happen to me? What if my suspicion was wrong, and he wasn't guilty? What would people do to me? And how could I live with myself if I accused an innocent boy of something like that? And maybe I still hoped for the chance that he'd ride up on his trusty steed with a wedding ring to rescue me from what he'd done to me. But now I don't care anymore. I guess I was unconsciously giving into it when

I blurted that out to you the other night. I must have thought deep down 'what the hell, go for it, see if that shakes something out.'"

"Obviously it didn't," O'Keefe said. "I told him what you said about knowing something far worse about him, and he still didn't hesitate to tell you to go pound sand. And that's because he knows it'll never stick, Bev. They won't even investigate it."

She sobbed a great gulp of a sob. After a long pause in which she kept trying to go on, trying to catch her breath amidst the sobs, she said, "Fuck it. I covered all this up, lived a lie, ruined Tim's life, my own, my kid's. I have to try to right things. This tree's gonna fall in the forest. Maybe nobody'll hear it, but it's gonna fall."

"Don't, Bev. Forget this shit. Get sober and clean, all the way sober and clean, instead of chasing this, or at least before you start chasing this. Let's go to a meeting."

"Fuck that. He'll be mayor in a couple of months. Another triumph for the rotten bastard. I just hope you were as decent in this as I believed you were. I hope somebody in this world has some fucking decency."

That was it. Nothing after that but the click of her phone hanging up. He was grateful he only had to hear her, grateful he did not have to see again those eyes stricken with scalding pain. He tried to call her back. The phone rang and rang. He tried to hope she had fled that tin-can coffin she lived in and had taken refuge in an AA or NA meeting—anything but facing alone the yawning gulf she would now have to leap over, the odds overwhelmingly against her landing safely on the other side. Or maybe she had already scored the next dose from her fixer. Maybe she had even kept some on hand for just such an "emergency" as this one and was already shooting up. He dialed her again. No answer. He did not let it ring on. No use tormenting her with a ringing phone. It was dark outside now. He decided to try to find her, do what he could to help her.

CHAPTER ▸ 10

DESPITE HIS FEAR of what harmful thing she might be doing to herself at that moment, O'Keefe, as he had done before, proceeded slowly and deliberately up the gravel driveway that ran through this lower section of the trailer park. He did not want to run over some kid out playing or some drunk passed out in the middle of the driveway, an event that might attract an angry mob of trailer park denizens. His headlights exposed her car still parked there. What did that mean since she had not answered her phone despite his several calls? Couldn't be good. He stopped at her trailer. He dialed her again. No answer. Not a good sign, though maybe she had unplugged her phone or was just letting it ring, not having any desire to speak to anyone during this dark night of her soul. He hesitated, thought about turning back, but he had to keep going. He could never face himself if it turned out he had abandoned her at the very moment when he could have intervened, whether she wanted it or not, and given her another chance.

~

HE WAS ABOUT TO give up for the night when O'Keefe came bounding out of his apartment in what looked like full-scale panic, jumped in his van, and sped away. Good. Maybe O'Keefe would be more vulnerable, less alert than usual. Maybe this would be the chance of pulling it off without complication, a lucky opportunity that might be long in coming again. He would not do something stupid like try to kill O'Keefe in his apartment or his office or any other of the guy's normal surroundings. He did not plan to do this thing until he could arrange or encounter the right situation or circumstances, at least until Robert gave him no other choice—an ultimatum: "Do it now, no more delays."

He had a tough time following O'Keefe, and hoped if one of them was stopped for speeding, it would be the lead car rather than his trailing one. His adrenalin started pounding in him when he realized that O'Keefe could not be headed anywhere but that trailer park. Whether O'Keefe was desperate for that piece of ass or had some better motive, the guy would likely soon be all alone with her in that trailer that hunkered all by its lonesome in the back of that trailer park where none of the residents were the type to be out in the dark catching fireflies. Not often did you do the hard work of meticulous planning and preparation and actually still get the chance to take advantage of it, executing your mission under near perfect circumstances.

The first challenge would be parking the car in the right place, away from any eyes coming or leaving, then approaching the back of her trailer through that brushwood jungle without mishap. On a dirt road running alongside the train tracks, his headlights barely illuminated the patch of forested darkness, darker than the moonlit night around it. He backed the car into a bare spot between the trees and tucked it partly behind overhanging branches. It would be difficult for anyone to notice the car there even in the daytime. He guided himself through the trees, scrambled down into and back out of a dry roadside ditch, and crossed the road. There were lights on in a few houses located a few hundred yards to his right and slightly upslope down the road. The trailer park spread across the hill, rising, first gradually then sharply, in front of him to his left and right. He could see a light or two in that direction as well but nothing to be concerned about.

Only a few yards of empty field separated him from what he had come to refer to as the brushwood jungle. He was pleased with himself that he always carried with him his night vision goggles. He adjusted the goggles and darted across the field while taking care not to step in a hole and twist his ankle.

Entering the jungle, he carefully picked his way to his left, through the brush and vines and stunted trees, until only a few yards of open ground separated him from her trailer. He could see O'Keefe's van parked there. Over his head he pulled a black stocking hat, holes carefully cut out to fit his eyes and mouth. From the elastic belt he wore across his chest like a bandoleer, he extracted a huge hunting knife he used to gut deer he had slain. Although right handed, he had taught himself to handle a pistol deftly with his left. With the knife in his right hand and a silencer-equipped pistol in his left, he cantered toward the front door of the trailer.

He planned to give the door latch a slow, quiet turn. If it was locked, he would just wait there until O'Keefe opened the door to leave, and then would slash O'Keefe's throat or plunge the knife into his heart in one quick stroke or thrust, then rush in and dispose of her. If it was not locked, he would have to burst in and do the work quickly because they might be in the front part of the trailer and see or hear the latch move on their side. He considered just waiting. That would be the least risky alternative, but he had learned that waiting just increased the chance of some third force or party intervening and conditions changing in a way not likely to favor him.

He slowly turned the latch. No resistance. But just as he was about to jerk the latch fully open, he heard a siren. Multiple sirens. Down on the road. A whole caravan. A fire truck, ambulance, and two police cars came speeding up the road he had crossed to get here. They turned right and seemed to be heading straight for this dump of a trailer park and would be blasting in here any second. Then he heard a heavy sound of movement inside the trailer. Startled, he lost his footing and fell backward off the little staircase that gave entry to the elevated trailer door. The door seemed to open, but he had scrambled up and was headed for the jungle before he could see anything else.

He ran hard until he reached the edge of the jungle, entered carefully until concealed, then looked back toward the trailer. A few moments later he could see through his goggles O'Keefe carefully come around to the side of the trailer and look toward the jungle, straight at him crouched there. He was sure he was invisible in the darkness. The approaching sirens indicated that something bad had happened in that trailer park. Then the ambulance and police car arrived at her trailer. The EMTs and police busied themselves with O'Keefe and whatever had happened inside that trailer. It wouldn't be long before at least a small crowd would gather. People might even migrate down to the scene from the upper portion of the park, behind and above him, on the other side of the jungle. Someone could stumble upon him there.

He moved swiftly and quietly deeper into the jungle and back out again and across the field, watching carefully for the possibility of another police car trailing in as backup. Lights had come on in one or two of the houses to his left. People might be wandering down toward the trailer park to see what had attracted all the commotion and might encounter him. But he crossed the road and the ditch without incident and found his way to his car. Time for a critical decision, maybe one of the most important of his life—should he get in the car and get out of there now or wait until the situation had settled down? He did not want to risk running into that possibly lagging backup police car on its way in, or the ambulance or police car going out, or some rubbernecker walking up the road to ogle the scene. But he also did not want to linger too long since daylight might expose his presence to a night owl or an early bird or just someone unable to go back to sleep after all the excitement.

~

O'KEEFE HAD KNOCKED on her door several times. No answer. He turned the latch. Unlocked. He had not armed himself. He could go back to the van and dig out one of the pistols or even the M-16. But surely there was no danger. Unless she had a gun in there for protection. That would not be unthinkable considering the person she had become.

"Bev!" he yelled. "It's Pete. You there? I'm coming in." And he kept saying "Bev?" as he entered the trailer, seeing nothing in the little front space with the photos of the son and those others turned face down. He said it again in the tiny kitchen where he had sat talking with her, and again as he moved cautiously through the narrow hallway past the empty bathroom stall toward a dim light in the sleeping compartment. His final "Bev" was a choked whisper, more of anguish than of call or warning.

She was sprawled out on the rumpled bed, clad only in panties, a spoon and an empty baggy next to her, a hypodermic needle protruding from the crook of her left arm. He knelt down to help her somehow if he could, but he knew immediately that she was beyond his aid. Still, he called 911 in case he was mistaken and something could be done. The police would arrive along with or soon after the ambulance. They would probably immediately suspect him of being her dealer or a fellow user. He tried to stay calm, to just carefully observe the scene, touch nothing, not even her, though he had to mightily resist the urge to sit down there and put his hand chastely on her cold flesh in a useless act of solidarity.

She had seemed more determined to stay clean than this scene evidenced. Most of all she seemed determined to do everything possible to bring Jensen down. Would she have given up so easily? But maybe she had meant only to drift a little, ease the pain a little. He could understand that thinking, foolish as he knew it to be. It seemed odd that the needle remained in her arm. He knew that sometimes even an experienced heroin user gets surprised by an especially pure and powerful dose, but could it be so powerful she did not even have time to remove the needle before the drug overwhelmed her?

He moved back through the tiny hallway to the front room. Nothing out of place. Too much that way? He returned to the bedroom and stared at her until it brought him to the edge of despair, which he overcame with anger—anger at all the bad luck, crimes, and mistakes, including her own, that had brought her to this fate. Tim, the pimp. Jerry, the rapist. Why did these men think they had the right? He thought of Kelly and how he must do everything he could to protect her from such an ending, not even the death so much as the suffering that had led to it. After he could no longer bear looking at her, he returned to the kitchen and stood there, wishing he could accomplish something other than just keep from fouling up the scene while he waited for the cops.

Then he heard two things at once—first a siren in the distance, then, barely above the sound of the siren growing louder as it came closer, a clicking sort of sound. Then a moment of silence. Then a thump. The thump seemed to come from outside the trailer's entry door. He cocked his head toward the door. The sirens kept growing louder, but he thought he heard something else. Maybe running footsteps? He moved to the door, opened it carefully.

No one there.

He moved quickly down the three steps of the stairway that led to the trailer door. Nobody there. He moved to the end of the trailer, then around to its butt end and stared into the tangled thicket of darkness behind it. Nothing.

The sirens were entering the park now, and the headlights of the ambulance and police cars spotlighted him in their glare. He resisted the impulse to flee.

The ambulance driver and the EMT leaped out.

"Where?" the EMT said.

"In the bedroom, all the way back. But she's gone."

The police car behind the ambulance skidded to a stop. O'Keefe saw lights blink on in various trailers. Doors began squeaking open. Muffled talking sounds. The two patrolmen, one on the elderly side, the other much younger, approached him with attitudes of squint-eyed skepticism.

"Go see what's up in there," the older one said to the younger one who hustled up the stairway and into the trailer.

"And you are?" the older cop asked O'Keefe.

"A friend."

"Name?"

"Peter O'Keefe."

"You were with her?"

"Not *with* her. I found her."

"That your van?"

"Yes."

"Doesn't seem to go with the place."

"We go...went...way back. I was trying to help her."

"When we check you out, will we find out you were her pusher?"

"If I was that, why would I have reported it? Why would I have stuck around? No. Just a friend. Trying to help her."

He did not want to identify himself as a private detective, at least not right then, which would create the implication he was there on detective business, which would lead to questions such as who he was working for.

The young cop came to the trailer door. He shook his head. "Dead. Overdose. Nothing to be done."

"Secure the scene," the older cop ordered.

"Did you do anything in there? Disturb anything?"

"Nothing."

"Do you mind if we search you, check your van?"

"I do."

"That doesn't speak so well for you. Something to hide?"

The weapons. Not all of them legal.

"When you check me out, you'll find I'm clean. Like I said, just a friend."

"We'll check you out and get a search warrant too."

It was getting complicated, not telling them he was a private detective, failing to mention his friends in the police department, but he still thought it best not to open that can of worms unless he absolutely had to. "All right. Go ahead and search, but you're wasting your time."

"I'll be the judge of that. You some kind of smart-ass?"

"Sorry. Really. I'm sorry. I'm shell-shocked. We went way back. I was hoping she could kick it. You'll find she's got a history."

"Any idea where she might have gotten the stuff? Be nice to put someone away for this."

"No clue."

They put her in the back of the ambulance. The older cop took down O'Keefe's driver's license and car registration information, said "stay here, please" to O'Keefe and "everybody stay back" to the park residents who had begun to crowd around and ask questions, then climbed into the trailer. O'Keefe studied the faces in the crowd in case he needed to come back and talk to someone, though he doubted he would have a reason to do that, and certainly he would not want to do that unless he absolutely had to.

"Is she dead in there?" asked a runt of a man standing in front of the rest of the small gathering. He was nearly bald and cursed with huge ears that protruded from his head like handles. Surely they called him Dumbo as a kid.

"Yes, sir," O'Keefe answered.

"Dope, I bet."

"Looks like it."

"Who are you?"

"Old friend of hers. Did you know her?"

"Not well," the little man said, craning his neck to watch. "Just saw her and her husband around. You could tell what they were up to. Bad killer shit. First him, now her."

"You live here, I guess?"

"Yes."

"Little Dumbo," as O'Keefe had silently named him, reached out his hand for a shake. Despite thinking it was an incongruous thing to do at such a time and in such a place and situation, O'Keefe shook the hand and mumbled "nice to meet you."

The young cop came out of the trailer and stood slightly in front of O'Keefe, inserting himself between O'Keefe and the crowd. From behind the crowd, toward the park entrance, came the sound of quick siren bursts, as if the siren operator was trying to politely create minimal disturbance, modestly warning of his incoming presence. O'Keefe lifted his gaze and Little Dumbo turned around to watch an unmarked car, a blue light flashing on its roof, drive up the gravel road toward them. The car stopped, and a man wearing a suit coat over a casual shirt made his way through the gauntlet of spectators, brandishing in his hand what O'Keefe guessed must be a badge, and saying, not loudly but with authority, "Police. Make way please."

When he reached the spot where O'Keefe and the younger cop stood, addressing the younger cop, the man said, "Lieutenant Ross. I was on the freeway and heard the reports on this. Thought I'd see if I could help. Who else is here?"

"Officer Nystrom's inside," the younger cop said.

"No detectives here yet?"

The patrolman shook his head.

"Any coming that you know about?"

"I don't think so."

With a gesture of his head toward O'Keefe, Ross said, "Who's this?"

"He found her."

"What's your name?"

"Peter O'Keefe."

"I'm going in," Ross said to the patrolman. "Keep him here. And move all these people out of here. They've got no business here. Crowds brew trouble."

The patrolman immediately set to shooing away the bystanders.

"Hey," O'Keefe said to Little Dumbo, "can we talk more sometime?"

"Sure. I like to talk."

"Which..." He stopped in mid-question. He did not want to say "trailer."

"Home," Little Dumbo said, filling in the blank. "Number Seven. My lucky number."

Soon after Ross went in, the older patrolman came out and joined the younger one and O'Keefe for a threesome.

"We're about done," the older one said to the younger one.

"Why is Ross here?" the younger one asked.

"Driving down the highway close to here when he heard the report. I've heard he's the super gung ho type. Always on duty. Ambitious. Butts in wherever he can."

O'Keefe decided to go fishing. "Does it look like it could be anything other than an overdose?"

"Ask Lieutenant Ross that," the older patrolman said, making a zipping motion across his lips.

As if on cue, Ross exited the trailer. "Secure it," he instructed the patrolmen who moved off in obedience.

"Does that mean it's a crime scene?" O'Keefe said.

"Not unless you did it and covered your tracks pretty well."

O'Keefe could not think of an appropriate response to that. It did not seem like an occasion for witticisms.

"I know your name but nothing else," Ross said. "What do you do, Mr. O'Keefe?"

No way to evade that one. "Private investigator. Sam Morrison knows me. He'll vouch for me."

"So what's a private investigator doing in a place like this and at a time like this? And how did he get in there to discover the body?"

He wanted to avoid the delicate issue of why he was really there, and who he was working for. He found a way to tell a truth that was actually a lie. "She and I went to high school together."

"Romantic?"

"A couple of dates. Nothing serious." *At least not for her.* He would try to skip over how they had become reacquainted and move past that as fast as he could. "I was trying to help her stay off the stuff. She'd been clean for a while. I called her a couple of times tonight to check on her. No answer. I got worried and came here. I knocked.

No answer. I yelled for her. No answer. I tried the door. It was open. I went in."

"Possibly a crime right there," Ross said.

O'Keefe ignored that one. "I found her and called 911," he said.

"Did you try to resuscitate?"

"No. She was obviously gone."

"So we won't find any evidence of you on her? Or *in* her?"

"None."

"Okay. Sounds legit. I may want to talk to you some more, but right now it looks like there's no reason. Looks like the only crime here was her possession and use of an illegal drug. And your possibly unlawful entry. But I do intend to ignore that."

He resisted saying thanks, didn't think he owed Ross that.

"Will there be an autopsy?"

"I'm not sure. Sounds like you suspect something. So I'll ask you the same thing you asked me. Do you think there was something more complicated here?"

"Not really. It would be nice to know for sure though."

"What makes you not sure?"

"Nothing really. It's just that she'd been clean for a while and seemed determined to stay that way this time."

"Well, we'll want to make sure we know exactly what killed her, so there'll definitely be an autopsy."

"Good."

"So you can go now," Ross said, which was more of an order than a permission.

CHAPTER ▶ 11

SITTING IN THE last pew at the rear of the church, O'Keefe listened to the priest try to maneuver around the delicate issue of how she had come to be dead at so young an age. Later, he listened, with grim satisfaction, to the choir sing the *Dies Irae: "Dies irae, dies illa, solvet saeclum in favilla."* Someone had realized that, despite the Church's move to the vernacular in its services, Latin was the only way this great ancient funeral dirge should properly be sung. The opening words matched his own mood and thoughts that morning, "Day of wrath, that day, shall consume the world in ashes."

When Bev's mother called him to ask him to help carry the coffin, she said she knew that he had been trying to help Bev because Bev, who did keep in touch despite everything that had happened to her, had told her mother so. "She seemed so..." The woman hesitated, groping for the right word..."not 'proud'...I guess I would say 'satisfied'...about it...almost like an old beau had come back to court her."

"It wasn't that," he rushed to say.

"Oh, I know, and I don't mean that she said that or meant it, but she had that excited lift in her voice when she talked about you. She had a lot of respect for you. Always did, as I remember. Spoke fondly of you."

That respect didn't do either of us much good. Love, or at least infatuation, would have worked a lot better.

The mother's voice choked then, but she pressed on. "She seemed so hopeful and determined this time."

"I'm sorry I couldn't do more."

"No. No blame on you. Everyone tried." She looked off into the distance as if there might be an answer far out there somewhere. "Maybe it was a mercy."

A surprisingly large number of people attended the ceremony, many likely just drawn there by the macabre scandal, more an expression of *Schadenfreude* than mourning. He recognized many of them, though he had drifted away over the years from the old neighborhood and this whole part of town and the people there, not with fully conscious intent, but a distancing all the same. He would need to be present at the cemetery, but he would try to leave as fast as he could, mumbling some work-related excuse, avoiding, as much as possible, the post-burial chatting and exchange of somber pleasantries and awkward reminiscences. He looked around and noted that no one from Tim's side of the family attended. Just as she blamed Tim for their downfall, his family blamed her and wished only riddance to her memory.

After the ceremony, the pallbearers gathered. One of them wore the uniform of the United States Marine Corps. Daniel. Her son. Jerry's son. When the pallbearers introduced themselves, the young man drew O'Keefe aside and, in a low-voiced, conspiratorial tone, said, "I hear you found her. Can we talk later?"

"Sure," O'Keefe said, not meaning it, caught by surprise again, not knowing how to say no. Everything seemed to be drawing him to the remaining broken fragments of her shattered world, now that it was too late to glue it all back together.

THE NEXT MORNING, after a quick knock and without waiting for him to answer, Sara came into his office with a secretive look and closed the door behind her.

"Guess who's in the waiting room," she said.

He indicated with a small upward jerk of his head that she should just tell him without requiring him to guess.

"Daniel Bronson. Just showed up out of the blue. Says you told him to come see you."

"I told him I'd meet with him. Guess he doesn't quite know what 'appointment' means. Send him in."

Sara opened the door for the young man, let him in, and quickly and gently closed the door behind her.

"Have a seat." O'Keefe said, gesturing toward a guest chair in front of his desk.

Daniel both walked and sat down in an angry slouch.

"Daniel or Dan?"

"Most people call me Danny, but I like Dan better."

"I understand. They used to call me 'Petey' until I made them stop. It's Pete. Not 'Mr. O'Keefe,' not 'Sir.' Okay?"

"Okay."

"When do you go back?"

"Tomorrow. If I go back."

"*If*?"

Dan responded with a sullen shrug. O'Keefe remembered how badly and how often in boot camp he wanted to "go over the wall" as they called it. He also remembered the military police marching captured AWOL soldiers through the camp to the brig, O'Keefe and the other recruits shuddering mentally if not physically as they watched the spectacle. O'Keefe guessed that they deliberately staged that scene to instill fear in the so-far law-abiding soldiers, confirming in them the resolution never to put themselves in a position to have to take that same walk.

O'Keefe did not know how to talk to a young man who had lost both parents within just a few months' span to heroin addiction—at least one of them to deliberate suicide, another to what appeared to be reckless, if not actually deliberate, self-immolation—a lost, abandoned boy, forced into the military to avoid jail and now on the verge of sliding even farther and far faster down the slippery slope toward total ruin.

"Can I buy you lunch?"

"I guess."

"Do you like hamburgers...cheeseburgers?"

Dan's head bobbed with an observable thrust of enthusiasm.

"You know, when I got my first weekend leave out of boot camp," O'Keefe said, hoping to establish a bond, "I didn't want to drink a beer, kiss a girl, any of that. I just wanted a *cheeseburger* more than anything in the world. There's a place right down the street that has some of the best in town."

"You were in the Army?" Dan asked, with a minute uptake of eagerness in his voice.

"Marines."

"Even worse."

"Yep. But I'm evidence you can survive it."

On the way out he said to Sara. "We'll be at Harvey's."

He could see her slight but noticeable tic of concern because that had been a favorite watering hole of his in the days before he had vowed to give up drinking. He still frequented the place. Too much, she thought.

"Just *lunch*," he said, aware of her concern. "Back soon."

O'Keefe had been a regular at Harvey's Bar & Grill from the first week after he reached the legal drinking age. He never tired of it, it always felt to him like the friendliest possible lair—dark wooden bar and walls, plank floors sprinkled with sawdust, a few large, but not overwhelming TVs sprinkled strategically around the front room; in the back room a jukebox and a small raised platform for occasional live music, comedy, or even poetry (left over from Harvey's beatnik coffee house period). Good sandwiches and other "bar" food, beer by the pitcher as well as bottle or glass, and a shuffleboard machine in one of the nooks, a game at which O'Keefe excelled when drink had numbed his nerves somewhat, but, to his chagrin, not so much when he was sober. Once they had seated themselves at a table in the always less-populated back room, O'Keefe ordered an iced tea, cheeseburger, and fries. Dan ordered a beer, cheeseburger, and a "50-50," Harvey's mixture of fries and onion rings.

"Cool place," the boy said. "So you went to school with her?"

"Yeah. High school. Same grade. I knew your dad too." *Yes, I knew both of your fathers.*

"What were they like?"

"'Your Daddy was rich and your Mama good lookin.' You know that song?"

Clearly Dan didn't know the song as he only stared back cluelessly.

"Your Mom was beautiful. Truly beautiful. And your Dad was handsome too, and pretty well off. At least his parents were."

"Not much good it did them, huh? What fuck-ups. I hate them." He said this with a brutal matter-of-factness, no doubt, hesitation, or emotion, even self-pity, in his tone.

"Life is hard. Sometimes people just get lost. They fall off the end of the world."

"Or jump off."

"It sounds like you're thinking about doing some jumping off yourself."

"You mean not going back?"

"Yeah. Really bad move that would be."

Dan lapsed into that sullen shrug again as O'Keefe continued, "That would be one of those life-altering things…a 'jumping off the world moment.' It could ruin you permanently. You'll have dug yourself a hole that'll be hard to ever climb back out of."

"I'm already ruined."

O'Keefe knew that a "you have everything to live for" pep talk would be useless, maybe worse. "All I can give you is that I had a weak, pathetic, drunken mother, a missing father, an evil stepfather, no college degree, and an addiction to drugs and alcohol. But here I am. Not exactly 'Mr. Wonderful' or anything…but good enough for now and with a chance at getting better all the time."

"Pretty interesting job you've got, huh?"

O'Keefe knew it was not the time for an answer describing the complex mixture of emotions that his work instilled in him. It was time to be positive without being a goofy Pollyanna even if a white lie or two had to be told. "Very," he said.

After lunch, as they walked back up the street toward the office, O'Keefe said, "Go back. Go back on time. Send me a card or write me a letter as soon as you can. I'll write you back. I remember how great it was to get letters when I was in what I thought was hell on earth. Lifelines they were. Literally. We'll stay in touch. You've only got a little more than a year now. No use screwing up the rest of a damn long life for a short period of time like that. Maybe I can help you out someday. Maybe not. But I'll at least try. You're not alone."

"Why would you care about me?"

"Some because I cared about your mother, and she cared about you, she really did. You need to believe that because it's true, and she deserved to leave a better legacy than she was able to. And some because you've had a rotten deal but still seem like a salvageable person who doesn't have to fuck his life up like you're thinking about doing."

The young man made no express commitment not to go AWOL but reached out his hand to shake O'Keefe's and said, "I'll write you," which seemed like it carried with it a broader affirmation.

LIEUTENANT ROSS called later the same day. "Say, I need to complete your interview. And the autopsy report's just in. You can have a look, along with the police report. Kill two birds with one stone, so to speak, no pun intended. Can you come tomorrow?"

The next day Ross met O'Keefe in the station waiting area, led him into a small office, and gestured toward a straight metal chair with a worn padded green vinyl seat on the visitor side of a small but uncluttered desk, containing only a coffee cup, a pen, a writing pad, a pair of reading glasses, and a small neatly stacked pile of papers near Ross's left hand. The office, and Ross himself—starched white shirt, expertly knotted tie, shiny belt buckle—presented in perfect order, squared away in a very military sense.

"You check out *fairly* well," Ross said. "Our guys say neutral to good things about you though there's a sheriff down in the southern part of the state that doesn't sing your praises...and then there's that...let's call him That Special Someone...that took a few shots at you last Halloween."

"All true."

"Ugly thing going after you when your daughter was with you."

"Very ugly."

"By the way, the word on the street is that he went ballistic when he found out they did that."

"I wouldn't give him any prizes for that. You unleash something like that you're responsible for the consequences."

"And how's your recovery from that shootout in the desert?"

"Goin' fine. Just random jabs of pain every once in a while." *More mental jabs than physical ones.*

"Any more encounters with That Special Someone or his people?"

"None."

"You know he just died down there in prison?"

"A beautiful lady told me once that 'Mr. Canada,' a code name for him back then, 'lives forever.'"

"The lady out there in Arizona?"

"Yes, sir." O'Keefe wanted badly to change the subject. "Were you in the service?" he said, lifting his eyes and head quickly up and around the office in an explanatory gesture.

"That obvious, huh? Yes. Navy. Four years. Shore patrol. That's how I got into law enforcement."

"Good for you," O'Keefe said.

"And I know you were a Marine," Ross said.

"'Fraid so."

"Didn't like it?"

"Hated every minute of it."

"Even when they weren't shooting at you?"

"Especially then."

Ross laughed as O'Keefe finished his thought: "Then they had nothing to do but torment *us* instead of the enemy."

"I missed 'Nam by just a year."

"Lucky you."

"I wonder if that's true. Nothing ventured, nothing gained."

"Nothing was gained."

Ross seemed to recognize that as a subject changer. He administered a couple of quick left-handed pats to the small pile of papers in front of him. "Here's copies of the autopsy report and the police report. But I don't think you'll see anything in either of them. Maybe you'll tell me something that makes a difference, but right now it seems pretty straightforward. Medical examiner concludes 'Undetermined—Accident versus Suicide.'"

"Not sure exactly what that means."

"It's a punt. He can't quite figure out whether she intended to kill herself or not."

"But not homicide?"

"There you go again. You cast suspicion on yourself that way. Who else do you think might have done this?"

This was running in a dangerous direction. He could find himself between the Ross rock and the Jensen hard place. But, at least for now, lies must be told, secrets kept. "I don't know. It's just that she seemed so determined to kick it this time."

"Junkie delusions maybe?"

"How about her supplier?"

"Well, that's interesting, because the one thing that stands out in the autopsy report is that the heroin she used was especially strong, not the normal street stuff."

Anger flared in O'Keefe, which, in O'Keefe, could quickly erupt into violence. He tried not to show it. "Any idea who he was?"

"None. And with that medical examiner conclusion my superiors won't want me to waste my time or any resources to investigate further...And you?"

"I doubt it. I have to make a living and nobody'd be paying me."

"Sometimes I wonder how many murders don't get solved because of that. Lack of resources....nobody paid to look."

Both sat quietly for a few awkward moments reflecting on Ross's question until Ross resumed. "Sorry to keep at it, but I need to confirm a couple of things. You went to high school together, you said?"

"Yes. Bishop Dolan."

Ross nodded his head in recognition.

"How about you? You grow up here?" O'Keefe asked.

"I did, but way across town from you guys. Grade school at St. Anthony's and high school at Christian Brothers."

"Scottish guy in Little Italy, eh?"

"Not quite. Ross was Ross-*i* at one time. Somebody back a couple of generations or so wanted to be somebody he wasn't and changed it. And we were north Italian, on the lighter complected and lighter haired side, so we manage to get away with "passing as white" when we wanted to."

"Interesting," O'Keefe said, hoping he had diverted the inquiry.

But he hadn't. "So I guess you were boyfriend-girlfriend?"

"No. A couple of dates, nothing serious." *At least on her side.*

"So what got you two back together?"

He would embed the lie in several truths. "She and her actual boyfriend had to get married. Shotgun thing. They moved away from here for a long time. They moved back recently. He killed himself not long ago. I heard she was trying to get straight. I have an addiction problem myself. Cocaine once upon a time. Mostly booze now but same problem. We're supposed to help other addicts if we can. So I reached out."

Ross seemed skeptical. "No romantic intentions? No igniting an old flame?"

He knew how to bring this to a brutal close. "Not a chance. She'd become a heroin whore. Snow White turned into the Wicked Witch." *Sorry, Bev, but I need to avoid Detective Ross's trap right now* .

"Too bad about that," Ross said. "If it means anything to you, you'll see in that report that there was no evidence she had sex with anyone recently." Then Ross looked at his watch and slid the papers across the desk, closing the interview in the same abruptly dismissive way he had ended their last encounter. "If you do find something," he said, "I'd appreciate you sharing it with me."

It was early evening but still light when O'Keefe left Detective Ross. Sara would likely be gone for the day. His office would be too empty and lonesome of a place for reading the autopsy report. He did not understand why, but he did not want to review the report at the office or home or any other place where he would be alone. A popular coffee shop in his neighborhood seemed like the right place.

"The body measures 65 inches in length and weighs 122 pounds," the report began. It noted the blonde-tinted hair that was darker "at the scalp." A scar on her lower abdomen was mentioned with no further detail provided. *Appendix or Caesarean?* O'Keefe wondered. Her brain weighed 1,540 grams. He could not help but picture it being removed to take that measurement. The weight of her gall bladder was also noted and that it "contained bile but no stones." The stomach contained approximately one cup of tomato and other vegetable liquid. The stomach also contained evidence of sleeping pill ingestion.

"The decedent" was found on her bed wearing only underpants, a needle containing heroin residue protruding from the vein in her left forearm. A ragged strip of cloth was tied around her arm above the injection site, "apparently used by the decedent as a tie-up to bring the vein more prominently to the surface." A small amount of cotton debris was found in her mouth. A spoon containing cooked heroin residue, burned matches, and tinfoil were found on the bed beside her. There was no evidence of recent sexual activity. "There is a toe tag on the left big toe bearing the name of the decedent." And, finally, "The examiner concluded that the death appeared to be an accidental or intentional heroin overdose."

He still could not believe she had intentionally overdosed. She would have left a note, told her story, done as much harm as she could to Jerry Jensen on her way out of this world. But an accidental overdose was certainly possible. It could have been that unexpected pure and powerful dose he had often heard about. But there were things in that report he did not understand and felt he needed to. He could try to interview the medical examiner, which probably would not be allowed, or find his own medical expert. But there was an especially knowledgeable expert that he most wanted to consult, and if he could find that expert somehow, he might be able to accomplish two valuable things at once—obtain useful information, and beat the living shit out of him at the same time.

CHAPTER ▶ 12

THE DAY AFTER they buried Beverly Bronson on one side of town, they buried Carmine Jagoda on another. Despite his Polish/Croatian/Jewish last name, Carmine was all Sicilian, fathered by a thug named Randazzo who died at age nineteen of a severed carotid artery caused by a slash across the throat inflicted during an explosion of street violence. His impregnated girlfriend, a runaway who had only recently embarked on an unpromising career as a street whore, was left with nothing in the world except a growing fetus and not even the means or, due to her Catholic upbringing, the mind, to obtain a back-alley abortion.

So she gave birth to Carmine and immediately dumped him at the public orphanage. He was unfortunately slow to attract adoptive parents, but finally, after too many years in the institution, a barren Jewish couple, desperate for a child, adopted him, bestowing on him their last name while leaving him his given first. Conferring their good name on him turned out to be a bad move on their part, as young Carmine set about besmirching it. Their little boy did not grow up to be a doctor, or even a dentist or a lawyer, as they had so fervently hoped. Whether due to unfortunate genes or the occasional brutality and constant lovelessness of the orphanage regime, he quickly followed on his father's stony path, serving his first stint in reform school at age thirteen for robbery at knifepoint. But even though he well knew his actual ethnicity and quickly fought his way into the local Italian street gang hierarchy, he never changed his name.

Some said he just liked the ring and rhythm of "Carmine Jagoda." Others said he liked the idea that the world, and especially the authorities, might be mystified at how a Jewish upstart had climbed so high in an organization in which the "made men" were all supposed to be Italian. Some of his criminal compatriots occasionally tried to hold it against him, and some were even brave or stupid enough to call him "Carmine the Jew," but his penchant for applying overwhelming violence to those who offended him stifled that right away. Not that he had anything against Jews—just nicknames. He admired the Jews, and even had some affection, in his limited way, for his adoptive parents, but he thought a nickname eroded his dignity, cheapened him, sapped away some of his manhood, which he would under no circumstances allow.

Columbus Gardens, the traditional Italian neighborhood, had been transformed in recent years by an influx of postwar South Vietnamese refugees and, even worse—much worse as far as the established inhabitants were concerned despite their own history of being discriminated against—a few African Americans on the outer edges. Those ethnic influxes, plus a general increase in the standard of living, had caused an outflux of many of the old-time families. But the neighborhood parish, St. Anthony's, still attracted many worshippers on Sundays and Holy Days, even including some families that had moved out of the area but still felt the magnetic pull back to the old unjustifiably romanticized community. Such emigrants, as if looking guiltily in the rearview mirror and in not-quite-conscious reparation for their abandonment of the old days and ways, were often especially generous with their financial contributions. It was especially the custom for the prominent "Outfit" criminals to be publicly prayed over at

St. Anthony's, and definitively ushered from this world at the nearby Resurrection Cemetery.

On this day St. Anthony's was stuffed to overflowing, even to the upstairs choir lofts, with everyone from Carmine's family members and criminal colleagues to several agents of local law enforcement and the FBI. Some of these spectators attended to pay respect in the old way and for the old reasons, but the majority were just typical Americans, with that special American fondness for the Outlaw—as long as they could keep a safe distance away, basking occasionally in a criminal aura without having to take any risk or pay any price.

The gawkers extracted special pleasure from watching Carmine's tiny but formidable family follow the priest and the altar boys in procession down the aisle to open the ceremony. Carmine's wife had died of pancreatic cancer some years before, so, by default, the matriarch was Rose, their daughter and only child, alone in front, followed by her husband, Robert, two steps behind with their two children, Steven, age nine and Sophia, age seven, one on each side of Robert holding his hand. Nobody else. No brothers, sisters, nieces, nephews, cousins, or in-laws, as if Carmine Jagoda had just hatched from an egg like a great bird of prey, devouring any siblings or others that had the misfortune to share the nest with him.

Since the words of the service meant nothing to Paul anymore, mumbo jumbo bullshit meant to conceal what the world is really like, he gave his thoughts over to remembering the past, analyzing the present, and wondering about the future. He was the youngest man in the second pew and placed on the aisle, privileged to be at that position because he was Robert's driver, which also meant Robert's bodyguard. A few old men and their wives filled the rest of the second pew—Carmine's inner circle, all criminals or supportive fellow-traveler financier types, including a Jewish real estate maven and an Irish banker. Behind the old guard the younger members spread out in less organized array. Out of fear of the Boss and, to a much lesser extent, the Boss's designated successor, Robert, or perhaps because their ambitions had waned along with their testosterone levels, none of the old men cared at this stage of their lives to try to succeed Carmine. Some of the younger ones might be imagining themselves in that position, but, for now anyway, they held back, unsure what unintended baleful, even fatal, consequences might ensue from a power play.

When the Boss decided not to appeal his conviction and instead just serve his time so he might get out with a few years left to enjoy his life (which, for him, simply meant the continuing exercise of power), he had left no doubt about who he wanted in charge in the interim—his son-in-law, Robert. But they all thought they saw through that. The only one in charge, even from behind bars, would be the Boss himself, and it was easier to accomplish that with his son-in-law in nominal control.

Robert was a "numbers guy" who had come up on the gambling, loan sharking, and general "white collar" side of the business. Not the rough part, the collecting part, just the "cooking up schemes" and "laundering the proceeds" part. But he proved awfully good at that. And he kept it all very much under wraps. Paul could see how smart that was, how much power Robert was building with his control of the money supply. And so far he had managed not to offend anyone and had even devised a few original and clever new initiatives that made money for a good number of the crew. Ronnie Reagan's people called this "all boats rising" or something like that. Robert's own boat lifted the most, which caused snarling envy among a few, but they missed the point. Robert's boat rose the most because Robert had been the one to make the waters rise. But any one of them could end Robert's reign with an impulsive act of irrational violence. Paul guessed that Robert being married to Rose, and the respect and fear of her father's ghost—and of Rose's own imperious presence—furnished Robert an extra level of protection. But that would only go so far. Some of these boys were real crazy motherfuckers.

An uncomfortable open question: Was Robert ruthless enough to do what had to be done in the way of discipline, which required, when necessary and sometimes just for the fuck of it, unblinking cruelty and implacable violence? This O'Keefe thing the Boss had ordered Robert to do might be a test of that. All their loyalties were based way more on greed and fear than affection of any depth. So far Robert had handled the greed part well, the fear part not so much. Paul hoped not, but there would likely be a time when he would have to either throw in his lot with Robert to protect him from others or join with others to overthrow Robert. And Rose complicated that calculus.

Paul's parents had escaped the perceived impending racial transformation of the Gardens when he was ten, moving only a couple of blocks away from the Jagodas in the suburban enclave to which many from the Gardens had emigrated. He thought he might have fallen immediately and irrevocably in love with her the first time he beheld her regally riding her bicycle down the street, no hurry, as if she understood instinctively even at that age that she was the Emperor's daughter and would—indeed must—act accordingly. Not like a petulant spoiled brat that families like hers so often produced, but with dignity, reserve, a deep-seated, almost Buddhistic detachment. That's the way she was as a kid, both on the outside and the inside too as far as he could tell, and she remained that way to this day. She seemed to proceed through the world in a slower motion—languorous and deliberate, but always alert, observant, intelligent—except for her flickering dark brown, almost black eyes, her father's eyes, that danced like flames and promised something wilder than did her exterior chilly affect. And now she was aging, and beautifully so. Even the few little pockets of fatty tissue and a varicose vein or two on her legs, even the blood vessels standing out more prominently and a brown spot or two on her hands, even the small crow's feet developing at the corner of each eye, the new slight weariness in her expression and more troubled knowingness in her gaze—all made her even more appealing to him. If he let himself think about her even for a sliver of a moment, he ached miserably for her.

He had pined for her in grade school, and in high school too, and even to this day despite years of trying to resist it. Things were even worse now since Carmine had chosen him for this current duty, which brought him in constant contact with Robert and, incidentally, much more into Rose's presence than he wanted to be—helping her carry groceries, or her asking his opinion on some household repair or improvement that Robert could not be bothered with, or her sitting in the back seat of the Lincoln as she did this morning on the way to church, as she would again later on the way to the cemetery, and then home—which only resulted in an initial seemingly uncontrollable surge of hopeless hope, followed quickly by the ripping off of the bandage, the reopening of the old wound of longing. No matter how much he berated himself for not letting this obsession go, no matter how many times he had mercifully bestowed on himself temporary reprieves—by clenching his teeth, steeling his will, and convincing himself he actually would probably dislike her if he knew her better, that she would be no good for him at all—any involuntary glimpse or thought of her reignited that forlorn, fruitless passion.

He cursed himself because he had always hung back, not just afraid of her formidable father but also of Rose herself, of the possibility that if he offended her by overstepping his bounds, she might freeze him in his place, never speak to him or even look at him again. Not as good looking as Robert, but he was handsome enough in a rough way, a good athlete, muscular, street-fighter tough and brave. So many of their crew were loud-mouthed, blustering buffoons; or oily punks like the snakes portrayed in the cartoons, predatory intentions obvious to all. He could not recall her ever associating with any of those. Her father was certainly not like any of those. So Paul pursued a strategy of projecting something close to his actual self—though a brutal criminal version thereof, a persona of quiet but deep strength, humility, dependability, a careful watcher and listener, someone who could be relied on in any place, time, or situation. His tactics—be silent, hang back, and hope she would notice him and one day be overwhelmed by his value and thus moved to confer on him her favors—had been an entire failure. If they were in the same room, she would acknowledge him, not pay much attention, occasionally direct a comment not even directly to him, only in his general direction, but otherwise show no interest.

They held the reception at the Whispering Hills Country Club, which would not have welcomed Carmine Jagoda himself as a member, nor would he have deigned to apply there. But Robert's family, long established in the restaurant and catering business and not at the time of their admission suspected to have any underworld ties, had been members there for decades, and the Club had automatically admitted Robert as a young adult before rumors surfaced that he had become associated romantically with the crown princess of the criminal clan.

Nothing of the 1960s or 1970s, including the women's liberation movement, had made any observable impact on this fanatically patriarchal subculture. Once the toasts were done (which were careful, tame, boring because they all assumed the place was bugged), and most of the men and several of the women were a little drunk, the men gathered around Robert and the women gathered around Rose while the teenagers flirted with each other and the children tried to find something to keep them occupied but mostly just whined that they wanted to go home.

Paul noticed how almost all of them, old and young, exhibited, apparently sincerely, the utmost respect and admiration for Rose, as if they recognized a source of strength within her to which heed must be paid. Given to observing and thinking more than most of the others, Paul wondered what the next chapter in the life of this clan would be, how the next phase would unfold, what bloodshed it might involve, and if any of the rest of them were similarly wondering. Or maybe they were plotting.

Maybe he should be plotting too. Their group had never followed the classic underworld structure. Carmine had not wanted or needed, and would not have tolerated, anything as close to an equal as a consigliere. There would never be a number two man, something well-understood from the beginning of his ascendancy. Now, notwithstanding the Boss's anointment of Robert, which, after all, could be considered to have been less than a vote of confidence but just a temporary stopgap pending the Boss's release, an ambitious man might believe he was the right one to fill what he perceived to be a leadership vacuum at the very top of the outfit.

Although everyone was expected to be willing, able, even eager to mete out whatever brutality the occasion might demand, there were special enforcers. Like hot-tempered Tony Farina. And there had been others—Otto "the Creep" Salerno, Karl "Dry Ice" Manzotti, and three more, five men in all—lost to this minor-league bozo O'Keefe, a thorn that had embedded under the Boss's skin and festered there, so much so that O'Keefe's extirpation had been the Boss's final wish, his last will and testament so to speak. Paul didn't get it. It didn't seem to be worth the risk or even the brain damage. Move on. It wasn't like the guy was doing anything other than trying to avoid causing them further trouble.

Sal Vagnino, looking weepy and worn out, big purplish black pouches under his eyes, said he had to go on home to his wife who had come down with the flu, too sick to attend the funeral. As Joe Marcetti watched Sal go, he said to the others, "Wife with the flu, my ass. She's home cryin' her heart out over that goddamn son of theirs."

"What?" one of them asked.

"Poor Sal. The son's a fucking queer."

"No! Sal's kid! How could that happen?"

Joe crossed himself as if it might ward off a curse. "A couple of years ago the kid actually moved to fucking San Francisco so he could be with his homo buddies. Now he's in a hospital no bigger than a stick dyin' of AIDS."

"Well, good riddance."

"That AIDS is gonna get them all before it's done."

"A toast to the AIDS!"

They lifted their glasses.

At one point, Paul went to the bathroom and Vince Sorvino joined him a few minutes later. Vince was an old soldier—steady, reliable, deadly as a rattlesnake, but, like the creature itself, only when provoked. Without being fully conscious of it, Paul had modeled himself on Vince, trying to follow his path.

Paul felt like he had to say something. "How goes it?"

"Good enough," Vince replied. "Probably better than we could expect at this point."

"Anybody makin' any moves? Anybody talkin' shit?"

"Not to me anyway."

"Well, nobody in their right mind would try anything without talkin' to you."

"Hope that's true. We don't need any shit comin' down right now. How's Robert? What's he sayin'...thinkin'?"

"I can't tell. He doesn't share much."

"You wouldn't be holdin' back now, would you? Not the right time to be keepin' secrets from a good friend."

"You're the last guy I'd hold back on."

"You ended up in a pretty important place, Paulie. You could get ideas about where you could go from there."

"Not a chance. Last thing I want is that. I think the Boss knew that. I think that's why he put me where I am."

"I'd say the rest of them are...let's say skeptical...not about you...about Robert...but willin' to let it play out...for a while at least."

"He's a damn smart guy."

"True. But that ain't enough. How's he gonna react when the feds come knockin' at this door...or some other outfit starts to muscle in on us."

"Agree."

"How's him and Rose?"

"Seem okay enough."

"What's that mean, 'okay enough'?"

"Just that. Not much passion there either way...but peaceful."

"Good. If he had a problem with Rose, that could upend things. No fightin' or anything like that between 'em?"

"None that I see."

"She's a hard one to read. Always has been. Him too. Meanwhile, I've only got two pieces of wisdom. One, you'd better be tellin' me everything. Two, watch Tony Farina. If there's a problem, that's where it's likely to come from."

~

PAUL DROPPED ROSE and Robert and the kids off mid-afternoon at their house. Robert lingered in the car with Paul while the rest of them trudged wearily to the front door.

"I saw you talkin' to Vince," Robert said. "What was that about?"

"I think he was just feeling me out."

Robert tensed up, his fear palpable. "Why?" he asked too eagerly. Not a good sign.

"Not for a bad reason. I think he wants no trouble at all."

"Good."

"I think all the old guys feel that way."

Robert looked fearful again. "And the young guys?"

"No worries."

Robert hesitated, as if he knew he might be about to make a mistake, then said, too meekly, "You'll tell me anything you hear that seems important, right? Anything you see. Anything you feel."

"Sure thing. No question about it."

"You can go on," Robert said. "I'm done for the day."

~

BUT ROBERT WAS not done for the day. There were things he didn't want Paul to know. From the picture window he watched Paul drive off as Rose sat on the couch, melancholy and exhausted.

"I've got meetings the rest of the day and most of the night too," he told her. "There's a lot I need to get done...a lot I need to stay ahead of with this crew."

"Is anything happening? Do you hear anything? Do you sense anything?" These questions did not seem to arise from any fear on her part. They seemed more like pressure on him to make sure he was paying the right kind of attention at this dangerous time. He understood this. He was probably more afraid than she was, which he was trying to keep from showing, to her or the others. A war, a civil war, stoked by someone's overweening ambition, might break out, might already be brewing.

"You want me to talk to anyone?" she added.

"No," he said, making clear by his tone that her question had offended him, "I've got it under control."

She looked up at him. He could not read her expression. "I need some love tonight," she said. "I'll make it worth your while."

~

IT WOULD HAVE been so nice to have dealt with O'Keefe that night in the trailer. He could not really hope to get another opportunity like that one. And what an odd way to lose the opportunity—the sirens converging on that dump of a trailer park and that woman's pissant trailer. He would need to find another way. Most important, he would need to stay patient, and he would need to keep Robert from becoming impatient. Ergo the meeting he had asked for—to make sure Robert knew that he was still engaged, still on mission. At the same time he wished something would happen to lift this burden off him. "Let this cup pass from me." Jesus in the Garden. He remembered it from all those Good Friday services attended in his youth. His upper body heaved upward slightly in an involuntary disgusted silent chuckle. Not quite the same situation and obviously not the same kind of person, but the same feeling. He had made that big mistake long ago and now he had to pay his dues. *"Don't do the crime if you can't do the time."* Still, maybe something would happen to free him from this, and he would be on the lookout to make something happen himself if any chance arose. And here was Robert, walking in the door looking uptight.

Robert stopped on his way to the table to catch the waitress and order a drink. He sat down at the booth in the shitkicker bar, so far away from the world they inhabited that no one from that world would ever imagine them in such a place, let alone encounter them there by chance.

"How was the funeral?"

Robert did not respond to that. Instead he said, "Must be something important to take the risk of another meeting."

"I was close to a perfect chance, but it disappeared as soon as it came."

"Find another one fast. This needs to get done."

"You wouldn't want me to be stupid about it, would you? He's managed to shove it back up even Mr. Jagoda's ass before. Not once but three or four times."

Robert said nothing to that, an acknowledgment that the point was well-taken. Despite his urgency on this, Robert was a careful man.

"I need a clean gun."

"You can't get one yourself? Why now? Why didn't you think about that before?"

"I thought I had a better way."

"Why not just blow him to bits? We're good at that."

"You'd know why if you'd think about it." *And if you'd ever done anything yourself other than count beans, you fuckhead.* "There are lots of reasons. But start with what I'd have to do to put it in place...all the components it takes and how easy some of them are to trace... the number of things that can go wrong from the installation to the explosion. And above all, possible collateral damage...innocent bystanders. You guys just blow up your criminal pals who nobody gives a shit about, so they don't investigate it hard."

"Well, you know what somebody said: 'Let God sort the innocent from the guilty.'"

"Like his daughter maybe? Someone made that mistake already. Last Halloween. Yeah, if you want to bring more shit down on your head than your bunch has ever even conceived, just torch an innocent bystander or two."

"Okay. Just get it done. The more time you take, the more I'll be thinking your heart's not in it…you might be procrastinating, playing for time, or worse. And that wouldn't be good for either of us."

"Don't forget how important this is to me. It's my way off the hook. But I sure don't wanna fuck it up."

He saw Robert rising to leave, so he quickly added, "And I need a silencer on it too." Robert gave him a slight nod that said, "I understand, it will be done" and headed for the door. As he watched Robert leave, he wondered why Robert was in such a hurry today, and it suddenly seemed like a good idea to follow Robert wherever he was in such a hurry to go. He threw more than enough cash on the table to cover whatever he might owe, and tried to affect a more casual air than he was feeling as he left the bar as quickly as he could without calling too much attention to himself. By the time he got to his own car, Robert's car was far down the road, almost out of sight. His guesswork would have to be good for him to have any chance of catching up.

DRIVING AWAY FROM the bar, Robert felt the weight of the day begin to lift. He had a long way to drive to his next destination, which was good. It gave him time to ready himself, let the layers of worry and dread evaporate off him in anticipation of the pleasure coming soon.

Besides, he would not want to arrive there before dark. He always made sure not to arrive before dark.

Rose had promised him something special tonight. Not that she was ever unwilling—she was almost always willing, and often eager, like today. But Rose was just not what he wanted, at least not most of the time. What he wanted—what surprised him that he wanted, sometimes wished that he didn't want, but couldn't seem to help wanting—waited in that small house in an obscure part of the city, gorgeously decorated on the inside though unprepossessing on the outside, both the house and the neighborhood having been chosen, respectively, for those very qualities of geographic obscurity and exterior banality. But all this exquisite pleasure came with an overlay of dread. What if they found him out? He must do everything possible to keep that from happening. As darkness slowly fell, he imagined the deliciousness of what would come soon: the chilled wine glass, the Pinot Grigio, a few tokes on the bong (sex was so much slower and sweeter that way), he had to be careful or he would come right there in the car.

Upon arriving, he began a ritual implemented on each visit, with slight variations sufficient to keep him from falling into a dangerous rut of complacency. He drove by the house first, and then beyond for several blocks, taking random turns deliberately here and there, stopping briefly sometimes to check behind him. At full dark, he completed the ritual. Pulling into the driveway, he pressed the garage door opening device and pulled in. He had been careless once about that remote, left it in the glove compartment, and Rose had dug it out while looking for something else.

"What's this?" she said.

After hesitating a little too long, he said, "Can't believe I left that in here. It opens a garage door down in the bottoms where we store some things...and want to get in and out as quick as possible...no fuss, no muss."

She accepted that, but he made sure it would never again be there for her to stumble across and provoke wayward thoughts or questions. He punched the button and the garage door closed behind him. In. He was in, in, in. Safe. At least as safe as the world he lived in allowed him to be. His life would have been so much simpler if he had not discovered what nestled inside that door he now eagerly approached. Keep your eye on the money, make enough of it to keep everyone happy, show up at the kids' soccer games, suck it up and fuck your wife once in a while and act like you actually want to. He daydreamed about finding a way to escape from *that* and into *this* permanently. He was working on it. He had been the de facto treasurer for years—in charge of the money, how to assemble it, spread it around, hide it, launder it, make it make more of itself. He had been skimming for a long time and working on his own private witness protection program. It would not take much longer to gather up enough to take care of them for the rest of their lives in some obscure place with a temperate climate, low cost of living, and cops with open palms and closed eyes.

CHAPTER ▶ 13

THERE WERE ONLY eight trailers in the lower section of the park, and he could see them all from near the park entrance where he stopped his van. Her trailer, to his left and all the way back near the underbrush jungle, seemed even more forlorn to him now, given what he knew had happened there. He planned to start at the front of the park, on the right side of the driveway, and work methodically up the group of trailers on the right, cross over at the end, skip her trailer of course, and work his way back down until he had covered them all. He lingered in the van for a few moments to screw up his courage. He only required a little courage to face the possible physical danger that awaited him from the occupants, but much more mental, emotional, and even spiritual courage would be required to face the squalor of the hard lives he would likely encounter in some of these places.

He had chosen 4 p.m., toward the end of the day but before nightfall and hopefully before dinner, to maximize the chance that people would be home and maybe willing to do more than just shut the door in his face or fail to answer at all. Nobody answered at the first trailer. No surprise; it looked abandoned, and he resisted taking a peek through the grimy window next to the door. As he walked up the driveway toward the second trailer, a young boy, around Kelly's age, ten or eleven, exited the trailer across the way with a little jump from the threshold to the stairway below, the metal stairway creaking with something like pain. One day it would surely collapse from the stress of the kid's enthusiastic little maneuver. He carried a basketball in the crook of his left arm and wore sweatpants and a hooded sweatshirt with what was likely the name of a college or an NBA team printed on the front.

O'Keefe said "Hi," but the boy only glanced back suspiciously and turned his attention to a rusty and dented, netless basketball goal affixed to a telephone pole stuck between two of the trailers. The goal sat low on the pole, not much taller than the boy himself—about an average man's height, probably about the height of the person who had attached it to the pole. The boy's shot banged off the shuddering metal backboard and down through the hoop. At the top of the stairway leading to the second trailer, O'Keefe turned back to find the boy staring at him. O'Keefe knew that the boy might be more able and willing to tell him about what went on in this place than any of the adults, but he could not risk approaching the kid, lest he be mistaken for a pedophile with who knows what consequences in this rough little rathole of the world.

He turned back to address a female voice speaking to him through the trailer door.

"What ya want?"

"My name is Peter O'Keefe. I'm an old friend of Tim and Beverly who lived up the road."

"Go away."

"I just want to ask a few questions."

"I didn't know 'em."

"How long have you lived here?"

"Go away. Leave me alone."

He took a new tack. "I'll pay you for your time."

"I'm calling the police right now."

"I'm working with the police," he lied.

No more voice from behind the door. He knocked again, not aggressively as he did not want to risk provoking a scene. No response forthcoming, he moved on to the next trailer, the boy stealthily observing him between dribbles, whirls, jump shots, and drives to the basket, followed by easy dunks into the short hoop.

At trailer after trailer he found nobody home, at least nobody willing or able to answer the door. Finally, he arrived at the trailer the boy had emerged from.

"They're not home," the boy said, the basketball crooked in his left arm.

O'Keefe walked toward the boy, keeping plenty of distance, and decided to risk the question that could…that should…arouse suspicion.

"When will they be home?"

"What do you want?"

"I'm an old friend of the people who used to live up in the last trailer," O'Keefe said, pointing at it. "I wanted to ask their neighbors about them."

"Never talked to 'em."

"Your parents either? Are you sure?"

The boy shrugged. "Larry might know," he said, gesturing toward the trailer next door, at the entrance to the park. "He's around *all* the time."

O'Keefe took one of his business cards from his shirt pocket. This version did not include his occupation, just an address and phone number.

"Will you give that to your parents and ask 'em to call me if they can tell me anything at all?"

"It's just my Mom." The kid had said "they're" at first. Probably coached by his mother to do that: Don't suggest to a stranger the absence of a male presence.

No father. O'Keefe thought of his own boyhood. Not unlike this kid standing here. Carrying a basketball the same way, similar sweatshirt, fatherless too, though his neighborhood had been a better one, with regulation-size basketball goals on the nearby school playground.

"You play on a team?"

The boy nodded.

"Are you good?"

"Pretty good."

"What's your position?"

"Forward. *Power* forward."

"Good luck. Will you tell your Mom I came by, tell her what I'm looking for, give her that card? If she tells me anything of value, I'd be glad to pay her something."

"Okay, but I don't think she knows anything. Larry's the guy who might."

"You think he's home?"

"He's always home."

Approaching Larry's trailer, thinking about the boy and what might happen to him in life, O'Keefe noticed that Larry's trailer was cantilevered so its front window looked up the driveway at the rest of the park. If Larry was there all the time, as the boy had said, his trailer was an excellent vantage point for continually observing the comings and goings into and out of the park.

O'Keefe did not have to knock. Larry stood in the door waiting for him. Little Dumbo.

"You remember me?" O'Keefe said. "Peter O'Keefe. The one who found Beverly—"

Larry, interrupting, held out his hand, and said, "I forget nothing and nobody. Larry Sims. Glad to see you again."

Larry stepped back and gestured to O'Keefe to come in. Larry's trailer was larger than Beverly's, and differently configured, though still quite cramped. The front window was big enough to furnish a decent view up the driveway all the way to Beverly's trailer at the end. A metal table sat in front of the window, a six-seater, two across and one at each end, with a chipped and cracked linoleum top on which numerous newspapers were piled in what seemed like purposeful arrangement, with a clearing for a placemat and another spot for a deck of cards laid out for a game of solitaire. A small television sat on a ledge on the left side of the table and a transistor radio on the right. Larry had built a crow's nest from which he could eat, read, view, listen, and distract himself with a card game while observing any activity in the park. Larry indicated that O'Keefe should sit down at one end of the table in a kitchen chair. O'Keefe did so and gingerly pushed the pile of newspapers in front of him slightly away, leaving just enough room to write in the small cub-reporter-type notebook he carried in his back pocket.

Larry, still standing, said, "I don't drink coffee this late in the day, Mr. O'Keefe, but I could offer you a Coke or an instant iced tea."

"Not a thing for me," O'Keefe said, and nodded his head out the window toward the boy madly dribbling his basketball. "That young man says you know everything that goes on here, Mr. Sims."

Mr. Sims laughed.

"Can I call you, Larry?"

"Sure."

"Pete, here."

"Yeah, Pete, I probably do know a lot. Just sitting here day after day. I don't work anymore. I was in the Navy twenty years and they pay me the pension payments. And when I came out, I worked on the railroad and fell off a train car ladder and hurt my back. So I get disability too. But that's all I've got, and even combined, it ain't much. I'm here because there's no cheaper rent in the whole city, maybe the whole damn world. Got no car. And nowhere much to go anyway. Got to husband my resources. Afraid I'll live too long. There's the TV and the radio, and I do pay for a newspaper subscription, and there's the solitaire that you see laid out here. And watching the not much going on around this place."

"I was a Marine," O'Keefe said, hoping to forge at least a slim bond of fellowship.

Larry only nodded.

"Did you know Beverly and her husband?"

"Tim was his name," Larry said eagerly, showing off his knowledge. "Too bad about him. Her too."

"Did you know them…talk to them?"

"Not much. I introduced myself when they arrived. But they kept to themselves. I guess we found out why. A lot of suffering there. As we saw. First him, then her. Drugs are evil."

"Have the police been to see you?"

"No. I thought maybe you were police."

"No. I happen to be a private investigator, but that's pure coincidence. I was a friend of theirs a long time ago. High school. I was just trying to help them out."

"Why would the cops care anyway? Just another junkie overdosing. Must happen all the time."

"Well, they might want to know who their supplier was."

Larry shrugged. "Apparently not."

"Do you know who it was?"

"Why would you think that?"

"The boy says you know everything."

"I'm not saying I know, but let's say I did. Let's say I know who the guy is that serviced them and some others in this place. If I tell you, and it leads to trouble for him, and he comes after me...I don't need that, nor deserve it."

"I understand," O'Keefe said, groping for something that might open Larry up, "and...I might feel the same way...but then I think about that boy out there...and wonder...if people like you and I do nothing, just sit watching, someday that boy might be getting regular visits from that same dealer."

Larry gave this a few moments thought, then said, "That's probably a fair point, Mr. O'Keefe. And, you know, if he comes after me, he might get a big surprise, because right under one of those piles I've got a loaded .45 with the safety off at all times."

Larry reached under one of the piles. O'Keefe tensed up since he knew nothing about this odd man or what he might be capable of. But all he pulled out was a spiral notebook, full of pages and pages of writing with sticky notes protruding from the edges, apparently marking places for later reference.

"My diary, sort of," Larry said, and flipped through pages with numbers on them along with a terse description of a vehicle beside each number. The last number on the list was the license plate number and a description of O'Keefe's van.

"A little hobby of mine," Larry said. "I always wondered if it would come to mean anything." He ran his finger down the page, stopped it, and said, "I don't know his name, but there's his license plate number. He drives a black Mustang GT. I suppose you can track him down from that since you're a private detective. But I haven't seen him here in a long time. He could've come to grief."

O'Keefe enthusiastically transcribed the numbers into his own notebook. *If he hasn't come to grief yet, he soon will.* "You're a good citizen, Mr. Sims. And a good man. If there's anything I can ever do for you in return for this, I'll do my best to help."

Larry looked at him, sizing him up, and said, "Ya know, if you mean that, there's one thing I'd like more than anything in the world."

Oh shit. I shouldn't have opened my mouth. He was afraid to say anything more.

"A police radio scanner."

Greatly relieved, O'Keefe said, "Sure thing. Happy to do it. I'll get one for you."

"Another thing."

Oh shit.

"Every once in a while I need a ride…to the doctor or even just the store to get a few things. It's a long walk to anything and no damn fun, especially in the winter."

O'Keefe reacted more slowly to this one, hoping that the hesitation would convey a message suggesting at least a slight warning of reluctance. "I'll do what I can," he said.

"Don't worry. I won't abuse you."

"Fair enough. In all that writing you've got in that notebook, do you think there might be anything else that might help me understand what happened to my friend?"

Larry considered this for a moment, then shook his head. "I really don't think so. Like I said, they weren't here that long, and they kept to themselves. But if I think of something, I'll sure get hold of you. I've got no phone, but someone here'll let me use theirs."

"And keep a good eye on that boy, will you?"

"Big job, but I'll try."

"You think there's anyone else here that might know anything to help me?"

Larry again pondered the question but shook his head. "I doubt it. Even when they're sober, they've pretty much got their heads down all the time just trying to survive."

CHAPTER ▶ 14

DEREK FAGAN RESIDED in a small house with no garage. He parked his black Mustang GT in the driveway, walked to his front door, inserted the key in the lock, turned the key, and had just began to push the door open when a force behind him drove his head into the door and shoved him inside the house.

Fagan managed to stay on his feet until O'Keefe, just like two Marine Corps drill instructors had shown him how to do by doing it to him, landed a side thrust kick to Fagan's solar plexus, then jumped on the sprawled, gasping man, seized Fagan's hair with his left hand and his throat with his right and squeezed hard, cutting off what air was left for Fagan to breathe with. He thrust his face close to Fagan's, hoping that seeing the hate that filled his eyes would make Fagan believe he was about to be murdered. He kept squeezing Fagan's throat until he thought the man was close to passing out, then let up, grabbed his arm, dragged him to a couch, and propped him up against it, his ass still on the floor. As Fagan struggled to suck oxygen back into his wheezing lungs, O'Keefe pulled up a straight chair close to Fagan and sat on the edge of it above Fagan slumped below.

"Here's your choice, Mr. Motherfucker. I need your help. If you don't help me, first I beat the shit out of you, which so far I've only *started* to do..." And before Fagan could even detect a slight movement, O'Keefe administered a clubbed fist to Fagan's left ear. "...and then I do everything possible, now and for the rest of your miserable life, to trash it in every way I can, starting with, but *only starting with*, sending you to jail for ruining all these people's lives."

O'Keefe observed Fagan trying to muster up a look of defiance, so he clubbed Fagan on the side of the head again.

"Goddamn, man. Who are you? What the fuck do you want?"

"Beverly Bronson."

"Oh no, man. Not me. I had nothin' to do with that."

This time O'Keefe slapped Fagan across the face with an open hand.

"You claiming that you never sold her any dope?"

Fagan, his hand on the side of his face as if it might sooth the sting somehow, said, "I didn't sell her *that* dope."

"We'll see about that, but even if you didn't sell her *that* dope, you had *everything* to do with it."

"So what do you want?"

"I'm so easy, Mr. Fagan. Not asking for much. Just a little advice. Nothing that'll incriminate you. Easy stuff. A lot easier than what you just experienced. That is, as long as you don't bullshit me."

"Like what?"

O'Keefe smacked him again, another stinger on the same side of Fagan's face. "That one was just to let you know that you don't have the right to ask questions. *I* am asking all the questions and you're giving all the answers. We will follow rigid adherence to that protocol, Mr. Fagan. And my first question, and you'd better understand that I'm a human lie detector, 'When was the last time you sold her anything?'"

"Months ago. Not once after Tim off'd himself. I didn't want anywhere near her after that."

"Mr. Fagan, are you aware of a concept called 'suspension of disbelief'?"

Painfully, wearily, Fagan closed his eyes and shook his head "no."

"It means that I'm gonna act as if it's possible that you are actually worthy of belief. Provisionally. Conditional in every way. So that we can proceed to other things."

"Other things?"

"So here's how easy it's gonna be, at least for now. I have Bev's autopsy report here. I want you to read it and see if you find anything odd in it. If you're telling me the truth that you didn't supply her that last dose, then you shouldn't have any reluctance."

"I'm no fucking coroner."

O'Keefe looked almost sad this time when he slapped Fagan again with his other hand on the other side of Fagan's face.

"Some rules, Mr. Fagan, should go without saying. In addition to no questions, no smart-ass comments. Like the song says, 'make this easy on yourself.'"

"Leave it here and I'll look at it."

O'Keefe drove his stiffened, outstretched fingers into Fagan's Adam's apple. He let Fagan finish choking and gagging, then said, "And you will not ever even begin to think I am such a dumbass that you can fool me that way."

"Ya know, I have associates that could make you answer for this."

"Mr. Fagan, you're only giving me incentive to do greater harm to you right now while I have the chance."

O'Keefe allowed a sullen silence to settle over them for a few moments, then said, "Where's your coffee pot?"

Fagan's look of alarm notched up a few degrees, as he seemed to be trying to imagine what torture might be administered through that device. "What for?"

"I'll have a cup of coffee or two while you read through it—very carefully, very studiously."

"Now?"

"Please note, Mr. Fagan, that you have now twice in quick succession violated the rule of 'no questions'...without me punishing you for it. And I will even answer your second question: Yes. *Right fucking now.*"

He helped Fagan up and patted him down. Odds were that Fagan would have a weapon on him or somewhere in the house. He would need to keep Fagan within arm's length and be on his guard.

In the kitchen he instructed Fagan on how much water and how many teaspoons to load into the Mr. Coffee.

"I'll tell you this," Fagan said. "She was too smart to overdose by accident. It had to be deliberate. Or just reckless. Maybe she just didn't give a shit anymore."

O'Keefe well knew the latter was very possible given her mental state the last time he had spoken with her, but he would not let Fagan in on that.

"You think that lets you off the hook?"

"I'm not *on* any hook. There's no way that whatever she put in herself was mine. Because when she went into rehab the last time, she had nothing left. Nada. She was out of money and maybe even the pussy to raise any more of it with."

Fagan seemed to react to the anger that O'Keefe knew had erupted in his face. He stepped backward and raised his hands to ward off the blow he expected.

"I'm sorry," Fagan said behind his hands, "but that's just the way things were when she and Tim ran out of dough."

"And how about you? D'you ever do a little bartering with her along those lines?"

"Never. I'm a businessman. And I'm not so dumb to stick my dick into junkie pussy. Even when it's fresh, let alone skanky and worn out."

O'Keefe grabbed Fagan by the shirt with his left hand and Fagan's throat with his right and choked him. For too long. He almost couldn't stop himself. When he did, Fagan raised his own hands to his throat and gagged for air.

"Another rule. We shall maintain a modicum of respect for the dead."

He waited for Fagan to retrieve his composure, then said, "You seem to require a large amount of governance, Mr. Fagan."

They moved to the adjacent dining room where O'Keefe sat drinking his coffee while Fagan read the report. After studying it for a few minutes, Fagan looked up. "This actually makes me sad."

"Really? I would guess you're around something like that a lot."

"Not. No deaths. Not one."

"I hope you're not expecting a medal."

Fagan gave a quick glance toward O'Keefe's hands. "No. Just that I'm not the worst. There are a lot worse."

O'Keefe shrugged contemptuously, and Fagan returned to the report. He read slowly and carefully, sometimes wincing, or clucking to himself, or shaking his head quickly, as if shaking away a fly. After he finished, he gave O'Keefe a wary look, leading O'Keefe to expect the worst. Nothing might come of his brutality.

"Do you have particular questions?"

"Could she have somehow gotten hold of a super-strong dose, something that surprised her, overwhelmed her before she had a chance to react? I mean, the needle was still in her arm."

"Well, there *was* a load of China White on the streets about that time. Super powerful stuff. And by the way, I didn't manage to score *any* of it. Pissed me off."

After a silence, as O'Keefe considered what he had been told, Fagan said, "Any more questions?" He seemed to want to probe the full extent of O'Keefe's knowledge and curiosity, like a lawyer in a deposition.

"Only one I can think of right now. The report refers to a hematoma that suggests maybe a stab or jab of more than usual pressure. Could that mean anything? Could it mean someone was holding her down?"

"Well, a lot of things, I guess. It could mean that. Or just clumsiness...in too much of a hurry..."

"Anger? An angry despair? Self-hatred?"

"Maybe."

The ensuing silence endured for too long. O'Keefe had read extensively about heroin addiction and its means, methods, and measures, but he had no more questions. The report had been a bust. This interrogation had been a bust. His brutality had only demeaned, not delivered.

"But that's not the important thing about the injection site," Fagan said.

"What's that?" O'Keefe said, with a hopeful timidity now.

"It's wrong."

"What's wrong about it?"

"It's wrong."

O'Keefe's anger rose in him again. "Are you playing with me?"

Fagan rushed to say, "The site is wrong. It's the wrong site."

O'Keefe's face was a question mark.

"There's all kinds of places in a body to inject. The movies always show it's the arm because that's more...what would you call it... *filmic*? But I saw her do it plenty of times, I saw Tim do it for her, and she even had me do it a time or two when Tim wasn't around—" Fagan flashed a look of alarm because he had spoken too soon without thinking, his hands jumped to cover his face, anticipating a punch from O'Keefe. But not this time.

Lowering his hands and looking relieved, Fagan went on, "And I don't believe she ever shot up in her arm. Not when I knew her anyway. Needle marks on arms are advertisements that say 'I'm a junkie.' She didn't want people, like her mother for example, like her son for example, to see that. The report mentions small scars on the back of her knees without connecting the dots. The coroner was as clueless as you are. That's where she usually did it. Other places too but mainly there. It's obviously hard to see the marks there. So if that needle was sticking out of her arm, she must've been desperate, or in a weird mood, or just didn't care anymore..."

Or she didn't inject herself. He had felt the need to run this to ground, not really expecting to find anything. Yet here it was, thanks to the wisdom of Fagan the Pusher Man.

"Is there more?"

"That torn rag around her arm. I guess it's not the right word to use, but she had more...I won't say class...more care or orderliness... than that. She used a rubber tie-up."

"I guess she could've thrown all that paraphernalia away once she decided to go straight?"

"Possible."

"Anything else?"

Fagan shook his head. "That's the only unusual thing I can see in there."

O'Keefe stood up, picked up the report from the table, tried to come up with an appropriate farewell, but could do no more than a sheepish "Thank you."

"You know, don't you...you're aware, aren't you... that I didn't have to tell you that? I could've kept it to myself as repayment for you knocking the shit out of me. You'd never've known."

"Maybe. But tell me the truth. Would you've told me any of this if I'd come bearing gifts instead?"

Fagan thought about it, smiled, and said, "Well, I suppose not."

"And I might've found out some other way…and then…"

"Just for the sake of a friendly discussion, will you permit me the small luxury of saying 'I doubt that'…that you'd've found out some other way?"

"I would permit that."

"So maybe I earned a reprieve there?"

"Not a chance. I wish I believed there was a Hell for you to go to. But since I don't, I intend to do my best to provide you the fullest experience of it on this earth."

~

AS A DETECTIVE, too often he learned things he'd rather not know, such as that needle dangling from her arm when she did not have a practice of injecting herself there. She could have made an exception this time, especially if she intended to kill herself or just didn't care any longer whether she lived or died. She could have just felt so alone and helpless it wasn't worth living another hour. Might as well go out feeling as good as she knew how to make herself feel. Yet she had seemed hopeful for her recovery, and, more important, angry and determined to have her vengeance. Yet, where did she have to turn once Jensen and Bowman called her bluff?

Difficult. It would be easy to rationalize the situation, resolve all doubts in favor of the accidental overdose or suicide theory and just move on to the many less quixotic and far more profitable things on his to-do list. But there were too many discrepancies. For example, the needle in the wrong place. For example, the needle she did not even manage to pull out of her vein before its contents killed her. For example, the residue of sleeping pills in her stomach. She would not have wanted to take the edge off the high that way. Which suggested at least the possibility she was chemically subdued somehow before the injection. And then the torn rag around her arm instead of a rubber tie-up, a rag that could just as easily have served as a gag in her mouth before it was wrapped around her arm. Most of all, the resolve she had expressed to him and he had *felt* in her, almost like a physical force. The resolve to stay clean and accomplish something—a legacy—for the son she had done so little for up to that point in his life—her declared mission to right the scales, to restore a balance to the world that had been disastrously tilted when a rape went unreported and a lie told that still festered and fouled her whole life—and Tim's life, and her son's life—and had enabled a rapist to escape justice, a rapist that might also be a murderer.

But where could he go with all that? As Ross had already said, the police wouldn't waste their time on the overdose death of this nothing of a person on the say-so of a marginal character like himself. Should he incur the expense of hiring someone to do forensics on the trailer? Maybe, but it would probably be a waste. Seek a more thorough autopsy or at least an expert review of the existing report? No, it appeared there was only one thing to do: Take the most direct approach—high risk in several ways including to the physical integrity of his own person and its continued earthly existence, but that is exactly what he had begun to believe might be required of him.

FIRST, HE ASKED Detective Morrison, the closest thing he had to a friend in the police department, to put in a good word for him with Lieutenant Ross.

"Ross, huh," Morrison said. "Ambitious guy. There'll have to be something in it for *him*."

Second, he made an appointment with Ross and carefully rehearsed what he would reveal and conceal. If he even got close to suggesting that Jerry Jensen—Ross's likely next ultimate boss as the soon-to-be mayor of the city, had something to do with causing Beverly's death, he would be branded right away as a nut case. Ross would see no percentage in bothering with such a flake. Later, if he came up with something more solid than he had now, maybe Ross would find it in his interest to take up the case himself. But, he had to be careful not to reveal certain information prematurely that might send Ross off in a misdirection that would solve a relatively meaningless part of the case and meander away from the more important part. For example, Fagan, and his visit with Fagan. He didn't even want Ross to know that he had identified Fagan as her supplier or what he had learned from Fagan about the injection site. It would be too easy just to nab the pusher man and leave it at that.

Ross greeted O'Keefe with a puzzled, mocking smile.

"I'm guessing there's no investigation going on in Beverly's case," O'Keefe said.

"Case? There is no case. Why should there be?"

"I'm not saying there should be, at least right now, at least from the department's point of view, limited resources and all that, like you said before. But I'd like to look at the evidence your guys gathered, however meager it may be…the needle and the other paraphernalia…maybe get access to the scene. I couldn't touch anything when I found her for fear of screwing something up. But I see discrepancies I'd like to follow up on."

"Like what?"

"Well, for example, that the needle was still stuck in her arm. Hard to believe she wouldn't've pulled it out before the dose killed her."

"Why do I have this feeling you've been carrying the torch for her since you were kids and just can't accept how she ended up?"

“Fair point. But there’s another angle that might be more interesting to you. I think for sure she was given some powerful stuff she didn’t expect. I’d like to find the bastard who sold her that. Who knows where that might lead? Maybe to a nest of vipers that you guys would like to burn out.”

“Only if it’s a whole chain of distribution. One pusher, who cares? Arrest him, another pops up. It’s like that game Whac-A-Mole. But I can let you look at what we’ve got…if we’ve still got it, that is.”

CHAPTER ▸ 15

SARA, HOLDING A newspaper, came into his office, not in her usual brash way but with a look of apprehension.

"I have a feeling you haven't seen the newspaper this morning."

"Why endanger a good mood?"

She opened the paper to the front page, set it in front of him on the desk, and stood waiting anxiously for his reaction. His eyes locked on a familiar name.

Bank Fraud: Attorney Michael Harrigan Indicted.

> The latest indictment stemming from the failure of Vanguard Savings & Loan was handed down yesterday against Michael Harrigan. The prominent local attorney is accused of participating in a scheme to misuse loan funds. The government alleges that the bank violated banking regulations by making a loan to a "straw" borrower who immediately re-routed the funds to companies owned by the bank's shareholders, Morris Manning and Mark Marcus. Earlier this week, Forest Marler, the former general counsel of Vanguard, and Edward Tremaine, a California businessman, were charged, pled guilty, and entered into a plea agreement with respect to the same charges. Morris Manning, one of

> Vanguard's owners and its chief operating officer, has been indicted, has refused to cooperate, and states that he intends to stand trial. Knowledgeable observers have speculated that one or more of the other defendants have agreed to testify against Harrigan. U.S. Attorney Kenneth Lord said "Where were the professionals? That is the question the public is asking. This indictment is a message that nobody is immune from being held to account." Mr. Harrigan could not be reached for comment.

Stunned, he had nothing to say. If he looked like he felt, it was like a deer in headlights.

"I'm so sorry, Pete," she said. "Do you believe it?"

"I don't know. I'll have to ask. If he tells me he didn't, then he didn't."

"Those others testifying against him..."

"Yeah, that's a big mountain to climb, innocent or not."

"I'll leave you alone. So sorry. I feel terrible for ever saying a bad thing about him."

He called Harrigan's office, but the receptionist would not let him through.

"He's not taking any calls, Pete. I'll let him know you called. I'll take the message in there right now."

Before long, Harrigan called him back. He sounded weary, defeated. "That prick Lord didn't even bother to call me, or even have one of his people call me, and tell me this was coming down," Harrigan said.

O'Keefe said nothing. His silence was a question, which Harrigan quickly understood. "Oh, and by the way, it isn't likely to matter, but I'm innocent."

"What happens next?"

"Nothing good. I'll try to keep from blowing my brains out. I'm meeting with my lawyer in a few minutes."

"Leclair?" O'Keefe guessed.

"Yes, the best. At least I hope he is. Maybe we can get together later at Harvey's. Don't worry, I won't expect you to drink anything, though I sure intend to."

O'KEEFE ARRIVED at Harvey's early. Harvey himself was doing bartender duty.

"You know about Harrigan?" he asked Harvey.

"Yeah. What a rotten deal. Can he duck it?"

"Don't know. Hard road."

"Well, if anyone can, he can."

"He's meeting me here in a few minutes. I'm goin' way in the back. Send him back there, okay? And do what you can to encourage people not to crowd us."

"Sure thing."

"Thanks."

"Shit, I wonder if he'll stop drinking now too," Harvey said lamely, trying to inject a little black humor to break the tension. "First you, now maybe him. I'll go broke before long if this keeps up."

As he waited, O'Keefe sipped occasionally at his rapidly cooling cup of coffee and smoked one Marlboro after another. No matter how this turned out, surely everything would change now. Selfishly, he could not help considering what Harrigan's downfall might mean to him and his shaky private detective business. He had Harrigan to thank for many things—rescuing him from the hellhole he had been digging for himself some years ago, providing him a fairly steady stream of work in the early days of his business to jump start the business, talking him up around the legal community, and down to almost that very day in the form of the loan Harrigan had helped arrange. *But if I can't fend for myself by now, then I don't deserve to be fended for.*

His petty concerns paled compared to the fate that had befallen his lifelong friend. He wondered what Harrigan would soon reveal to him. Was this a true tragedy, the consequence of a tragic flaw? Or just a melodrama? *Maybe some of both.* Despite his success, Harrigan had enough of 1960s anti-establishment thinking to be an uncomfortable capitalist. O'Keefe wondered if that discomfort, amounting sometimes to self-loathing about what he had become, may have made Harrigan reckless and encouraged him to indulge the outlaw part of his nature.

He looked up to see Harrigan marching toward him, a drink in neither hand, as if Harvey's joking prediction had come true. He sat down and lit up his own Marlboro.

"What can I do?" O'Keefe said.

"Maybe take me out back and beat the shit out of me for getting myself into this."

O'Keefe looked puzzled, trying to figure out if this was a confession, contrary to what Harrigan had told him earlier.

"No, I didn't do it, but I feel like I deserve it anyway. Hanging out with people our mothers told us not to. What good did I think could come of running with a skunk like Eddie Tremaine and a couple of hustler bankers? Reckless. Those guys can trade me for a suspended sentence. And the Feds'd make a pact with the devil to put a lawyer in jail. And for all I know I could've committed some kind of crime. Like I told you before, the criminal laws are broad and ambiguous enough to cover a lot of behavior if a jury decides they don't like you."

"I repeat: What can I do?"

Harrigan shrugged and closed his eyes in a kind of defeat, then reopened them. "Thanks for that. I really don't know. Maybe when I regain my balance I'll know. Or maybe Leclair will figure out what."

"How about Mary?"

"I don't know. She ought to dump me right now."

"And your partners?"

"At the moment they're making positive noises, but there's that look in their eyes. It'll be hard for them. I'll have to figure out whether I need to resign."

"Don't do somethin' hasty and Irish. Take a leave of absence or something. When will the trial happen?"

"Not sure, but it will be damn soon if I have anything to do with it. I won't put Mary and the kids, or my partners, or, whether I deserve it or not, even myself through this for any longer than necessary. If I'm gonna end up in jail, better go sooner and get out sooner."

But they both knew that delay tended to work in a defendant's favor. Time could cure a lot, change a lot.

"Fucking prison," Harrigan said, and the lids of his eyes closed shut as if he could not bear to see the images his imagination was presenting to him.

"You know what the answer is, Mike. Let's go to work. 'Chop wood, carry water.' No time for despair or even doubt right now. What's next?"

"Leclair's arranged a meeting with Lord and the strike force bunch. I'd like you to attend. Meanwhile, I have to figure out how to scratch the money together to pay Leclair. Damn lawyers are expensive."

O'Keefe said, "Maybe I could loan you some of that money I'm getting from the bank."

This amused Harrigan. "Is that a joke? Misuse of loan proceeds. That's what they're trying to put me away for."

"Not at all. No intent when I got the loan. No misrepresentation. No promise in those documents that I signed that I *wouldn't* use it for this...or that I *would* use it for anything in particular. Just promised to use it for business purposes. What the hell is not a business purpose about loaning money to my primary source of business...so he can save his ass and keep sending me business? You're the lawyer. Tell me what's wrong with that thinking."

Harrigan laughed again. "Okay, there's nothing wrong with it, or shouldn't be, except that it might make you a target for the same people that are trying to put me away...and I'm not putting you at risk to save my own ass. Plus, you need that money for the business. Hell, before this is over, you may have to hire *me*."

Now O'Keefe was amused. "It's like they say in AA. You might be your sponsor's sponsor someday."

"Don't mention that. It makes me want a drink."

"So, what can I do?"

"Okay," Harrigan said, seeming to recover himself somewhat, "let's start with finding everything we can to discredit these liars. Eddie Tremaine'll be easy. He's an obvious villain. Forest Marler'll probably be much harder. He's a decent man but probably shitting his pants from fear and would consider selling out his own wife right now, let alone a dipshit like me."

"On it."

Harrigan stood up. "So here I go. I need to learn how to walk down the street without hanging my head in shame."

"You didn't do it. You're the best lawyer in town, and you've got the second best representing you. And your best friend may not be the best PI, but he'll certainly work harder than anyone else...You can't lose."

Harrigan gave a skeptical cock of his head and turned to leave. As he watched Harrigan walk out, O'Keefe worried that Harrigan's streak of self-loathing might be his worst enemy in this crisis.

~

THE FEDERAL COURTHOUSE had been constructed fifty years before, during the Great Depression, using limestone from Indiana and concrete from local suppliers who had contributed to the right political campaigns, or better yet, hired the right relatives or friends of the local politicos. It made up for its ugliness with a promise of solidity and eternal life. O'Keefe, Harrigan's lawyer Ben Leclair, and a young male associate brought along to carry Ben's briefcase and take notes climbed the few steps from the sidewalk to the front doors of steel and tinted glass that continued the ugly-but-indestructible architectural theme. The Feds had recently installed extra security, including a metal detector, after an enraged client extracted a long-bladed knife from his briefcase and brandished it at the opposing lawyer who had just savaged him on cross-examination.

The chief U.S. Attorney, Ken Lord, had summoned them to a meeting and had bluntly suggested that Harrigan not attend. "He can come if he wants," Lord had said, "but I think we'll all be better off, especially him, if he doesn't."

"Seems to me a sign of weakness there," Leclair said when transmitting the message at a meeting in Leclair's office. "I recommend you let me handle it."

"Okay," Harrigan said, "but can Pete go?"

Leclair gave Harrigan a "so you don't trust me" look but said, "no problem."

As Harrigan later explained to O'Keefe, "It's not that I don't trust Ben. But I *don't* trust him. I don't trust any lawyer, including me, not to be pursuing their own agenda, even if they think it's for the client's own good. So any time that getting a different perspective is possible, it's worth it. Especially a layman's perspective, and a layman that I'm certain has my best interests at heart. Which would be you, get it?"

Lord did not make them play a waiting game. His secretary led them right in to his spacious office, the walls covered with diplomas, plaques of commendation, and photos of Lord with various local and national politicians including two different Attorneys General and President Reagan himself. Lord was photogenic handsome, tall and trim, streaks of gray in his black hair. He had the look of a United States Senator, which seemed to many, especially himself, to be his certain destiny.

A little birdlike man sporting orangeish horn-rimmed glasses and a yellow tie sat on Lord's right. O'Keefe recognized him as Max Trainer, which gave O'Keefe comfort. Harrigan had pointed Trainer out to him one day in the courthouse and said he considered Trainer a friendly acquaintance if not an actual friend. Max had never tried a case after his famously disastrous maiden performance long ago. He harbored not one theatrical bone in his sparrow's body, and his voice squeaked like a mouse under torture. But he was considered the best around town, and far beyond town, at preparing a case for trial. Lord did not rise to greet them while Trainer at least made a rising-from-his-seat gesture toward them, then sat abruptly back, as if trying to concede both to general courtesy and his boss's lack thereof.

Lord did at least offer a general, almost mumbled "good morning" and Leclair returned a similar clipped greeting.

"Who's this?" Lord said, indicating O'Keefe.

"His name is Peter O'Keefe," Leclair said, "he's our investigator."

"I'm not sure he was invited," Lord said, leaving that comment suspended in the air, waiting for Leclair to do something with it.

When Leclair failed to respond, Lord said, "I guess he can stay."

"What's up, Ken?" Leclair said.

"I wanted to give you a chance to plead him guilty for a much better deal than he'll get from Judge Montgomery once we convict him."

"Well, that's a mighty big leap you're making. I'd say world record big. We don't see a conviction in the cards."

"This case is just one manifestation of one of the most disastrous financial scandals in the history of our country. Hundreds of failures of financial institutions, and more to come. The losses have already been stupendous, and there'll be billions more down the road. The S&L rescue fund is insolvent. And the question has to be asked and answered: 'Where were the professionals?' They helped facilitate the transactions that resulted in all this. Will they just be allowed to reap all those huge fees from transactions they had to know were reckless at best and fraudulent at worst?"

"Practicing your jury speech already, I see. But I don't think the public thinks that at all. I think that's your own mantra. But much as you might wish so, lawyers aren't policemen, or FBI agents, or prosecutors."

"I have two witnesses testifying to your client's guilty knowledge."

"One of your witnesses is an obvious fraudster who'd sell his wife and children for his next trip to the whorehouse."

"You may be right about Eddie Tremaine, but Forest Marler will make Tremaine believable. Forest has been an upstanding lawyer and citizen all his life."

"And his particular thirty pieces of silver was the 'get-out-of-jail-free' card you gave him for his testimony. An old man at the end of his working life and with a sick wife to boot...and those tainted witnesses are all you have. You have no document or any other evidence that Harrigan knew where those loan proceeds were going."

"Given his *special* relationship with both sides of the loan transaction…the bank one of his top, if not his very top, paying client…and Tremaine not just his client but essentially his business partner…and given his reputation as a lawyer who has command of every aspect of anything he does, do you really think the jury'll believe he didn't know?"

CHAPTER ▶ 16

THE PHONE RANG, jolting both of them as they were watching *Watership Down* on the television. Hazel was just ascending to somewhere in the Great Beyond. Kelly was crying, and he was trying not to. So late on a Saturday night. Kelly gave him a look between a question and alarm. He let the phone ring, moved quickly to turn the volume down on the television and, in a couple of strides, he was standing next to his desk and expectantly hovering over the ringing phone. On the fifth ring his voice message answered the call.

"This is Peter O'Keefe. Please leave a message."

The voice on the other end said, "This is Fagan…"

O'Keefe quickly picked up the phone. "O'Keefe."

"…Derek Fagan. I assume you remember me."

O'Keefe felt his blood pressure rise and the stress pulse in his temples, just like on guard duty at the firebase in 'Nam and hearing a sudden unexplained noise or movement in the jungle. And this was certainly a creature of the jungle.

"I've got something you might be interested in."

O'Keefe's eyes narrowed into slits of curiosity. "What is it?"

"I don't talk on the phone. For all I know you record your calls."

Actually, he didn't. *That's a good idea. I need to get a device.*

"When?"

"Now. I'm in your neighborhood."

"Now? What neighborhood?"

"Where you live."

How the fuck do you know where I live, O'Keefe thought, but said, "It's Saturday night. I have someone here with me."

"Well, if you can't take a little break from bangin' the bitch to talk to me for a few minutes..."

After hesitating a moment, O'Keefe said, "It's my daughter."

Fagan stayed quiet for a bit, probably realizing that he had dug himself another hole with O'Keefe and perhaps contemplating what the physical consequences might be. "Sorry about that, but I'm in the mood right now, and I might not be later. Might be now or never."

"When?"

"I meant it. *Now.* I'm right down the street. Parked. I'll walk up and meet you on the sidewalk. And I'm armed, so don't think you can get away with beatin' me up again...Should I come?"

O'Keefe remembered Fagan's threat—the "associates" who could make O'Keefe "answer." A trap? He could taste the adrenalin as it flooded into his craw. Maybe Fagan knew Kelly was there, and this was a way to get O'Keefe out on the street to take his revenge. Or worse, maybe he knew Kelly was there and didn't care that she might be collateral damage.

"Are you there?" Fagan said impatiently.

"You're alone?"

"Yes."

"Okay. Come. And I'm armed too."

He hung up the phone and looked at Kelly. He chose to be honest with her.

"I need to meet a man out in front of the house. I'm not exactly sure what'll happen. I doubt anything will, but I don't know. Lock the door behind me. Then watch us from the front window. I don't think it will, but if something…bad…happens, call 911."

She said nothing, just vigorously nodded her head. He retrieved and strapped on his shoulder holster and noticed her eyes widen in fear. He turned off the front porch light he usually left on all night and took up watch on the front porch, trying to stay in the shadows. He did not have to wait long. Fagan was soon standing on the sidewalk in front of the house. O'Keefe moved slowly off the porch to the sidewalk, trying to open his senses to any possible sound, movement, or just a sensation.

"I'll make it quick," Fagan said. "I told you about China White. What you told me about Bev, which, believe me or not, I knew nothing about before your fucking assault…I hadn't seen her for months before that…well, it made me curious. I asked around about that big shipment that came in about that time. There was nothing on the street even close to as powerful as that, and nothing else that could have surprised her and killed her like that stuff. As I said, it pisses me off that I didn't even get any of it offered to me."

"I'm singing the blues for you."

"And it pisses me off even more now that I know who got it. It was a guy named Wayne Popper."

"Who's that?"

"I don't actually know him. And wouldn't want to know him. Wouldn't piss on him if he was on fire."

"So why are you telling me this?"

"First reason is that Popper and the guys he hangs with are redneck no-class violent punks that give people like me a bad name."

O'Keefe emitted a small breath of disgust.

"Hey, have a sense of humor. That was tongue-in-cheek."

"You're quite the wit." O'Keefe's shoulders lurched forward in a purely instinctual involuntary gesture of attack, but he quickly brought himself under control and Fagan didn't notice the movement.

"But really…guys like that do things that only bring the heat down on people like me."

"People like you, huh?"

"And I don't like the competition. I especially don't like that those idiots could score a load of China, of which I got zero. And so if you go charging in there and do your 'Rambo' thing on 'em, well, good for me."

"Why would I do that?"

"Well, I told you that China shipment was the only place she could've got a single shot powerful enough to kill her."

"That's not much to go on."

"One more thing. Popper and his bunch grew up in and still operate out of Bev's old part of town…your old part of town too. I bet she knew them, or of them. Bet she dealt with them before. I wasn't her only source."

O'Keefe was interested now.

"And there's another reason."

"I'm listening."

"I'm not as bad a guy as you think. I liked Bev. Tim too. I would never've done that to her. I've never done it to anybody."

"How wonderful. Move over, Mother Teresa. I'll write a letter to the Nobel Peace Prize Committee."

"All I want you to do is not pay me any more visits or make it your special mission to put me in jail or just fuck with me. I could've sent someone to see you who'd've done a lot worse than give you some useful information."

"Tried to…"

Fagan did not understand.

"*Tried* to do a lot worse. I'd've had somethin' to say about that."

"Touché. Fair enough."

"You know anything more about Popper?"

"Only that he's a piece of shit and that he's a bouncer at a topless joint out in the county called Cherry Pink."

Had the streetlight overhead been slightly brighter, Fagan would have seen a look of recognition on O'Keefe's face along with a slight, quick, startled snapback of head and neck.

Fagan turned to walk back where he had come from.

"Hey," O'Keefe said, and Fagan turned back. "I appreciate it... sincerely."

Fagan gave a nod of acceptance and satisfaction, turned, and walked on.

As O'Keefe watched Fagan's departing back fading into the darkness, he remembered how badly he had wanted to hurt Fagan on his first encounter with him. Had Fagan offered even the slightest physical resistance, O'Keefe was not sure he could have kept himself from badly hurting the man or done him even worse. He wondered if he suffered from an acute case of what they called "projection." O'Keefe himself had been poised on the verge of such a possible life. And he wondered if he hated Fagan so much because Fagan had reminded him, in an unconscious way, of the person O'Keefe himself had once been or could easily have become not all that long ago.

Kelly did not unlock the door until O'Keefe said "Okay, kid, you can open now." Once they tried to settle back down and resume watching the movie, he had a hard time concentrating and could tell she was having the same problem.

"Dad, what was that about?"

He wondered whether to tell her anything, or how to tell it, what to include and what to leave out. He decided to tell her the truth, some of it anyway.

"A lady I've known for a long time died of a drug overdose recently. I'm trying to figure out whether she did that to herself or someone did it to her."

She stayed quiet for a while, then said, gesturing toward the TV, "Dad, why are they always killing girls?"

Her gesture toward the TV...all those TV shows where the women were murdered...and it was true in real life too. Her question opened up so much he did not fully understand, let alone would be able to explain to an eleven-year-old. How much did she know about sex? How much had Annie or someone else covered it with her? And the violence. Not that he hadn't thought deeply about it, and for a long time and in many contexts, even painfully personal ones. He had thought about it when, a few times in drunken arguments, Annie had walked away and went wandering around in the night. He had not even tried to stop her. Once, the police had even picked her up and brought her home. Another time, on a trip out of town, she had walked off and later tried to come back into the hotel room. She did not have a key, and he had been asleep and so drunk he could not hear her knock. She was afraid to disturb the other guests or bring on the hotel employees by yelling or banging on the door too loudly, so she just left the hotel and wandered the streets of a strange city all night. The next day, once they had both recovered and somewhat made up, he said, "Please don't do that kind of stuff, and don't let me let you do it, no matter how drunk I am. Something horrible could happen to you." But that was advice only sober and rational people were likely to follow—not these two O'Keefes locked in desperate, mostly drunken combat.

Then Kelly had come along, giving him a reason to be fearful almost constantly. It would be so easy for a predator to take advantage of Annie, or more likely him, absent-minded and self-absorbed, failing to pay attention for a few negligent moments. How often did one of them leave Kelly alone, say for just a few minutes, when they were late to pick her up from school or somewhere else? It might not even be a stranger. It could be a schoolmate or a schoolmate's father or brother. And, yes, it would inevitably be a male. *Why do we think we have that right?* And he meant it when he used the word "we" in his thought. Twice, during those drunken arguments of theirs, he had hit her, in one case hard enough to give her a black eye. The second incident was just before he left home for good. He couldn't go on any longer when he could no longer assure himself that he would not do the same thing again. It made him feel like he was no better than the worst of men, taking advantage of their strength to beat or rape, or just hurt or force a creature less physically powerful—like Mary Jane Donovan and what she had to endure in her final moments of life. Or, now, Bev.

Finally, he said, "I have to admit that I really don't know why exactly, but you and every other girl or woman has to know it's there...somewhere deep within many boys and men. And there will almost certainly come a time when you're at risk...in real danger... and a decision you make at that moment may make all the difference (*whether you live or die, or live but live irreparably broken*). I don't know how to teach you how to make that decision."

"Geez, Dad, that's so scary." She visibly shuddered.

He wondered if he had been foolish to say what he had said to her, wondered if he had just done her a great disservice. She hadn't asked about herself. He had personalized it. But he felt he needed to warn her, make her feel deep down the danger that too often was right there, stalking her.

She jumped up and assumed a karate stance. "Maybe I ought to learn karate…like *The Karate Kid,*" she said.

That innocent gesture broke the spell. He laughed.

"Actually, that's a good idea. You know, Sara is doing martial arts."

"Really?"

"Will you really take some lessons if I arrange it?"

"Heck yes."

"Okay, Karate Kid."

But he would not let it end there. He thought and said something else, hoping it would stay with her and be with her at that fateful, decisive instant, the verge of horror and tragedy. "But that won't take away that moment of decision I'm talking about…that decision that gets you in or keeps you out of that situation, or deciding what to do if you get into it."

"How do I learn that?"

He wished he had an answer, needed to have an answer, but he didn't. "I have to admit I don't know. Just be careful. Be wise."

But it really seemed like too much to ask. He feared it would boil down to a roll of the dice, landing randomly on dumb good luck or the cruelest fate.

CHAPTER ▶ 17

"YOU GOTTA BE shittin' me, Boss. A strip joint called Cherry Pink?"

"So the job is right up your alley, George. Hang around naked women and get paid for it."

"Yeah, but hands off, I'm sure."

"'Fraid so."

"That's not a job, it's a punishment. What's the deal?"

"I need to know exactly what kind of bad things are going on in and out of that place and, most important, *who* is doing them."

"What's your theory?"

"At an absolute minimum, gambling and drugs. Surely there's some prostitution on the side too. Who knows what else? They operate in the county. Different government, different law enforcement, and different everything else than the city. They couldn't even operate that place under the city ordinances. They seem to be wired in the county, including with the sheriff's office. So be damn careful."

"If I hang around there as a customer, I'll end up a drunk with a dose of the clap or AIDS or somethin."

"You won't be able to do it for long. First, do all the background you can. Some of our old buddies in the neighborhood probably hang out there. Try the gambling angle. Your story is that you don't drink and you're not interested in sex you have to pay for, but it's football season, etcetera."

"Sorry, but you don't pay me enough to support a gambling habit."

"I'll give you enough to establish credibility, but if you don't win quick, or at least don't lose much, we're done."

"Who gets the winnings?"

"Same guy that gets the losings."

"Don't I get some vig? Or hazard pay?"

"Maybe. And you're right about hazard pay. These are some bad motherfuckers. Carry your weapon and be careful. Stay sober and stripper-free."

"Who're we working for here?"

"More bad news. We're working for the good of humanity unfortunately. And we may even be misguided about that."

"You'll have to do better than that, Boss."

So he explained the whole situation to George.

"How ugly. I can't believe Jerry would've done any of that. Bev's brain was probably Swiss cheese at the end."

"*I* can believe it about him."

"Why?"

He paused for a moment, wondering if he could explain it in a way that would effectively convey what happened. "One night a long time ago we double dated. Some older college guy buddy of his, they were trying to recruit him to the school, let us use his apartment. I just took my girl in one bedroom and made out some. I come out and he's there with his date, and she's sobbing, blood all down her dress. She was a virgin."

"He forced her?"

"Not sure exactly 'forced,' but he sure wasn't gentle with her... and showed not a hint of concern about what she was going through. After we took them home, we're driving along, and he laughs to himself, looking straight ahead, and says, 'Cherry poppin' time.'...I was done with him after that."

"He'll be the next mayor."

"That's one reason we need to run this down all the way if we can. Pay special attention to two people, one who I know is associated with the place, and one who might be. There's a bouncer named Wayne Popper. I think he's in the drug business. If you do nothing else, follow him close and see where he leads us. And if you run into or even hear someone mention the name of David Bowman, let me know ASAP."

"Fucking Bowman. I thought they put him in jail forever a long time ago. Or somebody just killed the prick."

"'Fraid not. Very much alive and still scary as hell."

TWO WEEKS LATER, George called a meeting at the office. The three of them gathered in the conference room.

"While we're all together," O'Keefe said, "let's talk about where we are on Mike's case."

George jerked his head toward Sara and said, "She's done most of the work so let her start."

Sara launched in. "The bad news is we've interviewed most of the bank employees now and haven't found any direct evidence or anything else to corroborate Harrigan's innocence. The good news is the obverse of the bad. We also haven't found anything that supports the prosecution's case."

"'Obverse,'" George said. "How you like them apples? Do we have an English major here?"

O'Keefe joined in the tease: "Maybe we need to look up 'opposite' in the dictionary and figure out why that word wasn't precise enough. Or maybe 'converse'...or 'inverse'...or 'reverse.'"

Sara blushed. "Okay, jackasses."

"And speaking of apples, Sara, our friend George here once misspelled that word in the class spelling bee. A-p-p-e-l according to George. The incident became famous."

"Shit," George said. "That's S-H-I-T."

Shrugging off the teasing, Sara said, "The important thing is the whole case is still only circumstantial. I really don't think they've got anything else."

"Well," said O'Keefe, "they've got Tremaine's and Marler's testimony. That's pretty damn direct."

"That's a whole other kettle of worms."

"You mean kettle of *fish*. It's 'kettle of fish' and *can* of worms. George, have you ever noticed that this obviously intelligent woman, with a vocabulary that includes ready recall and possibly proper usage of the word 'obverse,' just can't quite get her sayings right. Like, for example, one day she came out with the phrase 'he's no spring *puppy*,' thus transformed from the traditional spring *chicken*."

"Can we get on with this?" she said, her face reddening even further. "This is important. I read both of their statements first and then talked to each one of them on the phone, and what's really interesting is the chronology, the timeline of how they implicated Harrigan. Ben is really excited about this."

"How about the M&Ms?"

"I don't think Mark Marcus knew what was going on at all, and nobody's giving him up. He was never around. He was too busy on 'higher pursuits'—politics, and culture, and charity drives, and all that. Morris Manning had to try to keep the whole tottering empire propped up while Marcus was gallivanting around being a do-gooder. Morris was the architect of the whole scheme. He's not saying a word, taking the Fifth all the way."

"Well, let's hope he doesn't decide to buy a ticket on the Liar Train too. Two against one is hard enough."

"Here's the deal: In their initial statements neither of them mentioned Harrigan. Not a word about him the first time through. *Ken Lord's* the one that suggested Harrigan might have had some knowledge."

She noticed their sudden concentration on her words. "Yes, *Lord*. He suggested, separately and specifically to each of them, that they might get better treatment if they implicated someone else. They both immediately piled onto Morris Manning. But then *Lord* wonders out loud about Harrigan. He says to Tremaine 'Surely your lawyer knew about this.' And Tremaine says, 'Surely he did. He knows everything.' And as time goes on, and Tremaine sees a possible 'get out of jail free,' or at least 'get out sooner' card, his memory gets more and more specific, until by the end he remembers being in a conference room with Harrigan present with Morris Manning laying out how things were gonna go down."

"Did you get a date of that meeting?"

"I got within one of three dates, all within a two-week period, and George and I are reconstructing Harrigan's calendar and Tremaine's schedule to see if we can find a hole in that."

"Good. Let's hope he went too far trying to gild the lily too much. And Marler?"

"Again, the second time Lord interviews Marler, it's *Lord* who brings up Harrigan and asks about his role. And this was after he told Marler in so many words that he could earn some credit with the prosecution if he named others that might be involved. And all of a sudden Marler says, 'Sure, Harrigan okay'd it.'"

"Is that the word he used…'okay'd'…it.?"

"Yes. That's in the witness statement, and he used that word when I talked to him on the phone."

"It's one thing to 'okay' the loan...you know, from the legal point of view, the loan documents being correct and all that as far as the borrower is concerned. It doesn't mean he 'okay'd' or even knew how the loan funds were gonna be used. Lawyers usually have nothing to do with that."

"My thinking exactly."

"Might be a little tricky for a jury though. Most of them don't use words like 'obverse.'"

He and George had another good laugh.

"Funny ha-ha," she said.

"Is that it?"

"So far."

"Okay, let's talk about George's adventures in the skin trade."

"I think I'm done," George said. "They're not buying my line."

"How's the betting?" O'Keefe said.

"I've made two Saturdays worth of college bets and two Sundays worth of pro bets. Big bets. One good week and one bad. Same old gambling story."

"What else?"

"I hinted around trying to score some coke but nobody was snapping at that bait."

"Who'd you try with?"

"Mostly the bartender. Popper some, but it was hard to hang out with him. I stayed around late a couple nights until closing, but he disappeared. And I can't loiter around there forever not drinking or just drinking a little, trying to pace myself so they don't have to carry me out of there. I did feed the girls a lot of dollar bills but so did every hard dick in the place. Even that got old quick. I've had all I want of that for the rest of my life. Any more of that and I might swear off sex."

"That's it?"

"Maybe a couple other things. Lots of activity in the back room. The manager's office. I think there are people coming in and out of the back door. Popper heads back there every night at closing and leaves out the back."

"How about the liquor license...the ownership?"

"Well now there we start to get interesting. The license is in the name of Elmer Popper, Wayne Popper's uncle. And not his rich uncle either. He's eighty-four years old and in a nursing home."

"So somebody's got two levels between them and disclosure. Elmer, then Wayne."

"And neither Popper has 'a pot ta piss in or a window ta throw it out of,' as my mom used to say. And that damn place is no redneck scuffed-up dump. It's *nice*. It's *plush*. Somebody's put in a lot of money and keeps putting money in there."

"Drug money? A way to launder it?"

"Or mystery investors."

"Can't be. Not again. Not Jagoda."

"I doubt it. The Jagoda bunch wouldn't put their fate in the hands of a guy like Popper. Or Bowman either."

"What about Bowman?"

"I didn't see him around. I can only make a couple of connections, but they're damned interesting. First, he and Popper have been running buddies, thug buddies since high school...well, in their case, reform school. Second, Popper comes from this huge family out in the county with relatives sprinkled all over the county government from the council to the tax assessor to the sheriff's office. That's how they're able to keep that place—and all that goes on in it and out of it—running. The rumors are everywhere...the gambling but also drugs, some petty loan sharking, extortion when they get the chance, prostitution of course, and who knows what they do to those girls just for the sport of it. Those guys are lower than snake shit."

~

AFTER GEORGE LEFT, and after a long silence, Sara said, "You really want to get inside that place?"

"Hell yes," O'Keefe said and waited expectantly but soon wished he hadn't welcomed it.

"I'll apply for a job."

"What job?"

"Duh."

He knew his first reaction to this, emphatically negative, was not the right thing to express. He would need the indirect approach, coming around the long way. So he said nothing, just looked at her, with skepticism but not hostility.

She broke the silence. "You *know* it's a good idea."

He continued to keep his counsel.

"A job interview. How dangerous can that be? A lot less dangerous than marching into that drug house."

"As if that was a good idea," he said, having found a possible opening to a reasoned approach. "You know that wasn't a smart thing to do."

"It may have saved her sanity, even her life."

"And it probably could've waited just a few minutes until help, meaning me, arrived."

"Maybe. Who knows? But that's not the point. If I'm gonna do what you and George do, then I have to do things like this."

"But I'm not sure *I'd* do this, or that George would do it, or that I'd let George do something like it even if he was crazy...I repeat... *crazy*...enough to want to do it. This profession isn't supposed to be about putting yourself in danger."

"Well, then George is a wimp and so are you. I'm fond of you, I love working with you. I really like that business plan you've come up with. We can really make something here. But I can't keep playing the little sister..."

There it was. Use her or lose her. He didn't want to lose her even though her nearness was so often like a wound being reopened every day.

"At least let me think about it until tomorrow. You'd really quit?"

Her eyelids fluttered. She couldn't carry off a bluff with him. "I don't know. Just don't put me in that corner, okay?"

THE NEXT DAY, he didn't show up at the office at all. They talked on the phone a couple of times and not a word about the most important issue, to her anyway. On the following day he did not arrive at the office until mid-afternoon, like he was avoiding her. But he was carrying a box.

"Let's go in the conference room," he said.

He opened the box and extracted three small black devices.

"I've got a mad scientist buddy named Terry Lecumske. You'll probably be seeing him a lot in the future. He put this together for me. It's a device sort of like a pager, but all it does is transmit a signal over a short distance. No wires. It's a radio signal. You punch the button on one end, and it vibrates on the other. I'll have one at my end. I want you to take two...Stop grinning."

"Thanks," she said. "I thought when you didn't come in..."

Much taller than she, he looked down into her brown eyes, pools of sincerity, the slight blush in her cheeks, the gold hoops dangling just below the fall of her hair, the light peach blouse you could almost see through, her long slender fingers and clear-polished nails, the silver bracelet on her wrist. She had dressed today for maximum persuasiveness.

"That was a pretty powerful card you played...threatening to quit."

"I had to take a stand."

"And you won. I'll be scared shitless, but I'll try my best to let you do whatever I'd let myself or George do. But I don't trust you to stop where you ought to, so we might still butt heads about it every once in a while, and you can't threaten to quit every time."

"Fair enough. But, like they say, that devil's in the details."

"Anyway, you take two of these. One goes in your purse, and one actually on your physical person, well hidden."

"Why two?"

"Fail-safe. I'll be outside somewhere close, and if mine vibrates, I'll be tearing the door down to get in there. And George is also making up something that should pass on quick examination as a valid Alabama driver's license for one Tracy Fox who's gonna be calling up for a job interview."

Her brow furrowed.

"Didn't think about that, did you, Nancy Drew? That they might want to see your ID."

SHE PREPARED THE rest of that day and evening, and the next afternoon she called Cherry Pink. She asked for the manager, affecting a slight Southern accent and talking on the slow side, easy on the ear.

"I need to tell him why you're calling."

"I'd like to come to come work for y'all."

"Waitress?"

"On the platform."

"Hold on," he said, his voice jumping with sudden energy. "It may be a couple minutes."

And a couple minutes later another voice came on and said, "Marty Lansing."

"I guess that's your name?"

"Funny. Almost."

"I'd like to come in for an interview. I'm new in town and I need work."

"Why you think you're cut out for this?"

"I look great. I've got a great body. I like men looking at me."

"You and about a billion other chicks."

"They only *think* so. I've done it before…plenty…and I'm good at it."

"Where?"

"Birmingham…Alabama."

"Bush league."

"Well, what do you call *this* town? Sure isn't the majors."

"Name of the place?"

"Jewels." They had researched it and knew there was a joint still in business there with that name. But if he called there, the jig was, as they say, up.

"Your name?"

"Tracy Fox." They had researched enough to know there had been a stripper of that name performing at Jewels recently who had moved on. But if he called to check—again, that jig might be up.

"Can't be your real name."

"I'm ready when you are."

"When can you come in?"

"Say when and I'm in."

"Ditto that." He let that witticism sink in and then said, "One of the owners is gonna be here next Thursday night. We need two approvals to hire a dancer. Mine, and this owner's. He's got a nose for picking the right girls."

"I bet he's got something else for picking them too."

"Careful. We don't much like smartasses around here. You could've just lost the job right there."

Now was the time to show that vulnerability, that inner shame and self-loathing, whatever else it was that drove these women to abase themselves, often thinking they were achieving the opposite. "Oh, no, please. Meet me. You'll see I'm perfect for you."

"We close at 2 a.m. Come in at midnight or a little after, say 12:30."

A midnight job interview. Now *that* made her nervous.

CHAPTER ▶ 18

"OVERSLEEP?" SARA SAID, when he opened the door to the office on Monday morning.

"Took Kelly to school."

"Leclair called," she said, handing him the pink call memo slip for a reminder, which he didn't need because he quickly returned the call.

"When I got in this morning," Leclair said, "I had a voicemail message from a woman named Maura Davis. The message said, and I'm quoting it verbatim, 'I read the newspaper article on your Harrigan case. I might have some helpful information. Something Mike Harrigan and Ken Lord have in common.'"

"Odd," O'Keefe said.

"It's probably just an invite to a goose chase, but you never know. Can you give her a call?"

"On it," O'Keefe said, hung up the phone, and called George. "There's a woman named Maura Davis that I need to know more about. There might be some connection between this woman, Ken Lord, and Mike. The implication from the message I got is that whatever she has to tell us might help his defense."

George called back the next afternoon. "Maura Davis is a paralegal. Works at Foley and Schultz now. But her first paralegal job was at the U.S. Attorney's office."

"Was Lord U.S. Attorney then?"

"Yep. And by the way, she's single and a knockout. Want me to interview her?"

"Sorry to deprive you of an opportunity, George, but I'd better talk to Mike first. No telling what's going on here."

He called Harrigan right away. "Things get curiouser and curiouser, Michael. I don't know what this means yet, but does the name Maura Davis resonate with you?"

Harrigan said nothing for several seconds, then, "What the hell. Am I gonna have to pay for every one of my sins at the same time? What could she possibly have to do with my case?"

"What's the sin?"

"I had a thing with her when Mary and I were separated that time. Not a little thing. A big thing."

"And where did she work at the time?"

"U.S. Attorney's office."

"Ken Lord."

"So what. Coincidence."

O'Keefe told him about the message Leclair had received.

"I'm inclined to just leave it alone. Mary doesn't need that along with everything else she's goin' through."

"I think I should at least run it down. Stupid not to. Do you want to set it up?"

"Fuck no."

"Why not?"

"Because I'm a coward. She loved me. Or thought she did. Might still. It broke her up bad when I went back home."

"How come I never met her?"

"Those were your drug lord days. We didn't see much of each other during that phase of your drama."

"I'm gonna talk to her."

"Fine, but don't do one other thing without talking to me first."

"HELLO," SHE SAID, bright as a sunbeam.

"Is this Maura Davis?"

"Ye-e-e-s," she said hesitantly and not so brightly now.

He deliberately softened his voice.

"I'm sorry to bother you, especially at work, but I didn't know how else to contact you. My name is Peter O'Keefe. I'm a private investigator, but the important thing is I'm Mike Harrigan's best friend. From a long way back. We grew up together. I'm working with Ben Leclair on Mike's case. He asked me to follow up on your voicemail."

"Oka-a-y." No brightness at all now.

"Don't hesitate to look me up, check me out however you want. Don't hesitate to call Ben if you want. And we can meet in whatever public or private place you choose."

"What's your number? I'll call you later...maybe..."

He hung up, intrigued now and impatient for her to return his call, which she did not do until the next day.

"Okay, you check out okay. I have to admit that I had a few drinks before I left that message, and I've had some regrets. Now a private detective for Christ's sake! I'm scared to death. Where might this lead? Will I end up in the headlines...the scarlet lady in some huge scandal—"

He interrupted her because he thought that otherwise she might never stop. "Let's just take it a step at a time. I need to hear your story."

"Okay, let's get this over with. Can we meet after work tonight?"

"Sure."

"Do I have to do this? Should I get my own lawyer? What if I refuse now?"

"If you refuse, we may not do anything, but we probably will. Probably try to force you. That'll probably get in the papers."

"Well, I've dug myself a hole, haven't I? I guess we can meet. Where?"

"Would you be more comfortable at a public place?"

She went quiet, seemed unsure, so he helped her along. "Ever heard of Harvey's?"

"Yeah."

"Let's meet there."

"I hope a bunch of lawyers don't hang out there. I'd rather not take a chance on running into someone I know."

"No, this is a slightly higher-class bunch of predators."

He arrived early and waited for her at the door to minimize her anxiety and impress her with his solicitude. He had decided not to take notes. Dangerous, but it was worth it not to risk scaring her with that formality, possibly causing her to tailor her story for the notes. He wanted it raw and unedited. He was soon to discover this was an unedited woman all the way.

Wow. He could see why Lord and Harrigan fell for her. It would be hard not to. He steeled himself. This was no time for any of that.

Harvey, tending bar that afternoon, as well as several customers, said hello or otherwise acknowledged O'Keefe and approvingly checked out the lady as the two made their way back to a table at the far back corner of the back room.

Amused, she said, "Is this your clubhouse? Do I need the secret password?"

The waiter came right away: "Hey Pete, what can I get you guys?"

She said, "White wine for me."

"And iced tea for me."

"You don't drink?" she said.

"I'll put it this way. I've probably already had my lifetime quota, plus some."

"I get it. I probably ought to be drinking iced tea too," she said, laughing, her tousled strawberry blonde curls shaking back and forth, lapis blue eyes dancing and probing like searchlights. She wore no makeup, it seemed, except an assertive color of eye shadow—violet, he thought—and spotted, it seemed, with what he could swear were a few tiny specks of actual glitter. Her dress covered her right shoulder and angled down from there, stopping well above her breasts, not a hint of cleavage showing, but leaving her lovely left shoulder entirely bare.

"I like the purple," he said, referring to the color of her dress.

"Purple! That's aubergine, silly," she said, and mimicked a gum-chomping dame from a 1940s movie, "Ain't ya got no class, Mistah?"

"Not enough to know what aubergine means."

"Purple is what it means," she said and laughed again. "Eggplant actually, but that doesn't sound so sophisticated, does it? Eggplant!"

He needed to move on. This could quickly get out of hand. "So tell me about yourself. I know you're a paralegal."

She needed no more invitation or prodding than that, and it soon became apparent that she loved to talk. But she was entertaining and not overly self-absorbed. That brightness in her original "Hello" had returned now. He wondered at first how she could possibly have ended up with a dark, depressive type like Harrigan. He must have been looking for uplift at the time. She engaged you, made you smile and laugh a lot. She was twenty-nine now and had an eight-year-old daughter. Her marriage at age twenty ended by age twenty-two. "Nothing in common," she said. "Not one thing. What the heck was I thinking?"

In the years following the divorce she had "shacked up," as she put it, with a guy or two, but nothing lasted. Reciting each failed relationship, she became wistful and sad and vulnerable. No surprise that she had been a high school cheerleader. She had attended college for one semester but partied too much and flunked out. She started as a legal secretary, educating herself on the job and at junior college where she earned a paralegal degree. When the job at the U.S. Attorney's office came open, a government job seemed like a smart thing, with good health insurance benefits and lots of job security.

"And did you know, you don't have to pay into Social Security if you're a government employee? Crazy, huh? I thought I had it made..." She trailed off. They had come to the hard part, the reason they were meeting.

"It wasn't like I never had an office romance before Ken Lord—or worse, one of those drunken one-night motel stands with one of my lawyer bosses—not unmarried either, I *am* ashamed to say. God, I must seem like a real slut..." Pointing to her wine glass, she said, "This has had something to do with it. But I fall in love. I really do. I can't say that was true with Ken Lord though. That was pure...what's that word for wanting too much?"

She's landed right on my number. "Greed?"

"No. I'm not that dumb, I could come up with that myself. It's a bigger word than that."

"Craving? Longing?"

She shook her head "no," and her brain seemed to sizzle. "I think it begins with a 'C' though."

He thought for a bit. "Cupidity?"

"Wow. You got it. What a stud."

"No. I've got a special relationship with that particular human failing."

She looked at him, her face a question.

"Long story. Please go on."

At first she just thought of it as a way to advance in her career. Surely it couldn't hurt. It started slow, but as time went on, it became more and more regular and frequent. As things developed, she even conjured up the notion he might divorce his wife and marry her. The usual self-delusion. It actually happened once in a while, just often enough to make fools like her believe. But soon she realized he was way too much of a politician for such a wild and abandoned move as that. He bought her many nice things, everything from flowers to furniture, even gave her cash sometimes. Initially, she refused the cash because it made her feel like an actual prostitute, but he kept pushing it at her as time went on, and she felt more and more trapped. "I realized that's sort of what I was, a concubine at best, if not an actual whore, but at too damn big of a discount—so I started taking it…the money."

Because of "his position," Lord couldn't risk taking her out for dinner or anything else in the city. They took one trip out of town, during which he acted so paranoid that they both became so miserable they came back a day early. But despite the lack of commitment on his own part, over time he became more and more obsessed with her, and controlling. At the start she continued to date occasionally. He tolerated it at first but became more and more hostile. He never forbade her, just became meaner and meaner. He was a hard man to confront, but she tried.

"I said, 'how come it's okay for you to sleep with another woman every night, but I can't even go out to dinner with a guy?' And he said, 'I'm only sleeping with her,' as if that was all that needed to be said. So I had become literally a prisoner in my own apartment, and here's my daughter wondering if this guy was a new 'daddy' or what…more like *grand*-daddy actually.

"And the idea that it would help me in my career turned out to be about the most foolish notion I could've had. Typical of me. It went the other way. It became obvious really super quick he would bend over backwards *not* to be seen to help me. I'll tell you how uptight he was about the whole thing…not only did nobody in that whole office *know,* they never even *suspected.* So, man, did I want out of that situation, and I didn't see how except to quit the very job that had convinced me to try this thing in the first place…"

He was tempted to interrupt and ask her to move on to Harrigan but thought that would be a mistake, and so he let her go on and get to it in her own way. She was like a springtime torrent, but of the bubbly, fresh, soothing sort.

"…I started looking for a transfer within the government but didn't know how I could navigate that, how Ken might be able to kill that without me ever knowing. Meanwhile, he's showering me with these gifts, and I'm feeling more and more obligated and guilty but *not* grateful, feeling like a whore, etcetera. That's when Mike came into the picture. I'd stopped even trying to date but still went out 'with the girls' sometimes, you know—hit the bar after work. And one night he was there with some of the people from his office. I knew a couple of them, so I joined the group, and ended up sitting next to Mike. He didn't make a big deal about it but said he and his wife were separated and heading for a divorce. He didn't try to pick me up that night. Or ever really. We just fell into it. *Mucho* mutual. Looking back, and being honest, he was a way out for me. And I was something for him, or to him, I don't know what exactly. There was a time I really thought we were getting toward 'permanent' if you know what I mean. More delusion."

"Did Mike know about Lord?"

"No. I don't think *anyone* ever knew about him other than me and my little girl."

"But he knew about Mike. How did that come about?"

"Not sure. I juggled them for a couple of weeks. Only time in my life I've ever been unfaithful. Really. What a trick that was. Lucky, because Mike was quite polite when I told him I couldn't do a particular thing he wanted to do...go out or something. He was the opposite of Ken, very *un*-possessive. But later I realized that was mostly about making sure he himself had a way out if he needed it. But talk about crazy-making. And talk about feeling like a whore. If one of them was there, I was constantly afraid the other one would decide to drop by. It was only a couple of weeks, but I must have aged a year in that time period. And it didn't take but about five minutes for me to never want him, Ken that is, to touch me again.

"So, well, as I said, I couldn't take that juggling thing, so I put it to Ken as softly as I could. I said something like 'Ken, this is no good for me. Not only is there no future in it, but I'm like a prisoner.' And he was no dummy, he went straight to the heart of it. He said 'There's somebody else, isn't there?' I lied and said 'no' though it really wasn't a lie because, Mike or not, I needed to get out of that situation. I don't think he believed me. He was really mean about it. He could be a real ice cube, total frozen tundra, and that's what he was to me after that. We didn't work directly together much, he was too big of a deal for that. He didn't have a caseload..."

"Yet he's taken on Mike's case personally. First chair."

"Well, that's weird."

They both thought about this for a moment, until O'Keefe said, "Okay, I think we lost your thread there."

"Yeah. My threads tend to be loose. So one weeknight I'm home of course, and Ken calls me and asks if he can come over. 'Why?' I ask him, very wary I was. He says, 'I just want to talk about something. It will only take a few minutes. I don't even need to come in. You can come out to my car.' Which is what I did. He looked at me with these eyes that were both angry, and I guess the right word would be 'stricken' or 'pained,' not something I'd ever seen before from him, I'll tell you that. He was always in total command. Of himself and everyone else.

"He says, 'Isn't it bothering you to be around the office day after day?'

"Well, I'm always open, can't lie for shit, and I said, 'Frankly, yes.' And he says, 'You need to get another job.'

"I said, 'Well, easy for you to say, but it wouldn't be so easy to replace this job...the benefits and all.' And then he says, 'I'm told you're superb at your work. You could get a top job at several law firms, especially with my strong recommendation. The government might look good now, but it's a dead end for someone with your talent. You could go to law school, be a lawyer yourself someday.'

"I tried to act a little strong. I said 'I guess I could look around.' To which he responds, 'So that you understand very clearly, I'm not asking you, I'm telling you. You have to go. I'll make sure you get the best possible job.'

"And I said, 'Why are you doing this?'

"He didn't answer right away, I could tell he wasn't sure, but those eyes turned from mostly anger to all pain all at once. They flashed back again right away to anger, but I saw the other. Finally, he said 'I know you've got a new boyfriend.'

"I could tell he had a lot more he wanted to say, but his eyes told his story—accusations, threats, begging, you name it, but no words, just eyes. I didn't know what to say back, so I said nothing at all. Then he said, 'Start now. Most of the legal profession in this town want to please me. I'll make sure you're paid enough to make you better off than you are today.'

"So I said okay, and as I reached for the door handle, he said, 'Though I don't think you're the kind of person who would be so foolish as to try to cause trouble for me in the department, I warn you, for both of our sakes, that you *will* lose, and lose badly, if you take that route.'

"I said, 'You didn't need to say that,' and I left. I may have been imagining it, but I felt a sensation I thought was him reaching for me, an impulse, but withdrawing it as soon as it came. I've thought and thought. Was that a gesture toward violence or toward tenderness? What did he want to do to me right then?"

Maura took a long drink, emptying her wine glass. O'Keefe raised her empty glass and signaled the waiter for another.

"Thanks," she said. "I need another one for sure. What a mess. If there's a pile of crap somewhere, I'll be certain to step in it."

"What happened next?"

"It took a while, but he made his magic work, and I did get a great job…at Foley and Schultz, where I am still today."

"Doing well?"

"Top of the paralegal pile anyway."

"What about law school?"

"Well, I took the test and did well. The law school here admitted me. I'm sure the recommendation from Ken Lord helped a lot in that."

"How'd that come about?"

"I called and asked him. I'm sure he about crapped his pants when his secretary told him I was calling, him thinking 'Goddamn, I almost made a clean escape, and now she's got her hand out,'…and I'm sure he was super relieved when all I asked for was that recommendation letter."

"Any other contacts with him since?"

"None."

"You said he knew you had another guy. Did he know it was Mike?"

"I don't know for sure, but I can't believe he didn't know. Mike and I weren't advertising it around town, but we weren't keeping it a secret either. I didn't gossip about it in the office, not a bit, never would, but some of the lawyers and other people in the office knew about it. Mike was well-known around town even then. Heck, I guess Ken could've sort of even been stalking me. That's happened to me before. It's more common than you might think."

"Sorry to ask this if this is painful, but what happened with you and Mike?"

It was painful. She kept silent for an uncomfortably long time, then covered her face with her hands. Tears leaked through her fingers.

After composing herself, she went on, "It didn't last long. He went back home. He was as kind as he could be about it. But it broke my heart. I loved that guy, probably more than anybody ever. He was very dark but very deep, and I thought I could see something beautiful at the bottom of that well of loneliness, or whatever it is. I never quite got to see it, but there were hints and glimmers and images, unless I was just seeing my own fuzzy reflection in those dark waters. Stupid, stupid, stupid, always stupid. I apparently have to learn everything the hard way. This lesson was: Don't ever get hung up on a guy who's just separated, who's not divorced, and who's not prone to saying *mucho* nasty things about his ex-wife, preferably making death threats, and even better if the ex-wife has remarried."

The interview seemed to be over. He shuffled through his brain to try to identify any loose ends he needed to tie up. But there were only ones about her personal life. It would be good for her to think he cared. And he did care, but it might be good for his client if she actually knew that he cared.

"And how are things with you now?"

"Not much happening these days. It's all getting old. Or maybe it's just me that's getting old. I'm not all the way over him, if that's what you mean."

"No, I wouldn't've asked that...directly or indirectly."

"It's gone from constant heart-stabbing pain to a too-frequent dull ache, but it's still there. You know, I never left any of them. Except for my husband and Ken, they all left me."

And that one stabbed *his* heart. He groped awkwardly for a change of subject, looking for something positive. "How about law school?"

"Well, I got accepted but didn't go. It's hard enough working and taking care of a kid. Now, how do I add law school, even if it's night school and a limited schedule, onto that? And it's expensive. What if I start out and run up a bunch of student loans and then have to quit?"

"Tough. Working mothers are the real heroes of this world."

"Well, thanks, but I wish that hero thing had better pay, hours, and benefits. They really set us up to be a sort of combo concubine and maid to you guys, and if we end up without one of you to support us, we're S-O-L."

He thought of Annie struggling now to find a career that could reduce her dependence and maybe even provide a modicum of dignity. He said, "You ought to go for a scholarship. Maybe your law firm would help on the cost."

She did not look hopeful about her prospects.

"And how's your eight-year-old?"

"Now that's the one thing that seems to be going just right, cross my fingers and knock on wood and pray to the devil if I have to... 'cause she'll be in her teens before long and that's a whole new thing. Dangerous, dangerous waters, those."

"Yeah, I've got one of those myself...daughter."

"Hmm...I don't see a ring."

"Divorced."

She offered him a look that managed to combine seductive come on with an amused, sardonic "here I go again" self-knowledge. Which meant it was definitely time to close the interview. Neither of them could afford the distraction and especially the risk of taking a next step and seeing where this might lead.

"Can you think of anything else I ought to know...anything that might help, or hurt, Mike?"

She pondered this, her eyes focused and brow furrowed in concentration, then said, "Can't think of anything."

"Will you call me if you do?"

He could tell she would like to say "no," remove herself from what this situation could develop into, because it was hard to see how it could be anything but a bad deal for her.

"I wish I could say no, but I can't. You think it'll really happen. This thing could cost me my job."

"I can't say for sure, but I can't envision a situation where Lord won't know about it. How public it gets, I'm not sure."

"God! What a cluster-fuck, excuse my *English*."

He walked her to her car and stood by the driver's side door as she scratched around in her purse for her keys.

"My God, even a gentleman," she said. "I think this is where I should say 'Call me sometime.'"

"Save yourself. You're wonderful by the way, and I mean that, but I'm just another heartache waiting to happen."

She gave him a "well, thanks but no thanks" look and said, "But then 'no risk, no reward' either." After a sharp conclusory nod of her head, she scooted into the driver's seat as he closed the door. She started the car, and, after a quick upward glance, Maura Davis drove off as he watched her and wondered why she couldn't get someone worthwhile to love her in the way she seemed to deserve.

CHAPTER ▶ 19

"I'VE GOT A grenade for you," he told Leclair.

"Jesus, I hope you haven't pulled the pin already," Leclair said, half joking but half serious. "Maybe I don't want you to hand it over."

He told Leclair the story of Ken and Maura and Mike.

"What's she like? As a witness, I mean."

"Completely candid. Completely engaging. She'll have a tendency to wander all over the place but is smart enough to know what could hurt and what not."

"Promiscuous?"

He really didn't know how to answer that. "I don't know. Depends how you define that. But she has this basic...I'll call it innocence...certainly that's the affect...and the effect too...overwhelmingly so."

"So I'll ask what the Judge will ask. How is this relevant?"

"Are you kidding? We know that Lord's the one that actually suggested to Tremaine and Marler that they implicate Harrigan."

"Well, in the end, so what? Mike either knew, or he didn't know."

"It goes to the credibility of their testimony."

"That Lord led them there is relevant. That he may have had a malicious reason for it may not be relevant."

"But for that malicious reason, there probably wouldn't be any prosecution here at all. It taints the whole thing."

"But now there's two witnesses that implicate him. It may have been a witch hunt, but they think they found a witch."

"Let's call Mike. This could decide his fate."

"Sure."

They found Harrigan at home and got him on the speaker phone. O'Keefe let Leclair explain it, without interrupting him once, and had to admit to himself that Leclair laid it out fairly, after which Harrigan said, "I can't have this conversation from here. I'll be down there in thirty minutes."

Leclair and O'Keefe stared at each other for a few uncomfortable moments until Leclair said, "If you don't mind, Pete, I want to confer with my partner about this."

Harrigan arrived before Leclair returned and said, "I couldn't have this conversation from home."

"Mary?" O'Keefe said.

"Yeah, it'll be just another stab in her heart. We were separated at the time, but the separation was my doing so that's not gonna ease the pain."

"Here I come with the best news we've gotten so far, possibly the trump card, and you two lawyers are pissing all over it."

Leclair rushed in, excited, as if he'd discovered buried treasure somewhere down one of his hallways.

"You see the problem, right, Mike?" he said.

"Yes," Harrigan said in disgusted resignation.

O'Keefe couldn't control himself. "Problem? You guys kill me. It's not a problem, it's the fucking solution."

"Hear me out," Leclair said. "If Judge Montgomery has the same reaction to this as I do, that it's irrelevant, he's likely to go ballistic that we pulled this stunt to try to blackmail the U.S. Attorney's office... bringing scandalous shame and disrepute on the Department of Justice and effectively the entire federal government...and let's remember he was the U.S. Attorney himself before he became Judge Montgomery. But maybe we can have our cake and eat it too."

"File under seal?" Harrigan said.

Leclair, looking satisfied with himself, said, "Exactly."

O'Keefe, severely agitated, asked, "Does that mean it may never be public, never see the light of day?"

"Well, if he does rule it to be irrelevant, he may put a gag order on us."

"And if you file it under seal, you're just inviting him to do exactly that."

"Well, if he does, that'll be a major issue on appeal and a bargaining chip for negotiations with the U.S. Attorney's office on sentencing."

"Jesus, you're assuming conviction. This will keep a conviction from happening. Would that gag order apply to me? I'll take it to the press myself."

"Hell yes, it would apply to you," Leclair said. "Contempt of court. He'd throw you in jail, fine you, and do everything he could to make your life miserable."

"It might be worth it if it gets Mike off the hook. Just file the damn thing. The press'll pick it up, and it'll be too late for him to do anything about it."

"I strongly advise against it. And, Mike, I'm sorry to say, if you reject that advice, I'll have to consult with my partners, and I might have to ask you to find other counsel."

O'Keefe leaned forward toward Leclair. "It sounds to me like this is more about you and your future in the courthouse than it is about your client here."

"Who do you think you are to make an accusation like that? To do other than I'm suggesting is just reckless. It's a boomerang that could come back and cut Mike's head off."

O'Keefe intended to continue arguing, but Harrigan raised his arm and hand in a gesture of restraint. "Thanks, Pete, but I have to go with Ben. Let's show him the gun without pulling the trigger. Save the bullet for later, especially if it might be a blank. If we go public with it and the Judge says it's irrelevant, we've created a public scandal for nothing. He'll hate us, and he might do everything he can to punish us for it. And he can do that in subtle ways, through all kinds of rulings, gestures, and expressions of attitude to the jury that won't be possible for us to appeal..."

"Absolutely," said Leclair.

"...and we'll have caused trouble and pain for other people."

"You mean Mary."

"Mary, yes. And Maura too. Staying out of jail isn't worth it."

"Bullshit. Tell me you're not saying we shouldn't file it at all."

"No. I'm saying let's file it under seal and see what happens. Play it by ear from there. But be careful of unintended consequences that hurt bystanders. You should remember all about that."

O'Keefe's jaw clenched. He well understood the dig about last year's tragedy in Arizona and O'Keefe's own complicity in that tragedy. But he pressed on anyway. "What if the Judge says it's relevant?"

"We'll cross that bridge then," Harrigan said. "No use making a decision before we have to and before we have all the facts and circumstances in front of us. Who knows, maybe when Lord sees this, he'll stop."

"You think that self-righteous asshole won't be able to rationalize and justify this?"

"Well, maybe he will, but maybe his superiors in the Justice Department won't."

Leclair, who had lapsed into an angry silence, said to Harrigan, "So you agree with my advice?"

Harrigan nodded his head.

"And I have to tell you, Mike, I don't know that I can work with this man any longer. I can't tolerate someone attacking my integrity like this."

O'Keefe wanted to reach out and smack the sonuvabitch, challenge him to a duel, or something. *God, I'm in a Dickens novel. Typical hypocrite of a lawyer advancing his own interests at the expense of his client.* But he could not overcome Harrigan's own reasoning and resolve not to wound others just to save his own ass. O'Keefe realized he was probably wrong; and right or wrong, he needed to retreat damn fast to have any chance of staying on the case and proving useful to his friend.

"Ben, fire me if you want, but I do apologize. Stupid of me, but heat of the moment. Please remember this guy is not just a client, he's my blood brother."

Leclair began to puff himself up like a cobra in further righteous indignation, but Harrigan intervened. "Give him a pass, Ben. We've got a good team here. Let's not disrupt it. Besides, he's cheap."

O'Keefe and Harrigan laughed. Leclair stood up and extended his hand, requiring O'Keefe to do the same. "Okay," Leclair said. "A pass. A Mulligan as we say on the golf course."

He's a fucking golfer too, O'Keefe thought as he extended a weak handshake and a fake smile.

As they rode the elevator down to the street, O'Keefe said, "Mike, tell me you're not holding back on this just out of shame."

"I don't know. I hope it's not so selfish as that. I'm just so tired of being a goddamn pinball banging and bouncing around off everything and everyone, just waiting for the Big Tilt to put us all out of our misery."

"Not sure you should be so unselfish when you're staring total ruin in the face."

"Even if I calculate it on purely selfish terms—the one way, let's call it the O'Keefe way, I bring myself, to quote Ben, into further 'scandalous disrepute'...expose and hurt innocent bystanders...maybe with the result of keeping me out of jail, but maybe not...maybe pissing the Judge off so much that I actually hurt myself, and end up in jail anyway. *The other way,* maybe Lord backs off, or the Judge or his superiors make him back off, and I win without all the drama."

"Lawyers!" O'Keefe said. "How did I get tied up with you characters?"

"The hard way, remember. The extremely hard way."

THEY FILED THE MOTION, supported by affidavits from O'Keefe and Maura Davis, under seal. The next morning, Judge Harlan Montgomery summoned both sides to a meeting in his chambers late that afternoon. He stipulated that only two lawyers from each side be present. Leclair sought and received permission for O'Keefe to attend in place of a second lawyer given the critical role he had played in gathering the facts supporting the motion. One of Judge Montgomery's young clerks, fresh out of law school, assembled the group in his chambers. "He's in the courtroom right now," the clerk said, "but there'll be a break soon." As they waited for the Judge, almost nothing was said, none of the meaningless small-talk courtesies that usually opened such meetings, no time-filling chatter or banter, only an excruciatingly uncomfortable silence. Ken Lord looked like he had just learned of the death of a close family member and was angry at the news. Leclair seemed afraid, on the verge of hyperventilating. Max Trainer was nervous too, as he sat poised on the end of his chair, notes on a legal pad in his hand, ready to champion his cause.

The Judge swept into the room still in his robes, which made a rustling sound as he sat down and quickly surveyed the group. He was in his fifties with a large forehead, gray curly hair that stood up somewhat in a short, wiry pompadour, and colorless eyes that seemed like they had seen too much of the wrong side of the world. He was famous for his mastery of civil and criminal legal procedure—and for his impatience, including occasional witheringly contemptuous dressing-downs in open court, with those lawyers appearing before him who failed to meet his high standards in this regard.

"I assume this is Mr. O'Keefe," he said.

"Yes, Your Honor," both Leclair and O'Keefe nervously blurted out at the same time.

"I have to get back out in the courtroom," the Judge said. "Certainly I can make a pretty good guess, but what is the government's position on this motion?"

Max Trainer ventured forth: "Your Honor, even if the facts stated in the affidavits were true..."

The Judge interrupted: "Let's cut right to it, Mr. Trainer. *Are* they true, Mr. Lord?"

Lord gathered himself with a long pause and a deep breath, then said, "The basic allegation...the relationship with Ms. Davis...is true. The inferences being drawn from that fact are untrue and slanderous...beneath contempt."

"And did you know about her relationship with Mr. Harrigan?"

"I did, Your Honor."

"How long have you known about it?"

"For several years."

Trainer tried to intercede. "May I say something, Your Honor?"

"Just wait, Max," the Judge, said, then turned to Leclair: "It may be unfortunate and troubling in certain respects, but it doesn't seem relevant. I think your filing under seal is effectively an admission of that. Or at least your discomfort on that issue."

Trainer jumped in, trying to make himself relevant. "Our position exactly, Your Honor." The Judge ignored him as if he were an irritating fly buzzing around his desk.

Leclair said, "We have fully set forth why it's relevant in our motion and brief in support."

"And I've read it, and I'm not so sure. The issue is whether Mr. Harrigan had knowledge of the use of the loan proceeds and whether that knowledge violated the law, *not* why Mr. Lord may have taken a special satisfaction in bringing on the prosecution."

O'Keefe noted that the Judge flashed an angry look at Lord, which preserved in O'Keefe a tiny shred of hope—for exactly what, he wasn't sure.

Leclair straightened up in his chair as if bravely facing a firing squad. "Your Honor, we point out in detail in our papers that Mr. Lord's conduct went far beyond that. As we show, Mr. Lord went fishing with Mr. Tremaine and Mr. Marler in an attempt to catch in his net a third fish… Mr. Harrigan. And he dangled some powerful bait in front of them in the form of reduced sentences or even probation. We think the jury should be made aware of that."

"So now he's attacking standard prosecutorial procedure," Lord said.

"That damn procedure is dangerous at best and sure as hell shouldn't be used in the service of a personal vendetta."

O'Keefe thought for a moment Lord might come out of his chair at Leclair. The Judge looked at his watch and out toward the courtroom where they were waiting for him. "Mr. Leclair, I'm denying your motion. Mr. Trainer, by tomorrow sometime, I want you to file a motion, under seal of course, requesting that I order the defense not to in any way bring this issue into the trial. I'll grant that motion promptly after you file it."

Leclair, bravely again (and O'Keefe silently withdrew his previous accusation of self-servicing cowardice against the lawyer) said, "We'll need to work with the court to make a proper record for appeal based on your ruling here, Your Honor."

"That's assuming you'll need to appeal, Mr. Leclair. Look at the bright side. Your man might be acquitted. But in the meantime I will not have this become a public scandal. I'm imposing a special order. A gag order. Not one word to anyone outside this room. I want an affidavit from each of you and Mr. Harrigan and Ms. Davis disclosing anyone you have told this to. And I'll want affidavits from each of *those* people as to whom they may have told this to. We'll arrange to have a phone call with each of them in which I will issue the order directly and explain to them what the penalties are for violating that order. And those penalties will be severe. And we will use the full power and resources of the U.S. Marshall's office to track down any leaks, so nobody had better try to get cute."

He stood up. "I need to get back in the courtroom."

"Your Honor," Lord said, "I want to apologize for my lapse in judgment."

The Judge said nothing in response, but O'Keefe noticed the Judge's jaw tighten in anger. Once again he hoped that meant something to hope for.

CHAPTER ▶ 20

THE CHERRY PINK had established itself in a fading commercial district a few square blocks long and spotted with small, old, low-rise warehouse buildings, many of them vacant. It was the only place in the area open after regular working hours. Sara and O'Keefe arrived separately just before midnight, she in her car, he in George's because the van would be too conspicuous. He parked on the next block over, parallel to the block on which the club stood, close to a walkway between two buildings. He checked out the walkway and could see that he had a clear path, allowing him to dart down the walkway and across the alley to the back door of the Cherry Pink. He conducted a practice jog down the walkway as far as the alley behind the club and satisfied himself there was also a clear path from the club's back door to its front if he could not gain entry the back way. He showed Sara where he would be parked so she would know how to find him if it came to that.

O'Keefe was no meditator, but he did occasionally employ one mantra he had picked up from a book, and it occasionally had even helped him with his CPTSD: "I can see peace instead of this." Waiting anxiously in the car, hoping to cool down his boiling brain, he tossed the mantra up in the metaphorical air, but it came crashing back down at him like a shuttlecock in a windstorm. Peace was a ridiculous concept at that moment. If Derek Fagan's information was true, Wayne Popper and maybe others associated with Cherry Pink had likely murdered Bev. Now Sara had parachuted into the middle of them. Two of the pagers should be plenty, but what if she could not get to either of them? Or the one she could get to malfunctioned? They had tested the devices over a longer distance than the one that separated him and Sara now, but how competent was Terry Lecumske really? And so much else could go wrong. He only knew he could never forgive himself if something bad happened to her. He should have tried to call her bluff, even let her quit rather than risk this, and he wasn't at all sure about his motives for keeping her around at all costs.

On a couple of occasions, as headlights beamed in his direction and moved down the street toward him, he thought it best not to take a chance of being noticed there in the dark car on the empty street at this hour, so he ducked down each time. He wished he had found a better observation post, a place where the building he had parked in front of did not block his view of the club.

~

ON THE SIDEWALK, approaching the bouncer, who matched O'Keefe's description of Wayne Popper, Sara took a deep breath and did her best to summon up not a different persona but a part of her persona she normally suppressed. She had worked hard to look sexy, but not too much—not "all whore" as she phrased it to herself. She thought she needed to look somewhat but not too much on the hard side, so she polished her nails red, ratted her hair a bit, wore a sleeveless silk red blouse that fit tight over her breasts, and a short black skirt that showed off her legs and ass.

"I'm Tracy Fox. They're expecting me."

"Yes, they are." Based on his exceedingly lecherous up-and-down and double-take, Popper seemed well-satisfied with Cherry Pink's possible new hire. "Good luck," he said, "and if I can be any help anytime, you just holler, honey."

Once inside, she walked toward the bar, doing a quick inconspicuous visual scan of the customers. The place was packed, overwhelmingly male but also a few women. Some of the dancers cozied up in booths with their customers, a half-full drink and a small pile of currency in front of them. In one booth a dancer writhed on her beau's lap, and he looked very much like something was about to erupt. Wilson Pickett's "Midnight Hour," which she guessed played every night about this time, blasted from the speakers. The dancer on the platform, well into her set, had nothing on but a black bikini bottom and high heeled black pumps. She caressed her breasts, cupping a hand under each and squeezing. She dropped to her knees, whipped her head and body back and forth a few times in sync with the music, then laid back on her elbows, pumping her crotch in "stick it in and fuck me" gyrations. Men were lined up along the rail around the stage, their hands stuffed with bills, some whooping and hollering, some silent and fiercely focused. Some shouted her name—"Gigi"—which also flashed on a neon sign on the platform.

I too could have my name in lights.

Several of the men still sitting at their tables or at the bar noticed Sara and openly set about appraising her assets, apparently awarding them a high valuation, though she couldn't be sure of the quality of their judgment. She took a stool at the bar in the middle of two other empty stools. She reached in her purse for a sequined red lighter and a pack of Kools and looked around for an ashtray. The bartender brought her that, as well as a pleased expression and a small cocktail napkin that he sat in front of her for the drink he expected her to order.

"You have to be Tracy Fox."

"That I am."

"I'll tell Marty you're here."

He moved back to the cash register area, picked up the telephone receiver, and punched a button to engage an internal line. As he talked, he turned away from her as if he wanted to make sure she could neither hear him nor read his lips. He hung up the receiver and came back to her as she made herself look eagerly expectant.

"You'll meet with Marty back in his office in a bit. How 'bout a drink?"

"I'll have a Coke with a lime."

He smiled. "I said 'drink.' This ain't Chuck E. Cheese."

"No thanks," she said. "Maybe later."

"You uptight? Might be good to loosen up some."

"No, I'm plenty loose...always." She tapped the side of her forehead with her index finger. "But need to be clear-headed. For now. Later...that's another matter."

He got the point, provided her a knowing little smirk. "Not sure it's ever good to be clear-headed around here. Better to be at least a little high all the time."

On her second Kool, one of the men sitting at the tables, a large man, large enough to stand out prominently not just from his tablemates but from the entire rest of the crowd, carrying some extra pounds but not what she would call fat, sat down on the stool next to her. She tried to drive out of her mind the image of him on top of her. It was an unpleasant image and even more unpleasant that her mind had conjured it up.

She had inadvertently briefly locked eyes with him on her way to the bar, and this apparently encouraged him, which annoyed her because it deprived her of the opportunity to watch Gigi and possibly learn something that would help her in the interview. But she showed no displeasure, just the opposite, a gentle smile. For all she knew this could be the "owner" who would be interviewing her. Somewhere in his fifties, he had a tanning-bed tan and a full head of black hair overlaid with sweeps of silver. He was clearly some kind of businessman or lawyer, his tie loosened and pulled down from his unbuttoned collar, his initials emblazoned on both his shirt pocket and each of his French cuffs. His cufflinks looked like gold coins. She wondered if they were real gold. He looked good enough except that his facial features—eyes like little black beans and a smidge of a nose—seemed too small for the size of his body.

He looked at her near-empty glass. "Can I buy you a drink?"

"No thanks. I'm coasting at the moment."

"So how is it that someone lookin' as good as you is in here with her clothes still on?"

"Thank you, sir. Interview."

"Oh yes," he said as if he had special information. "Interview."

"Wish me luck."

He wobbled a little drunkenly on his stool. "With what you've got you won't need luck. You might need something, but luck it won't be."

Gigi had finished her performance and was replaced by a duo, billed as the "Twisted Sisters" with a dual lesbian-incest theme that ignited a sensation in the crowd around the stage and beyond, including the gentleman caller on the stool next to Sara, who couldn't help but watch.

The bartender came over. "Another *Coke*?"

She shook her head no.

The bartender looked in a pointed, meaningful way at her new companion. "She'll be goin' in to meet Marty in a few minutes."

I see. That look meant "Scram!"

A slight facial tic indicated the large man understood the message. When the bartender left, the man said. "Hope to be seein' you up there," gesturing toward the platform, "and other places too."

"Ditto."

Shouldn't have said that.

"When you're done, why don't you join me at my table?"

My fault. I encouraged him. She produced a look that she hoped said "maybe, I'll think about it." Again she pictured him lying on top of her. *Not a chance, big fella.*

After the big man left, the bartender returned and said "Better get you in to see Marty, honey, before you attract all the flies in the place…"

"Well, that would be my job, wouldn't it?"

"Hey, Judy," he said to a waitress at the bartender station waiting to pick up drinks. "This is Tracy. Take her back to Marty's office, okay?"

On the way back the waitress said, "Dancer, I assume."

"Hope so."

They passed through a doorway in a partition wall that separated the club proper from the warren of rooms in the back. On her left, she glimpsed the dancer's room, crammed with short rows of plastic swivel chairs, each pulled up to a cubby featuring a large mirror, separated from the next cubby by a partition a few inches high, not enough for privacy (and they probably preferred to be able to cross-chat down the line anyway), just a necessary territorial demarcation to discourage careless or intentional imperialist expansion from one cubby to the next. The counter spaces in front of the mirror were mostly junked up with an individualized miscellany of cosmetics, tissues, brushes and combs, sprays, hair clips, cigarette packs, ashtrays, tampon boxes, magazines, paperback books, soft drink cans and plastic bottles, each a carelessly curated collection that, if one undertook to study each space carefully, likely revealed much of significance about the personality of the occupant.

On the right, down a short hallway, was a raised platform where the next-act dancers waited at a door from which they entered the stage for their sets. Empty now. The Twisted Sisters might be the last act of the evening.

Down another hallway a double door just said "OFFICE" in large gold lettering. As she knocked, the waitress said, with a sarcastic edge, "Break a leg."

"Come in" said a voice beyond the door.

And just as she opened the door to let Sara in, the waitress said, "Take care."

Sara tried to evaluate that last thing from the waitress while also summoning up a proper mix of perky and lascivious with which to greet Mr. Marty Lansing. Was it just a harmless way to say goodbye? But "take care" seemed ominous, might mean there was something specific and significant to worry about. But the waitress had not gone all the way to "be careful."

The appearance of the man sitting behind the desk gave the lie to her imaginings, as did the elegant ebony desk he sat behind and the tastefully decorated, spacious, even luxurious office he presided over like some exotic potentate. No silk shirt unbuttoned halfway down the front. No neck chains. No bracelet, silver or gold. No Rolex, real or fake. No contemptuous, snarky expression. He looked more like something out of the softer side of the '60s. Wire rimmed glasses. Dishwater blond hair pulled back into a short ponytail. Although his shirt was black, and silk, it was a preppy button-down.

As for the office, the partition wall behind him, which included a doorway to someplace, consisted of rich, dark brown wood paneling with black streaks. In front of his desk two sleek Eames-style office chairs. Against the side wall to her right, a wooden straight chair, painted with many layers of royal blue. To her left and his right, a short nook of a hallway and another door, leading, she guessed, to a bathroom. The office walls, other than the rear partition, were covered entirely, giving almost a wallpaper effect, with erotic but not pornographic art prints and posters by everyone from Modigliani to Warhol. Many reflected an Art Deco "Weimar" aura—the women's bodies—as well as their physical surroundings—dark, sharp-edged, abstract shapes—the women's facial expressions more alarmed than sultry, on the edge of anguish, even hysteria. Closer on her right, a marble-topped conference table and four more Eames-like chairs. On the left wall, a massive, exceptionally comfortable looking overstuffed couch, covered in green, black, and red abstract fabric. *Too comfortable.* No telling how many girls had been fondled, fucked, or who knows what else on that thing, a reaction that must have been obvious on her face because it provoked Marty Lansing to greet her with "It's not a casting couch. It's a napping couch." She thought about responding with a "Too bad" but didn't want to brand herself that way right off the bat.

"Have a seat and tell me what you'd like me to know about you."

She gave him the same details she had provided on the phone and a few more in that same vein.

"What makes you want to live this particular crazy life?"

"The money. How about you?"

"Let's see. The money yes, and…the pussy, the dope, and maybe most of all, the *edge*."

"Well, I guess that's quite an appealing foursome."

"For example, item one: If you do start working here, I'm likely to be wanting to fuck you pdq, with protection for both of us of course. This AIDS thing's got everyone scared shitless. Just not as much fun as it used to be."

"But not on the couch, I guess."

"No. I do have slightly more class than that. I'd at least take you home. And my home's pretty nice, something like this," and he made a flourishing circular gesture in the air, referencing the style and ambience of his current surroundings.

"Now for item two, the dope." He opened a drawer in his desk and pulled out a tray with four fat blunts carefully arranged on a small silver tray, which he held out to her in offering.

"Maybe later."

He pulled the tray back, gave it a brief longing look, and returned it to the drawer.

"So you've refused both drink and dope. Are you Mormon, Muslim, or what?"

"Just professional. Don't judge me until you get to know me after work hours."

"You think this is a profession?"

"I do."

"We'll see about that. I consider it more of a lifestyle, an ethos, an existential choice and statement, a special stance in and toward the universe."

"Heavy shit. I like it."

~

AN HOUR OR so after she had gone into the place, O'Keefe left the car, jogged over to the walkway at the side of the building that led to the alley and observed the club's back door, which was illuminated by a small outside light. He thought about staying there so he could see the door at all times, but he couldn't just lurk around there, or some security person or even a sheriff's deputy might notice and detain him. If that happened, then she would be entirely on her own. He hurried back to the car and sat looking at the building in front of him, wishing he had Superman's X-ray vision to see right through it. So he failed to see a large black SUV drive down the alley and park in the back of Cherry Pink, and a thin blade of a man, with peroxide blond hair that shined in the night like a reflector, leave the car, walk to the back door, take a key out of the pocket of his leather jacket, unlock the door, and slip into the building.

~

"YOU DO ANY hooking on the side?" Marty Lansing was saying.

"Is that expected here?"

"I wouldn't go that far. Let's say 'not discouraged'...as long as we get our...let's call it a finder's fee."

"I won't say I haven't accepted money from a few admirers but not a direct quid pro quo. Not yet anyway."

"Got crabs, the clap, or worse? Certainly not AIDS, I hope.

"AIDS?"

"It's not just gays that get it."

"I don't have any of them. Not now, not ever."

"We'll test you. Initially and periodically after that."

"I didn't know they had a test for AIDS."

"Just coming out."

"I saw lap dancing out there."

"Definitely expected, at least with special customers. You have a problem with that?"

A noise from somewhere behind him interrupted. Her brow furrowed while Marty Lansing smiled. "As I said—the pussy, the dope...and here comes *both* of items three and four, the money *and* the edge."

The doorway behind Lansing opened, and the anorexically thin, pale man, with a rooster comb on top and duck tails left over from the 1950s on the sides of his head, fit O'Keefe's description of David Bowman.

Lansing and Bowman did not say hello but nodded to each other like frequent companions. Bowman took her in quickly, all the way in, grabbed one of the straight chairs standing against the wall, carried it over to the side of the desk, positioned the back of the chair facing Sara, straddled the chair, and sat down with his arms resting on the top. He exuded an intrusive manner and aura, an unwelcome intimacy, seeming to be closer to her than he actually was, filling not just the space he inhabited but all the space between them.

"To sum it up," Lansing said to Bowman, "she's from Birmingham, has danced before, refused both a free drink and a free joint, takes herself a little too seriously, says no venereal problems—"

"No poisonous pussy, eh?" Bowman said.

"No, sir," she said, the politeness not fake in the least. This man instilled fear if not respect. She recognized all this "pussy" talk as softening her up, probing to see how open she might be to being taken advantage of, exploited, degraded.

"You mind standing up?"

She stood up.

"Turn around for me."

Which she did.

"Nice enough," he said. She guessed that meant she could sit down now. Which she did.

"You maybe wonder why we had you come meet us this time of night?"

"A little."

"It's almost closing time. Maybe you could do an audition for a few special customers. The staff too. They've got a good eye for talent."

She hoped she was not hesitating too long. She tried to convince herself to agree to his suggestion but failed. She thought she could pull off a decent erotic dance but wasn't sure. Anyway, she was only willing to go so far with self-abasement for this mission.

She reached for something. "Good idea…I'm game…but not tonight."

"Disappointing," Bowman said. "Maybe fatal to your hopes and ambitions, Tracy Fox. What's the problem?"

"Well, I'd like to be able to prepare a little better…mentally, ya know…it's too big of a moment not to give it my best…"

Lansing interrupted, "She considers herself a professional."

Bowman's lip quivered upward in contempt.

She seemed to be faltering with them, and it came to her to add, "And it's that time of month."

"So what?" Bowman said. "Surely you don't plan on taking a week off every month."

"Oh, no. But it's a real…gusher…" *Jesus, where am I going with this?* "It just complicates things. Mentally, I mean. Being able to do my best out there."

"Well, let's see if it's even worth you coming back for that."

She thought she knew what he meant but wanted to make damn sure so she shot him a questioning look.

"Yeah. We need to see you."

She stood up and, with all the insouciance she could fake, kicked off her pumps, showing them what she hoped they would see as wild, fascinating abandon, used both hands to rip open her blouse, buttons popping off and bouncing on the floor. Lansing laughed merrily and even Bowman smiled with approval. She had worn a red lace bra that revealed a lot underneath it. Their smirks told her they liked that a lot. Her skirt, which zipped down the side, was soon off and on the floor. Her panties matched her bra. Her legs were bare. Nothing on now but bra and panties. Bowman gave her a nod that said "go on, you're not done yet." So she pulled down the left cup of her bra and showed them a handful of ample breast. Then she showed them the other. Unclasping the bra in back proved a little awkward, a demerit against her performance, but then there she stood, nothing on but the red lace panties, just like she would appear on stage.

"Very nice," Bowman said, "but, eventually, we'll have to see how you dance."

She noticed Bowman direct a quick look and a flicker of the chin at Lansing.

"Need to go close the place," Lansing said. As he walked past her, he brushed his eyebrow with his finger which she took as a gesture of either affirmation or farewell or both. She also picked up a disconcerting twinkling in his eyes, which told her his departure was a bad sign for her.

Bowman stared at her for a few more seconds, then moved casually toward her as if taking care not to cause her to panic. She retreated until her back pressed up against one of the Weimar ladies on the wall, life imitating art. She could not withdraw any farther. He eased up to her, placed his left index finger under her right nipple and flicked it gently, and lightly squeezed her other nipple between his right index finger and thumb, "Besides a dance, you've only got one more thing to do to get hired. I'm okay with the gush if it's okay with you, but a blow job'll do just fine too…for now."

"I bet you say that to all the girls."

"Actually, I do."

He moved his left hand down and gently cupped his hand on her mons.

A sudden startle in his eyes. "What the…" as he recoiled from his shock at feeling metal where he thought he would be feeling the softest flesh. O'Keefe's mad scientist device. She had taped the second one around her lower waist and stowed it inside her panties. Bowman froze in confusion. Despite her fear, she almost laughed out loud. She gave him a quick hard shove with both hands that sent him stumbling backward and falling down and punched the pager as he struggled to his feet to come back at her.

This was the moment for her to apply one of the many jiu jitsu moves she had been learning, but this wasn't the dojo, and she had blanked it all out. She pressed the pager button again.

~

"FUCK!" WAS O'Keefe's reaction when his device vibrated. *Vietnam. Soldiers out there to rescue.* He rolled out the door and sprinted from the car, down the side of the building, down the walkway, across the alley, grabbed the back doorknob. Locked. He threw himself against the door, trying to break it open, but the door didn't budge. He would need to try the front. If the front door was also locked, as it probably would be now after closing time, no telling what might happen to her. He ripped the pistol out of his shoulder holster as he ran.

~

SHE SAID, "That was a pager, and it just called the police," which halted Bowman's forward progress for a few moments.

But then he said, "I own the fucking police in this county."

She grabbed her purse, left her clothes, and ran. Out of the office, down the hallway, and out into the club where Marty Lansing and some of the staff, including two or three dancers and a few "special customers" allowed to linger after closing hours, huddled around the bar. Before they could understand what was happening and just as Bowman came charging out of the back, yelling "Stop that cunt!" she was at the front door, Bowman and Popper not far behind her. *Please, O'Keefe, be here.*

And there he was, standing on the sidewalk. She instinctively crossed her arms to cover her breasts.

"What the fuck?" he said, startled at her nakedness. "You have your keys?"

She shook her head vigorously "yes."

"Get out of here as fast as you can."

Jaybird naked as she was, she had to acknowledge that it was a good idea to get to the car, but no way she would leave him there alone. Unlocking her car, she looked back at a standoff: O'Keefe on the sidewalk, pistol in hand but not pointed, both arms straight down at his sides; Bowman a few yards away on the sidewalk; Popper remaining behind at the door to push back at the people wanting to get out of the club to rubberneck.

Just above the low CPTSD rumble in his ears, O'Keefe heard Popper keep saying "Get back, stay there, he's got a gun," but he focused on Bowman, waiting for Bowman to lunge, semi-consciously calculating at what point he could just shoot him in self-defense. Or would he need to forgo the firearm and grapple with Bowman mano a mano? He had a flash of a wish that he had joined Sara at the dojo for martial arts lessons. Even more so, he wished he had the M-16 instead of the pistol. He recognized this as CPTSD mode—his mental world lightly painted over with yellow haze, flashes of gunfire in the night sky of his mind, adrenaline surging. He knew he would not hesitate to shoot Bowman dead right there and suspected that might be exactly what he hoped to do.

Bowman finally spoke. "O'Keefe. Seems like you're lost."

"I know you killed her."

"Who?"

O'Keefe saw Popper moving toward them and raised the pistol, pointing it directly at Popper. "Stay right there, asswipe."

Bowman said, "This is the county, O'Keefe. This is *my* territory. Maybe I'll have you arrested for this little conspiracy...this assault. I didn't do anything to that bitch of yours. She took off her clothes on her own. Voluntary. An audition. You two tried to entrap me. You failed. My word against hers. And my manager to support me."

Sara's car pulled up beside them.

"I'm letting you go this time, O'Keefe—"

"I guess you're confused about who's got the gun and who doesn't."

"If I ever see you again, even feel your vibrations anywhere close, you'll pay."

"I'm not letting go."

"You won't be the only one to pay. Better think of others, starting with your cunt there. Any more of this shit from you, and you'll be worse than dead."

~

IN HER CAR HE tried not to look as she drove him to George's car. Neither of them seemed to know what else to say. Uncomfortable with her nakedness, he stripped off his shirt.

"You need to put this on. I doubt it's a good idea to drive around topless."

"Don't worry about it."

"And think about how you get from your car to your apartment. I've got extra clothes in the car for me."

It was a lie, but she accepted it, pulled up next to George's car, and put the shirt on. He wondered if he would ever see her that naked again.

"You okay?" he said.

"I think so. It won't hit me until later."

"Not sure *I'm* okay," he said.

"Well, those are some evil motherfuckers."

She told him her story and, at the end, said, "I hope I accomplished something with all that."

"A lot. Now we know for sure that Bowman is connected with that club. George wasn't able to find that out."

"What's next?"

"We need to find out who's the money behind that place. I don't think it's Bowman. Can you do that? Or is that too dull for you now?"

"I have to admit I was scared to death back in that office alone with him."

"Good. That means you've got at least a touch of survival instinct in you. I want you to think hard about whether you should quit."

"No way."

"I'll follow you home."

She started to shake her head. "Indulge me," he said, "it's for me, not you. I'll wait out front, and when I see your light blink twice, that'll mean—and listen carefully—that you've checked every possible place in your apartment that someone could hide."

"Come on, they couldn't've got their act together enough yet to pull that off."

"Make it a habit. I want you to do it every time from now on."

"Well, you can't be driving me home every night. I want a weapon and some firearms training."

"Done," he said. "And *I* want some martial arts. Introduce me to your dojo guy."

"Agreed."

"Do they work with kids?"

"They do. Kelly would be welcome. I'll tell you though…it did me no good at all in that office. I forgot every move they taught me. I need daily practice in real world situations…Maybe you should start sneaking up and attacking me."

"Oh, sure. Like Inspector Clouseau and Cato."

"I'm serious."

"Cato didn't fare so well in those contests as I recall."

She smiled. "I'll only hurt you a little."

CHAPTER ▸ 21

SARA PREPPED O'KEEFE for the interview with Forest Marler, who was fifty-nine years old and at the twilight of a legal career that, while not particularly distinguished, had been uncontroversial—until his recent and unfortunate plunge into the headlines and the clutches of the U.S. Financial Crimes Task Force. He had served for many years as a low-level partner at one of the better firms in the city that advised financial institutions on matters large and small. He did decent work but had no talent for originating legal business or even engendering more than tepid client loyalty—a competent man destined for mediocrity, due not to anything negative in his personality but to an absence of something sufficiently positive. When he reached his mid-fifties in a firm where ambitious Baby Boomers in their thirties were demanding more responsibility and compensation, his partners searched for the most charitable way to move him out. Marler himself was not inclined to quit and not in a financial position to do so, his investment decisions having been no more distinguished than his legal career. The firm solved this by persuading Mark Marcus and Morris Manning to take him "in-house" at Vanguard Savings, which they agreed to because they thought they could save a large amount of money by assigning work to an in-house counsel whose salary would cost far less than the high hourly rates outside firms charged them.

"Guess what," she said. "He went to Bishop Dolan High."

"I'll be damned."

"Yeah. Your alma mater."

"Twenty-five years earlier."

"He was a decent athlete in several sports, but nothing spectacular. Never anything spectacular with this guy, just competent, everything B- to C+ including college and law school at local universities. He's been married for thirty-eight years. His wife is not doing well. Emphysema and congestive heart failure. Prognosis not good. He has one daughter and two grandchildren who live in California."

"What a sad way to end an otherwise decent life," O'Keefe said.

"Want to hear something really sad? I visited the school because it turns out they keep all the old yearbooks there. His graduating year, they had a short quote from each senior answering the question, 'What do you plan to accomplish in your life?' Marler's answer: 'I intend to be a lawyer and serve justice.'"

"Old yearbooks. I'd say that was damn thorough, ma'am."

"Thank you."

"One more thing. Find out if he still goes to church."

"How do I do that?"

"Find out the hours for Mass on Saturday afternoon and evening and all day Sunday in his parish church."

"Saturday?"

"Yeah. These days they give you Sunday credit for the Saturday afternoon and evening Masses. But not Saturday morning. Only a few hours separating you from a mortal sin and an eternity in hell."

The following Sunday morning Sara called: "Sure enough. He came out of his house and drove to early Mass."

~

ARRIVING PRECISELY on time for the interview, he suspected that Marler's house told the story of Marler's adult life. Bought more than thirty years ago by a young lawyer at an elite law firm, making the kind of first-job salary that pointed him toward rising into the upper middle class and maybe even beyond. A "starter" house in a neighborhood of homeowners much like himself. But where it began, it also ended. All these years later and the same house in the same neighborhood. Still a starter. No ability to go anywhere else without getting in over his head in debt, since he had no justifiable hope of achieving the large future bumps in income that would allow him to earn his way into comfortably making the payments. But the mortgage had probably been paid off for a long time, and his law firm probably had made a decent annual 401k contribution over many years. If Marler had invested, not spectacularly, but at least carefully, he and his wife probably could survive financially until their deaths—as long as they remained thrifty, watching every dollar, hopefully avoiding any health issues that Medicare wouldn't pay for, a too-long slide into their graves, their spirits progressively depleting along with their bodies and bank accounts, leaving just enough at the end so their daughter would not be forced to bear the burden of funeral and burial expenses.

When Marler opened the door, he brought his forefinger to his lips in a silencing gesture and whispered, "Wife is resting now. She isn't well." He was top-heavy, a bulky torso above skinny legs. He enjoyed a luxuriance of gray hair and had done a poor job of shaving that morning. Hunched forward at the shoulders like people often do as they age (observing that, in sudden alarm O'Keefe straightened his own posture), Marler led them through the living room and the kitchen to a room in the back of the house that they probably referred to as the "family room," which had once been a large back porch that had been enclosed at some point. Here the occupants lived most of the time—ate their dinners at the round table just large enough for two, watched television night after night and sometimes in the daytime too, and never disturbed the books in the built-in bookcases along the walls that had been read once a long time ago.

A pitcher of water and two glasses waited for them on the small table. Marler gestured toward a chair for O'Keefe and then sat down himself, his face reflecting pain as he did so.

"I'm afraid I need new hips," he said. "What a nightmare. One invalid around here's enough."

He looked questioningly at O'Keefe, expecting O'Keefe to take the conversation the next step.

"Thanks for seeing me, Forest."

Marler only nodded.

Looking for a way past Marler's resistance, O'Keefe said, "We haven't worked together in a while. Not since you were at the Cutler firm."

"Yes, sir," Marler visibly softened a little. "I remember. That check kiting deal at First National."

"Turns out we grew up in the same neighborhood."

"With that name, you surely went to Catholic school."

"Yes, St. Jude's."

Now Marler softened even more, "Good ol' St. Jude's. Our big rivals. I lived just on the other side of the border line. St. Cyril's parish. How about high school?"

"Bishop Dolan. Same as you, Forrest."

"I'll be damned. This town's always been the smallest of worlds."

"In our trial prep we went back and looked at your yearbook for your senior year."

"My God, that's thorough."

"You said you wanted to be a lawyer and 'serve justice.'...Nice thought."

"And look where I end up."

"One mistake does not a lifetime make."

"Tell that to Ken Lord. 'Where were the professionals?' he keeps prattling."

O'Keefe liked to hear that word, "prattling," and the tone of resentment in which Marler said it. He moved onto the details of the loan at the heart of the case, opening his larger notebook, not asking Marler for permission. He could not take the risk of relying on his memory and wanted contemporaneous notes that would refresh his recollection and support his memory if challenged on the witness stand.

Gently confirming various items that Sara had established in her earlier interview, O'Keefe tried in that process to create as much of a rapport as opposing parties on an important legal matter could reasonably establish, which brought him to the destination he had intended to arrive at from the beginning. He carefully and in full detail reconstructed Marler's interviews with Ken Lord, trying not to give away his primary goal. Marler affirmed that he had not mentioned anything about Harrigan at all until Lord brought him up: "When Lord said that to me, I thought, Why should I be the only lawyer scapegoat in this deal?"

"And you said..."

"I said, 'Harrigan okayed it.'"

"And Harrigan was representing Tremaine, the borrower. Right? Not the bank?"

"Right. We always signed a conflict waiver allowing him to do that on Tremaine's deals even though he usually represented us."

"And what do you mean by 'okayed' the loan?"

"I mean he or someone in his firm reviewed the papers. I called and asked him if everything was 'okay,' and he said 'yes.'"

"Do you know if it was him or someone else in his firm that did the actual review?"

Marler thought about it, eyed O'Keefe suspiciously, and said, "Can't recall. I'll think more about it though."

"Will you let me know if something more specific comes to you?"

Marler hesitated, but seeming not to know what else to do, said "Alright."

"Anything else, Forest?"

"As I recall now, that's it."

"And, again, I'd appreciate it if between now and the trial you'd let me know anything that might come to you after our talk today."

Marler had recovered himself enough to hedge this time: "I may have to consult Lord about that."

"Whatever you need to do, but I'd appreciate the head's up."

They sat for a few moments in uncomfortable silence, until O'Keefe continued, "Is it typical for a borrower's lawyer to review the actual use of loan proceeds by the borrower?"

Marler knew where O'Keefe was going with that, and his face might as well have flashed a yellow caution light. "Probably varies. But probably not for the most part. Probably no more than to review a closing statement to make sure the fees and expenses being deducted were correct."

"But not to follow what happens to those proceeds once they hit the borrower's bank account?"

"That's probably right, but remember…Harrigan was more than Tremaine's lawyer. He had ownership in the deals."

"Very small pieces, right? Ten percent. Like a tip, not a partnership."

Marler said nothing but gave him a look of acknowledgment and concession.

"Anything else about that conversation?"

"No. I just asked if the loan was okay…"

"The loan itself or the documents?"

"I can't recall exactly. I think it was a question, something like, 'Everything okay?' Simple as that."

"Seems like a close call to me...what he meant by 'everything' and 'okay.'"

"I know what *I* meant."

"I hope you're sure about all this, Forest. Your testimony is likely to send Mike Harrigan to prison, and they won't be going easy on him, sentencing-wise. I know they've put you in a helluva spot...your wife sick, no job, and your law license probably about to be revoked. But I know where we both came from, and I think I know what kind of a decent person you've always been ... and I don't believe you'll do anything but hate yourself if you ruin his life by convenient remembering or outright lying."

Marler absorbed that as if it were a kick to his solar plexus. "Some might think you were here to tamper with a witness or suborn perjury to save your buddy's rear end."

"If persuading a witness to tell the truth is tampering, I plead guilty. And I'm concerned that perjury has already been suborned—by Ken Lord. And yes, it's about saving Harrigan's ass, Forest, but it's also about saving *your* soul."

~

THE NEXT DAY Leclair called. "I wouldn't worry about it much, but Lord called me this morning complaining about your interview with Marler. He said, and I quote, 'From what Marler told me, your man O'Keefe crossed the line yesterday. I'm tempted to open a witness-tampering investigation.'"

"Jesus," O'Keefe said. "Do I really need to worry? That guy is vicious."

"Fuck him. You must've gotten somewhere. Can't wait to read your report."

When they hung up, Leclair was laughing while O'Keefe's heart was beating fast, and not for joy.

CHAPTER ▸ 22

AS ON ANY other typical weekday morning, O'Keefe rose at 5 a.m., turned on the Mr. Coffee, went to his exercise room, put something by Bach on the CD player, and performed the simple but strenuous exercise routines he had learned in the Marine Corps. While getting dressed, he drank a cup of coffee and smoked a Marlboro. He did not read the newspaper or linger around the apartment but headed straight out the door to work so he could get an early start on the day, before the phone started ringing and other people began to control his time and agenda. Although he had access to the decrepit garage at the end of a driveway that ran alongside the house, he never parked in it other than in the winter to save himself from having to brush off the fallen snow and de-ice the windshield. Instead, since he had tenant seniority over the upstairs renter, he just left the van in the driveway while the upstairs guy parked on the street.

As soon as he opened his front door, he realized he hadn't dressed warmly enough. The first frost of the season coated the front lawn. When he climbed into the van and inserted and turned the key in the ignition, several things happened, seemingly all at once. He sensed in some instinctual, unconscious way that something about the turning of the key was unusual, wrong. Only a micro-moment later, before his brain had any chance to process that initial sensation, a fireball flashed from the dashboard in front of the steering wheel and engulfed him. *Vietnam! Cover!*

He grabbed the door handle, which seared his hand, which he automatically pulled back, the scalded skin now dangling in strips. Trapped there, momentarily inert, he understood somehow that hesitation could be fatal, that he had to endure whatever pain it would take to escape *right now.* He groped for the door handle again, and since his nerves had been burnt away the first time he had grabbed it, it didn't hurt the second time. He pulled up hard on the handle and threw his left shoulder into the door, forcing it open, and rolled out, rotating to his right, reeling but still on his feet when he landed on the pavement, and feeling tremendous heat on his left side. Looking down, he saw flames sprouting along his entire left arm and hand and leg. He threw himself onto the ground hard, wondering after he crashed if he might have broken his arm. He rolled over and over until he thought he had smothered the fire consuming him, then staggered to his feet. But only for a moment—until the blast energy from the explosion. He felt it before he heard it. It knocked him back several yards, and he skidded like a hockey puck across the pavement.

At the end of his skid, lying there and looking back at the van, now nothing but the burned out hulk of a chassis, debris strewn around the driveway, his front yard, and even some in the neighbor's front yard, he only knew he wasn't dead, but he wondered why not. And how could he be suffering such pain and not be dead. Surely he would be dead soon and that would be okay, because whatever was left of him was surely not worth living. Oddly, at that moment he remembered he had decided to get rid of the van anyway. Too conspicuous. Sara called it "the Blimp."

He managed to stand up and realized that the skin on his left leg and arm hung in strips, and his blackened, smoldering left hand looked like the claw of a bird. He felt a strip or two of skin hanging from or around his left ear. He sat back down again, and that's how they found him—seated, in shock, unable to speak, a twisted, blackened human charcoal log plucked from the fire.

They told him later that he was delirious though mostly quiet in the ambulance but that he screamed in agony as they cleaned his wounds in the emergency room until the morphine took full effect. For the first couple of days, it was the infection that almost killed him, until the doctors and nurses brought it under control. He remembered cloudy images hovering in his consciousness in those early days in the hospital faces it seemed they were, but none he could recognize. They said he entertained everyone with various amusing hallucinatory utterances during that period. He seemed to believe himself back in Vietnam some of the time. At other times he seemed to believe that his entire world had become a rather chaotic game of basketball in which he competed with strips of skin streaming from various parts of his body.

When he regained coherent consciousness, he found himself in a hospital burn ward, beds lined up along each wall of a long room, foot to head, only a few yards, maybe five, separating them, one after another. At various times, often in the dead of night, much noise—stomping, banging, loud talking—would signal that a patient was dying and that resuscitation efforts were failing. In the daytime they would wheel patients, still immobilized in their beds, past him for their skin grafting surgery, or to the "tank" for the daily dreaded debridement (a fancy word for a torture administered without any drugs whatsoever involving a wire brush scraping dead skin from seething, pulsing raw flesh). He learned not to look. It only took one view of a young girl passing by with a face out of a horror movie to teach him to keep facing straight ahead. He had seen such sights before but thought he never would again. Night after night he dreamed of Vietnam, of stretchers, of fireballs, of deafening explosions and screaming men—and of himself, the helicopter door gunner firing his machine gun madly into the jungle, not knowing whether he was killing animals or humans, the innocent, the guilty, or anyone at all.

As for his own face, the doctor talked to him about that as soon as he was free enough of drugs and pain to participate in a coherent conversation. "Your face is bandaged now, and it doesn't look good, but it *will* be all right. That part of you just got 'flash fried' so to speak... meaning a super-fast WHOOSH of fire that didn't linger, so it didn't destroy the skin. Except for a few places, mostly around your left ear and along your left jawline close to your ear, we won't need to graft on your face, and you won't be permanently scarred, except, again, somewhat along your ear on that left side. Your left arm and hand and leg are another matter. You probably don't remember, but you've already had operations for temporary grafts. There'll be scarring, and you'll have to work hard in physical therapy to regain your range of motion...but you will."

When he opened his mouth to speak, the skin on his face felt stretched drum tight. Initially, he struggled to form understandable words. "Even my hand will be okay? It looked like a claw."

"It will be okay as long as you do the physical therapy and keep using it. Use it or lose it. The scar bands will be trying to pull your fingers back into your palm for the rest of your life."

"When do I get out of here?"

"Don't rush it. A few days ago you were a human fireball."

"I've got work to do. Do they know who did this?"

"That's a question for the police, not me."

He had plenty of visitors, so many that the hospital had to control access. Harrigan came almost every day, as did many others, and everyone from various lawyers he had worked for to Beverly's mother. Maura Davis wished him well with a giant get-well card festooned with her own peppy exclamations and drawings of hearts, smiling faces, the sun and its rays with an accompanying rainbow, and even bunnies, all in violet ink.

"Damn," said Sara, who attended on him more than anyone else. "You've got more friends than any other introvert I know."

After a week, his face looked acceptable enough for them to take the bandages off. The nurse gave him a mirror to let him see himself. Then she showed him a photo of his face right after the explosion. Glad he had not seen it then. What would it have been like to go through the rest of his life with such a face, a face that people could not help but recoil from in startled disgust, before they caught themselves and felt ashamed of their reaction, just as he himself had done in such situations? Or the frightened little kids asking their mothers what was wrong with that man over there? He thought, as he had done so many other times in his accident-prone life, how lucky he was to have done so many stupid things and still survive them, and how unlucky so many others were, the innocents cursed to endure life with such disfigurement.

They kept Kelly away until his face had largely healed. Sara brought her in to see him—now purplish of face, peeling as if from an extreme sunburn, and swathed in bandages around the left ear; in a temporary cast from the top of his left shoulder down his left arm and hand to the tips of his fingers, the only thing that protruded, his thumb, oddly the only unburned digit on his hand. Kelly started crying right away and scooted to his left side to embrace him. When he recoiled, she realized she had chosen the wrong side and raced around to the other and just laid her head on his rib cage, sobbing, as he rested his hand on her head.

On her way out of the room Sara said, "Her mother brought her. She's outside waiting. She'd like to see you when you two are done."

Kelly stood up straight, surveyed him with a cooler eye, and said, "You think you'll still be able to play basketball with me?"

He laughed, glad she could think of normal things at a time like this, a hope and promise of a stable world despite everything. "They tell me so."

They talked aimlessly for a few minutes. He asked her about school.

"Three B's and two A's."

"So you only need three more."

"Three more *A's?*" she said, exaggerating the word in a high voice and sticking her neck out at him and bulging her eyes to register the outrageousness of his suggestion.

"You'll need them."

"I'm in *grade* school!"

He smiled. "You don't think I'm gonna let you off easy, do ya? You need to get in the straight-A groove early."

She shook her head in exasperation. "Did *you* get straight A's?"

"Never. But it was a different world...And look what's become of me."

They remained silent for a time while she surveyed his cast and bandages and the tube that led from a bottle on a slender silver pole and hooked into his arm somewhere.

"Does it hurt a lot? I burned myself on the stove once. It really hurt."

"That stuff in that bottle helps a lot."

"Drugs?"

"Morphine. For the pain. I pump it in myself when it starts hurting too much. Best thing since sliced bread."

"Mom's worried about that. She says you used to be hooked on drugs."

"She told you that?"

"No, I heard her talking on the phone."

"You little sneak. You need to mind your own little girl business."

"What's such a big deal about sliced bread anyway?"

Things got quiet again. They needed something else to talk about. He asked her about her last two basketball games since he had been in the hospital and missed them. They had lost, but she had scored a few points in each game.

"How was your defense?"

"Pretty good. Except I fouled out one of the games."

"A little *too* good, huh? Better than letting them get past you. How about rebounds?"

She looked evasive.

"Rebounds," he said. "Rebounds. Rebounds! More important than points even. And rebounds will get you more points. Position, position, position. Block them out. Be tough. Bill Russell."

"Okay, Dad, okay...When do you get out of here anyway?"

"They won't tell me. I hope in another week, at most two."

Restless, she walked over to the window and looked out, came back to the side of his bed with a stern look and said, "You need a different job."

He wanted to say, "You got that right, kid." But that would be what the lawyers called an "admission against interest" so he kept it to himself and said instead, "You think so, huh?"

"That's what Mom said."

"I'll talk to her about that. Should she come in now?"

Kelly nodded in agreement.

"You come back and see me more often now, okay? Every other day at least?"

"You bet." She went to the door, took a last look back at him, and left.

When Annie came in, he could tell she had taken pains to look even better than usual, and her usual was always impressive. She would pass up no chance to remind him what he was missing. And old good feelings did indeed pop to the surface. They had been good at making love if not conversation. He often thought of trying to put things back together, but he was not sure she would take him back after all this time, even if he begged, which he would not do, and he had little faith that they could avoid falling into the same civil warfare that had always plagued them, two strong-willed combatants who never really understood why they were in conflict but could still never make peace, only an occasional truce.

She entered with a look of disapproval that quickly turned into tears. She came to the bed and kissed him chastely on the forehead. Her lips were soft and left a moistness on his brow. She smelled fantastic. Her auburn-tinted hair fell to and covered her shoulders. Golden hoops dangled gypsy-like from her ears. Brown eyes penetrated him. She perched on the side of the bed with one leg on the floor and the other hanging in the air.

"What are we gonna do about you?" she said.

"Buy more insurance if they'll sell it."

She laughed. A raucous laugh. Her laugh always revealed something joyful in her that stayed mostly hidden.

"They say you're gonna be okay. Pretty much okay anyway."

"Are you worried about the money?"

"Of course I'm worried. But I'm not here to hassle you about that. I'm almost through with the classes. I'm sure I'll pass the license test. But I'm a long way from the first commission check."

"I can still make the payments for a while. I have a small stash."

"You might not be so anxious to pay me when you hear what I have to say. But I have to say it. I said it last Halloween. You may love her to death, but you're a danger to your daughter. Here I am, just one year away from the last time, visiting you in a hospital."

"Kelly wasn't near it this time."

"But she easily could've been. Those Mafia people aren't gonna forgive you. And they don't go away. And who knows what they'll do to get at you? What if they do something to her to get at you?"

"They don't do that kind of thing. And it wasn't them."

"That's not what the newspaper thinks."

"They've got their head up their ass. It wasn't them."

"How do you know that? How *could* you know that? That's what they do. They blow people up."

"That's what someone else wanted to make it look like. If it was really them, you'd be visiting me in the graveyard, not the hospital."

"Oh, that's real comforting. So there's somebody else who wants to kill you now? She's now in double danger?"

He started to argue but stopped himself, knowing she was right. The same thing had occurred to him a number of times, but each time he had let the thought swirl away into the haze of terror, morphine, and constant pain of the burn ward, with a powerful assist from welcome self-delusion.

"I can't let her be with you anymore unless there's an armed guard there and maybe someone tasting your food, and starting your car with a remote device, and who knows what the hell else. It's horrible, but I don't know what else to do."

No more self-delusion. Now he had to acknowledge and reckon with it, and the reckoning made it hard for him to breathe. Just a few moments ago he might have been alone with his daughter for the last time for the foreseeable future. He may have played the last game of "Around the World" with her, might not be able to attend any more of her basketball games, her grade school graduation, and so much else. The luck he had so often reluctantly congratulated himself on having more than his share of had run out, and in the worst way.

"I'll do whatever you want," he said.

"It's not what I want. Not at all."

"It's what's right. How could I have thought any other way? I'll try to make it up…to everyone."

"Sad, sad, sad," she said, weeping and moving her head slowly from side to side.

He had an impulse to take her in his arms, or arm, his good arm, and comfort her, but he suspected it was himself he most wanted to comfort.

"I'll try to make it as easy as possible, but I have to protect her… take no chances. I haven't told her yet. It will break her heart."

"We'll make it work somehow."

"I have to go. This is too damn much."

It seemed the right time to deal with something else. "I've been thinking…a lot…about those times…I hit you…"

"My God, why?"

"I'm sorry and ashamed that I did that to you."

"You apologized then. We were both drunk. And I provoked you. Wouldn't stop when you asked me to, then you *told* me to stop, then…"

"Don't take *any* of it on you. That didn't justify it. Nothing justifies it."

"Why now?"

"Long past time."

Her hand on the door, she looked back at him. "The hell of it is that I'm sure, crazy as I am, if you'd have ever wanted to come back, I would've said 'yes, yes, yes—'scared to death but as excited and eager as I was on our wedding day. But now even that idiot fantasy is dead. What horrible sin did we commit that the malicious fucking gods put us together?"

KELLY WAS NOT the only one in danger. Sara. Even George. They both hung around the hospital a lot, arranged a private room for him, and rotated the security guards George had hired for the new line of business outside O'Keefe's room on a twenty-four-hour basis, which the hospital allowed on the condition they be in mufti, not uniform, and with no weapons visible.

"Probably a good idea, I can't argue with it, but that means they're not out making any money for us," he told them. "You guys need to quit babysitting me and get back and get us some business. Thank God I popped for health insurance, expensive as it is, but that doesn't give us any cash flow."

He made them also station a twenty-four-hour security guard at the office, and George agreed to temporarily overcome his aversion to an office environment and work from there anytime he did not absolutely need to be on the street. Sara began an extensive course of firearms training, obtained a carry permit, and started toting a small pistol at all times. She also increased her martial arts classes.

"Despite the stories in the papers, and I'm meeting with Oswald Malone to straighten him out as soon as I get out of here, we *know* it wasn't Jagoda's people, right? Why do we know that? Because you're talking to me and not my tombstone."

Nobody disagreed.

"Find out everything about Bowman and Popper, especially Bowman. Follow Popper. He's the one likely to lead us to Bowman. As soon as we find Bowman's lair, surveil him. And we've got to figure out who the real owners of that place are."

"Not sure how to do that last one, Boss," George said.

"Me neither," O'Keefe said, "But put your heads together...and any other heads you can find. Working hypothesis is that the owner, or one of them, is Jerry Jensen. And Sara, get on your running shoes. You'll be following Jensen."

"Rumble in the jungle," George said.

"You bet. Except for the surveillance, don't be secret about any of it. I want everyone in town to know we're looking at this...turning over every rock. Shake 'em up, baby."

"'Twist & Shout,'" George said. "We sure will."

"You guys really ought to quit."

They each looked at him with a "get a life, dickhead" expression, so he shrugged and relented. "This Bowman-Jensen thing was always 'no pay' and now it's become an actual black hole sucking in both our money and our time. Hell, I'll be bankrupt anyway before long, and you'll *have to* quit."

"Watch us," Sara said. "Your butterflies are roaming free to pollinate now. 'Freedom's just another word for nothin' left to choose.'"

O'Keefe and George looked at each other and smiled.

"What?" said Sara.

"I believe most certainly, Sara, that it's nothin' left to *lose*, not choose."

"There she goes again," George said, and he and O'Keefe laughed harder while Sara blushed and said, "Enjoy yourselves, assholes."

HE HADN'T EVEN settled his rear end comfortably into the seat of the booth when Robert said, "What the fuck. I thought you were *not* gonna bomb him. I've got the gun in the car. You couldn't wait or what? And then you fucked it up..."

"Spare me that shit. It wasn't me."

"Then who was it?"

"I don't know, but don't insult me by even thinking I would've done such a crappy job as that. If I'd've done it, they wouldn't even be able to find little pieces of him."

"Everyone is thinking it was us anyway. Like that newspaper article. We'll have the FBI up our ass and down our throat."

"Not my fault. Should we put it on hold?"

"No. What we need to do is figure out how to get the story out that it was someone else, that someone else is after that guy. If we can sell that, then it's perfect. We do him in, and everybody thinks it was whoever else. Can we figure out who that might be? Would help to know. We might want to help them along…without them knowing we're helping of course."

"This is dangerous enough without trying to hook up with the idiots who fucked up that car bombing."

"Let's just get it done."

"While this giant spotlight is on you? Seems like the worst possible time."

"Those fuck-ups might try something else that'll put even more heat on us. And some of my people are saying, 'If we're getting blamed for it anyway, let's just do it.'"

They sat there thinking, both quiet, both trying to figure out how to make the most of this bad situation. Eventually, Robert shrugged and said, "I have the item in my car. Come on out and I'll give it to you out there. Then I've got to get to an appointment."

Another appointment. A pattern.

At the car, Robert opened the passenger side door. In the seat sat a festively wrapped and beribboned package in a box far larger than a pistol.

"Happy Birthday. How do you like that? I wrapped it myself."

Really? You wrapped it. A surprising talent, Robert. I would not have predicted that.

He took the package, walked briskly to his car, and waited until Robert drove out of sight. He had decided to gamble that Robert would end up in the same place as Robert had the last time, which would not require him to follow close enough to risk Robert noticing him. So he took every opportunity he could to push the speed limit and take shortcuts to arrive there ahead of Robert. He avoided the street Robert had traveled down the last time to reach the house. He needed to avoid the possibility that Robert might drive past him and recognize the car. It was the kind of neighborhood in which any strange car would likely seem out of place and provoke the curiosity of residents. Fortunately, he did not need to linger long. All he needed to know right now was whether Robert visited this place a second time. He would be able to find out later who resided there and whatever domestic arrangements had been established.

Sure enough, even though he had parked too far away to be able to give an honest eyewitness identification of Robert in the car driving up to the house, into the driveway, and into the garage after opening the door remotely, he knew, with absolute confidence, that he would be able to testify under oath, if, God forbid, it would ever be necessary, that it was the exact car that Robert had parked at the shitkicker bar and from the front seat thereof had extracted the gift-wrapped firearm, and in which Robert had driven rapidly, even excitedly, away. That remote opening of the garage door—so settled, so cozy, so proprietary, so Ward Cleaver—impressed him as the most significant, the most telling fact of all. Yes, the conclusion seemed inescapable that Robert had something serious going on there on the side, and as he drove away, he considered yet again that husbandly adultery, and even the maintenance of a regular sugar baby, might be typical, winked at, even expected in the "Rat Pack" cultural waters in which Robert swam. Yet Robert's bride was not some inconsequential chippie or spread-assed matron that nobody knew or cared about. It was Rose Jagoda, Mafia Princess, the only daughter of Carmine Jagoda—now deceased but still projecting a long ghostly shadow—and she, all on her own a formidably regal presence in that world. There had to be serious risk in betraying such a woman. Again, maybe meaningless, but good to know—a situation pregnant with possibility.

CHAPTER ▸ 23

BEGINNING THE SECOND day after the explosion, while O'Keefe was still delirious, and continuing every day afterward, Lieutenant Ross tried to interview him. O'Keefe kept putting off the interview, mainly because he did not know how much truth he should tell. But it became increasingly clear that just sitting waiting for something to happen—not just to him but possibly to Sara or George, or Kelly, or Annie even—who knew where they would stop—could no longer be tolerated. He needed to do his best to bring the situation to a climax soon. One way could be to engage law enforcement.

"Looks like I've become your keeper," Ross said, as he pulled a chair up to O'Keefe's bedside. A younger detective accompanied him, introduced himself as Billy Rankine and after that said not one word, just sitting close to Ross but out of his way and furiously taking notes. Ross himself took a note or two but nothing compared to the expert stenography of the younger detective. O'Keefe wondered if the guy knew shorthand, which reminded O'Keefe that he wanted to take a course in shorthand so he could take more thorough notes at interviews.

"Have you figured anything out yet?" O'Keefe asked Ross.

"Not really. We know what the bomb was made out of, but it's common stuff, hard to trace. We've interviewed all the people on your block and a couple of the adjacent ones. You'd think that someone would've seen something, but apparently not."

"I might not be able to prove it, but I know who did it."

"Not the 'unknown person' all the way from the grave?"

"No. And you know why as well as I do."

"You're alive."

"Exactly." He told Ross the whole story including the involvement of Wayne Popper, David Bowman, and the likely next mayor. The only thing he left out was Derek Fagan's role. He thought he owed Fagan that.

Ross was not happy. "First, fuck you for not telling me any of this before. Second, it's too wild, especially the Jensen part. All you've really got to support your theory is that Wayne Popper may have scored some China White that may have somehow ended up in Beverly Bronson…maybe involuntarily…maybe voluntarily. That, my friend, is about as close to nothing as you can get."

"How about the injection site?"

"Interesting. Even suspicious. But still not much."

"How about Cherry Pink? If there's ever been a den of criminal iniquity, that's it. Gambling and drug distribution for sure. Some prostitution no doubt, and probably worse. Who knows what they do to those women just for the hell of it."

"That's the county. I've got no jurisdiction out there."

"How about a call to the sheriff's office to ask for some help with an attempted murder—mine—in *your* jurisdiction?"

"I might do that. From what I know about them, they won't help, but it might shake things up some."

"Exactly what I want to do."

"Keep me informed this time. I might be able to help, and you damn well need it. And break the fewest laws possible." He quickly turned to the younger detective. "No, Billy. Don't write down that last sentence."

AFTER THE SECOND week of what he thought must be the modern equivalent of medieval torture, O'Keefe left the hospital with a daily physical therapy appointment and a prescription for Percocet tablets. The primary goal of the physical therapy was to restore the range of motion in his left arm and hand, and, especially, to keep the scar bands in his hand from curling up. If this failed, his hand really would end up a claw—or worse, just a club. Each day a pleasant young woman would dip his hand in the hottest paraffin wax he could stand and let it congeal over his hand and soften the grafted skin; then, so much stronger than she looked, she stretched his hand and fingers, causing him great pain but nothing—he kept telling himself with teeth gritted—compared to the wire brush over raw flesh, *sans* pain killers, in the tank at the hospital.

Chop Wood, Carry Water. Although it wasn't easy to function, he headed to the office the day after the hospital release because there was so much to do even beyond the Bronson-Bowman-Jensen situation, including the rapidly approaching Harrigan trial and just trying to take in and manage enough work to keep his business alive. His "butterflies" were pollinating well, but he needed to do his part too. The Percocet enervated him, and he learned they were highly addictive though he couldn't understand why anyone would want to experience more than once the way those pills made him feel. He soon stopped taking them, which left him in constant pain that made it difficult to concentrate. He spent a lot of time on the couch in his office, just resting, not sleeping, because any part of his wounds that didn't hurt itched like a bad case of poison ivy.

OSWALD MALONE had eagerly accepted his invitation to a meeting.

"Can I bring a photographer?"

"Yeah, but I'm not guaranteeing I'll let him take any photos, and I want approval of any you intend to publish."

When Sara announced their arrival, O'Keefe told her to keep the photographer in the waiting room and bring Malone into his office. Malone was the lead business and financial reporter for the local newspaper, the *Herald*, but his editors valued him so highly they allowed him pretty much a roving commission to investigate other things that attracted his interest. O'Keefe wasn't sure of Malone's age—somewhere in the late thirties or early forties. He seemed to have evolved his persona to match his first name. He gave off the air of a dandy, including extravagant bow ties and flashy plaid suits and sport coats. He was fastidious, even prissy, though not effeminate. One could easily picture him, like John Steed in *The Avengers*, in a derby hat and brandishing a long, cane-like umbrella, though he never wore the one or carried the other. Many suspected he was gay, but nobody could say for sure. He was usually the smartest guy in the room. Nobody called him "Ozzie."

They had met the year before when Malone covered O'Keefe's mink farm Ponzi scheme adventure, which had originated in the hill and lake country in the southern part of the state and ended in a deadly firefight in the Arizona desert between O'Keefe and soldiers from the Jagoda "family." The relationship had evolved from the professional to the personal as O'Keefe introduced Oswald to Harvey's, which well-matched Oswald's quirkiness.

Malone tendered the obligatory concern and condolences to O'Keefe about his unfortunate injury and thankfulness that O'Keefe had managed to survive it all. "It made me a lot more comfortable to see that security guard out there," he said.

"And we have a bomb sniffing dog visit us every morning too."

"Really?"

"Yep. The cops are loaning it to me. Office, home, auto. Blanket coverage. Like insurance."

"So you've got something for me?"

"First, I understand why you came to the conclusion you did, but that story connecting the bombing to the Jagoda people was off base."

"Why?" Malone said, "because you're still sitting here talking to me?"

"Exactly."

"I've been wondering about that. I couldn't get to you when I needed to since you were otherwise in the throes of an apparent infection-caused delirium at the time."

"I've recently managed to stir up another hornet's nest, but this time of less well-known scumbags. You've heard of the Cherry Pink?"

"I have. Only slightly, however. Only enough to hope you're not one of its customers."

"Illegal gambling, prostitution, drug dealing, at a minimum. Probably many other and far worse things. And they have what appears to be a free pass from law enforcement out in the county. It's a scandal, just waiting for the crusading reporter."

"It's a bit far off my beat, geographically and subject matter-wise too."

"Stay with me. It's hard to figure out the ownership. The liquor license is in the name of Elmer Popper, who is the uncle of the *bouncer* at the place. Elmer is eighty-four years old and in a nursing home. He's never had two nickels to rub together in his life. The nephew, Wayne Popper, who's definitely a drug dealer by the way, has been running since he was an adolescent with a bad news hoodlum named David Bowman, who I think you'd discover, does some odd jobs, really odd jobs, for a certain well known public figure."

"I'd of course like to hear about the public figure, but I still don't see my connection."

"This place is plush. Lots of capital has gone into it."

"Drug money?"

"Probably. And maybe some outside, 'silent'-type partners who the world might be shocked to know are involved. And I believe one of those is...are you ready?"

"All ears, my friend."

"Jerry Jensen."

Malone tried to maintain his cool, disguise his shock. "That would indeed be news-worthy. What evidence do you have?"

"Nothing concrete. And I can't at this point even tell you all that I do know, don't ask me why, but if we shake a few trees, I guarantee you something is gonna fall out, and it won't be an apple or a pear. I think it's gonna be Jerry Jensen. If it is, he damn well ought to be exposed before he becomes the mayor. And if it's not him, it'll be somebody else you'll be glad to've exposed."

"The paper has to be careful...libel and all that."

"I have a couple of ideas. First, do an interview with me, right here today, a follow-up to your story. I don't name names, but I steer you away from the Jagoda people and suggest vaguely about some bad people I've run into out in the county. Then, separately, you start an investigation into the Cherry Pink and its liquor license...maybe try to get an interview with Elmer Popper in his nursing home?"

"Not sure about the second thing. I need to talk to the higher-ups about that, but let's do the interview right now."

~

THE NEXT DAY an article appeared in the *Herald* under Oswald Malone's byline, titled "PI O'Keefe Back on the Hunt," with a photo of O'Keefe, his arm prominently positioned, and a burn scar visible on the left side of his face. After sketching the background, including last year's firefight in the Arizona desert, the recent van bombing, his injuries, medical treatment, and ongoing recovery, the article concluded:

> Asked who he thought might be responsible for the attack on him, O'Keefe replied, "It was too amateurish to be organized crime. I've been doing some work out in the county lately. There's some rough dudes out there." Asked to provide more details, O'Keefe refused. "I'm not at liberty to discuss that right now. Maybe soon though."

A FEW DAYS later, O'Keefe, George, and Sara gathered in front of the small TV in the office breakroom to watch an event organized by the Jerry Jensen for Mayor campaign, at which the candidate made a short speech, then took questions from the press. Near the end, Oswald Malone raised his hand, and when recognized, asked, "Mr. Jensen, have you had any financial or other involvement in a business known as Cherry Pink?"

O'Keefe wondered if anyone else in the world but he, George, Sara, and Oswald Malone noticed Jensen's face abruptly change for a moment before he recovered himself, "What's that? Never heard of it..." and moved rapidly on to the next questioner before Malone could follow up.

"Shake 'em up, baby," O'Keefe said. "Everyone be extra careful from now on."

"Twist and Shout," said George and Sara in near unison.

CHAPTER ▶ 24

LOOKING UP AT the high ceilings and massive windows, the bland, chilly nothingness feel of the granite and marbled walls and floors, the dull brown walnut of the wooden trimmings including rows of pew-like benches, almost like church, for the spectators, O'Keefe said, "Monumental."

"Yep," Harrigan said, "monumental and majestic…the nation-state reminding you that it enjoys the monopoly of force, which seems to be bearing right down on me at the moment. I'll be frank with you guys, I'm scared to death."

"We'll win," Leclair said, and O'Keefe hoped the lawyer wasn't just blowing smoke.

O'Keefe asked Leclair, "What do you think the Judge really thinks about all this?"

"I can't exactly tell, but I'll tell you for sure he'll always be several mental steps ahead of everyone else in this courtroom."

"Where do I sit?" O'Keefe asked. "At the counsel table?"

"No," Leclair said, "only the lawyers and the parties to the case are allowed there or anywhere within the bar of the court."

This "bar" appeared to be merely a dark wood-paneled partition slightly lower than waist high, with swinging doors in the middle, that created an enclosed space in which the combat ensued.

"Part boxing ring, part altar," O'Keefe said. "Where's the tabernacle?"

But Harrigan and Leclair were too distracted to respond as the jury was just now being paraded in and seated. O'Keefe wished he had brought a seat cushion as he took his place on the bare wooden pew on the first row behind the bar, and on the same side and behind the defense counsel table so Leclair could jump up and quickly confer with him if necessary.

Mary Harrigan arrived and looked relieved at seeing a familiar face, even a somewhat scarred one, and that there was even room next to that face for her to sit. She made her way to him, wobbling slightly on her high heels as she navigated down the narrow space that separated the pew from the bar partition. Unlike many people these days who showed a definite aversion to coming too close to him, she nestled in, getting very close as if for warmth and security. "I'll prove my bravery," she said, "by sitting next to the human target. How are you feeling?"

"Hurts like hell and damn awkward, but functioning better every day."

She reached up and gently touched the scar on the side of his face as if that might help it heal. Although her usual manner tended to the aloof, composed, even what might be called snobbish, he could tell she was trying to present a different side of herself, still dignified but much softer, to the citizenry of the courtroom—in the way she dressed, the way she arranged her hair less Junior League than usual, and in how often she smiled, except when beaming scorn at Lord or any witness who said anything negative about her husband. But her real feelings often broke through her carefully composed veneer, which were more like those of a deer in headlights than a cuddly bunny.

She had not signed up for this, or most of the rest of the life Harrigan had plunged her into. She had been born into and stayed in a socially conformist *moyenne bourgeois* mold all her life with only one inexplicable exception—Mike Harrigan. Her parents had recognized him as trouble right away and campaigned against him, but she would not give in to them on this point though she had acquiesced to them on every other thing over the rest of her young life. Harrigan brought something out from within her that she had otherwise suppressed—a magnetic attraction to a force of special intensity and even danger. The parents were forced to move from hostility, to skepticism, to we'll-have-to-make-the-best-of-it acceptance.

But after the beautiful wedding, Harrigan not only didn't "grow up," he became even more of himself—a workaholic, a heavy problem drinker if not an actual alcoholic, alienated from most of the world including himself, desperate to succeed but disdaining every achievement as soon as he achieved it, and, yes, most hurtful of all, an occasional one-night-stand adulterer when he could make time away from work for it. Although he had provided her a sufficiently abundant material life, as good or better than that of her parents—the house, the cars, the clubs, the vacations, the handsome children, the private schools, the charitable and cultural events—the unhappiness, the insatiability in the deepest core of him corroded everything else. All of this produced in her a confusion of hurt, anger, disapproval, and a love that was closer to unconditional than was good for her.

O'Keefe had known her for a long time, since they were in high school. They were not particularly close but never hostile either. She seemed to accept him as some part of Mike that was not as unpleasant as some of the other things that came along with Mike. He wished now that they were closer so he could understand a way in, a way to find out what she was really thinking, and maybe even a way to comfort her. He wondered if she would divorce Harrigan at the end of the trial no matter how it turned out. Or did she feel trapped, afraid to let go?

"How you doin'?" he said, hoping to open something up. And he did.

"Devastated," she said. "We were in trouble anyway."

Now that he had opened it, he didn't know what to do with it. Copping out, he said, "How's he?"

"I can't really tell. He's been very sweet. He seems to apologize to me every other day about something. Big things and small. But he's lost. I think he's just put himself in Ben's hands and yours, and whatever happens will happen."

"Maybe that's good."

"Maybe."

She looked at him, a look of recognition, realizing that a major unasked question hovered over them, which she proceeded to answer. "I decided I was going to help him in this…no recriminations… accepting whatever happens, even prison, even losing everything. Despite all these years together, I don't think he knows me. I don't think he knows what love is either, so I don't know if he'll be able to accept what I'm offering. But I'll stay with him if he still wants me… and if he'll stop hurting me…I really am done with that."

Good for you, Mary. Which made him think of Annie—both women flawed, surely, but no more and probably much less so than the men to whom they had tendered their marriage vows—and he wondered how he and Harrigan could have been such fools as to fail to cherish these special creatures that fate had placed in their paths.

The Judge entered the courtroom with a robed flourish and the bailiff's announcement of "All rise!" *Where's the trumpets? There should be trumpets, a fanfare of trumpets.*

He had been involved in enough litigation that he understood most of the rules, procedures, and protocols, some of which seemed ridiculously arcane. Opening statements were supposed to be non-argumentative, "just the facts, ma'am," like Jack Webb would often say on *Dragnet*. Of course the lawyers tried to escape those constraints. Ken Lord described the national financial debacle called "the S&L crisis"—how corrupt practices like the ones the jury would learn about here had bankrupted hundreds of financial institutions and enriched the high rolling real estate developers and other swashbuckling financial pirates, *and their lawyers,* requiring bailouts funded by hard-up taxpayers who received no benefit from the mountains of cash that might as well have been thrown into a furnace and burned to ash. He mentioned Tremaine, mainly to emphasize the closeness of the relationship between Harrigan and that confessed criminal. He rang loudly his "Where were the professionals?" bell, dwelling for a long time on Forest Marler and his otherwise exemplary life, tragically capped by this one mistake, but who would now cleanse himself by not only admitting his own wrong but telling the whole story, not being like some schoolboy unwilling to "tattle" on his equally culpable peers, like defendant Michael Harrigan.

Leclair, laboring under the constant hostile eye of the Judge when he went anywhere near the Maura Davis issue, painted a picture of Tremaine as essentially a crook, who, to avoid a jail term, would sell out his parents, wife, children, and everything else that an honest man would hold dear. And even Forest Marler could not be expected to tell the truth when faced with the choice between the prison house and staying at his own house caring for his sick wife. Harrigan was just a scapegoat, an innocent, selected by the prosecution to be sacrificed for the sins of others, especially, and most shockingly unjust of all, the sins of the very men falsely testifying against him.

Lord called an FBI agent first, who reconstructed the loan, the use of proceeds, the participants. It was a neutral enough presentation, just laying down the facts. Leclair simply pointed out on cross-examination that not once had the agent mentioned the name of Michael Harrigan in his entire direct testimony. "And in all the records you mentioned—the bank ledgers, the correspondence, the memos, the transcribed voicemails, Michael Harrigan was not mentioned once, was he?"

"No, he was not."

Eddie Tremaine was up next. No surprise about Lord's tactic in presenting Tremaine early and definitely before Marler. If Tremaine did not perform well, Marler would be left to tidy up some of the mess and dull jurors' memories. Lord skillfully spent considerable time on direct examination establishing the especially close relationship between Tremaine and Harrigan.

"I thought of him as my partner," Tremaine said.

As for the decisive issue in the trial, Lord asked, "And, Mr. Tremaine, you were fully aware that the loan proceeds would pass through your entity and end up with a company owned by Messrs. Marcus and Manning, correct?"

"I was."

"And did you know that this...*diversion*...was for the purpose of trying to evade banking regulations that prevented a direct loan to the Manning/Marcus company?"

"I did."

"Why did you agree to do it? Is it your practice, Mr. Tremaine, to borrow funds that you are liable to repay and then give those to others?"

"Well, these guys did a lot for me. Morris asked me, and I was happy to help. Besides, they said they'd pay me back, and if it ever came down to it, I thought I could just offset what I owe them against it."

"Any other reason you went along with this?"

"Yes. Since my lawyer knew about it and didn't raise any red flags, I didn't think there could be much wrong with it."

"So Mr. Harrigan knew where those monies were going after they were loaned to you?"

Leclair objected, "No foundation, pure speculation, Your Honor."

"I'll allow it," the Judge said. "Mr. Lord, there had better be some basis for this statement or I'll strike and tell the jury to disregard."

"Why do you believe Mr. Harrigan knew?"

"He always knew everything. That's the kind of lawyer he is. That's why I made him my lawyer."

"That is an insufficient foundation, Your Honor."

The Judge kept silent for a few moments, his uncertainty clear to all, but then, in a tone of reluctance, said, "Overruled."

On cross-examination Leclair beat hard on Tremaine, dragged him back and forth through the slop of his life, pointed out his past history of defaulted loans, bankruptcies, fraud lawsuits from investors, and according to both of his former wives, hiding assets in anticipation of divorce proceedings. Leclair asked in every way he could exactly how Tremaine knew that Harrigan "knew everything," but Tremaine just retreated into "I don't remember exactly, but I know he did."

Leclair saved for last what he hoped would be best. "In your initial statement to the U.S. Attorney's office you didn't mention Mr. Harrigan at all, correct?"

"No, I didn't."

Leclair glanced at the Judge, and the Judge glared back at him as Lord edged to the lip of his chair in order to be ready to leap up and object.

"In fact, the possibility of Mr. Harrigan's involvement was suggested to you by Mr. Lord, correct?"

"Yes, but—"

Leclair thundered, "You've answered the question, Mr. Tremaine. No more!"

Lord said, "He should be allowed to explain."

The Judge said, "You can get that explanation on re-direct, Mr. Lord."

"And immediately following Mr. Lord's suggestion that Mr. Harrigan might be involved, he further suggested that if you named others who might be involved in this scheme and otherwise cooperated with the government, the government would look upon that favorably in connection with your own sentencing for your own crimes, correct?"

"I don't know that those were his exact words."

"But they were his exact message, right?"

"I interpreted it as 'if you come clean and cooperate and tell the truth, we'll go easier on you.'"

"And although Mr. Lord specifically mentioned Mr. Harrigan, he didn't specifically mention anyone else, did he?"

"No," Tremaine said reluctantly, looking at Lord for any help he might be able to give him.

"Mr. Lord can't provide you the answers, Mr. Tremaine. Hasn't he provided you enough answers already?"

Again, the Judge anticipated Lord's objection. "The jury will disregard Mr. Leclair's last statement. It was improper. Mr. Leclair, consider yourself warned."

Leclair continued, "For example, he didn't mention Mr. Mark Marcus, who was both half owner of the bank with Mr. Manning and also half owner, with Mr. Manning, of the company that ultimately received these round robin loan proceeds, correct?"

"No, he didn't mention anyone else."

Leclair asked the Judge if he could approach the bench. Later he told Harrigan and O'Keefe what occurred there. "I asked him to reconsider his Maura Davis ruling…how important it would be if the jury could be told and be allowed to consider Mr. Lord's special interest in Mr. Harrigan to the exclusion of others, including even Mr. Marcus who was much more likely to have known about and approved and desired that outcome than Mr. Harrigan. The Judge said 'no' of course, but he looked guilty about it."

Throughout the trial and especially during Tremaine's testimony, O'Keefe had observed the jurors as much as he could without offending them with his prying eyes. But he couldn't tell where they stood after Tremaine's testimony.

"That'll be all for today," the Judge said. "Who's your next witness, Mr. Lord?"

"Forest Marler, Your Honor. First thing in the morning."

Harrigan, Mary, O'Keefe, and Leclair gathered briefly in the hallway outside the courtroom.

Mary asked, "How do you think it went today, Ben?"

Leclair gave it a few moments' thought, as if being very careful about how he worded his answer, and said, "As well as it could have, I think. As well as we could've expected."

After Harrigan and Mary left, O'Keefe asked Leclair the question he knew Harrigan would have asked if Mary had not been present: "I understand you were being careful with Mary, Ben, but that wasn't much of an answer. Are we winning or losing?"

Leclair shrugged. "I don't really know, but to be perfectly frank, I think we're behind by a neck."

Since Marler seemed certain to come off better than Tremaine, that seemed like very bad news.

O'KEEFE HURRIED to the office to catch George and Sara before they left for the day. He gathered them in the conference room, looked at them expectantly, and said, "So who owns the Cherry Pink?"

"Still nothing," Sara said. "They've got the county people, both the liquor licensing and law enforcement people, zipped up tight. Can't find any records anywhere."

"How about Jensen?"

"Nothing to report there either," she said. "No fun following a politician running for office. But he's gone nowhere close to the club or anywhere else interesting."

"I've got some good news," George said.

"Give it up," O'Keefe said. "I'm in need."

"Popper finally led us to Bowman. No surprise, he lives in the county...his own little homestead off the road and surrounded by fields of unplowed ground."

George flipped open a notebook in front of them and showed them a map he had drawn of the property. "Long driveway, really a road, gravel, from the road to the house. The house is hidden by a line of trees on the left. You come out of the trees into a big open area. Clear line of sight from the house to where a car would come out of the trees. There's another line of trees on the right but a long way from the house. Hard to see anything inside the house from there. I didn't have binoculars."

"Is he alone there?"

"Looks like it to me."

"Not even any dogs? Seems like a guy who would keep pit bulls."

"Not a bark or a growl."

~

ROBERT AND HIS colleagues seemed dangerously impatient to administer last rites to O'Keefe with the public spotlight already glaring on them. Maybe the Jagoda bunch would be blamed anyway, as Robert had said, but that would not implicate him; if whoever else had it in for O'Keefe succeeded, he would not personally be involved. But if he moved forward now and accomplished the mission (not a sure thing by any means), and they turned the bloodhounds loose in earnest, who knows who they might ultimately sniff out? And if Robert and his crew would get their heads screwed on straight instead of bringing trouble on themselves by jumping the gun, they would find a way to convince the bloodhounds that someone else had dispatched O'Keefe. Surely if Carmine were alive, he would counsel patience in this situation, no matter how much O'Keefe had gotten under his skin.

Unless a near perfect opportunity presented itself to terminate O'Keefe's existence without risk of either failure or detection, an occasion he would be looking for and open to but doubted would occur, he needed to delay, and to develop plausible reasons to justify that delay to Robert, meanwhile looking for a more permanent escape.

Since it was not far from either his house or his office, he had taken to driving at random times through the neighborhood of Robert's love nest. He never paused, only drove a little slowly, not enough to cause someone to notice and wonder. The first several times there had been nothing to see, but then, on a bright Indian summer day, he drove by and someone in a sleeveless T-shirt and short-shorts stood in the front yard, leisurely raking up the latest fall of leaves. That someone sure did not look like a yard man.

CHAPTER ▶ 25

9:32 A.M. O'KEEFE hoped he would not be late for the start of the trial that day. They said Judge Montgomery was a stickler for punctuality. He tucked himself into an already packed elevator. Luckily, his floor was the first stop. He hurried through the near-empty corridors leading to the courtroom, his echoing footsteps reverberating off the limestone floors like a warning. The only person waiting outside, sitting alone in a corner—Forest Marler—was bent over, forearms against his inner thighs, hands on his knees, staring at the floor as if it might tell him a secret. Hearing O'Keefe's footsteps, he looked up.

"Hello, Forest."

Marler nodded in recognition and quickly returned to whatever he was pondering. O'Keefe thought it best, especially due to Lord's previous witness-tampering threat, to leave it at that. In the courtroom Harrigan and Leclair were hunched over at their counsel table, whispering to each other animatedly. Lord sat in his chair. with his usual perfect politician's posture, staring ahead. The spectators, more of them than usual for a criminal trial, sat quietly in the pews, waiting for the arrival of the robed priest of justice to enter and commence the ceremony. Mary sat alone and looked relieved to see him. But Oswald Malone was also in attendance. Much as Mary might welcome the comfort of his close presence, he needed to talk to Malone. Stopping by Mary's pew, he bent over and said, "Mary, I'm gonna spend a few minutes with the *Herald* reporter back there. Save my place."

Malone, seeming glad for the company, especially of so rich a potential source as O'Keefe might be, scooted over to make room for him.

"Slumming, are you?" O'Keefe said.

"The conjunction of finance and crime is too irresistible. What's going to happen here? Does Harrigan stand a chance?"

"Off the record?"

"Of course," Malone said, as if the question was unnecessary, which O'Keefe well knew it wasn't.

"Neck and neck, and they might actually be a neck ahead."

"Damn. I always liked Harrigan. Pulls no punches, tells it like it is, no puffery, and only slightly prima donna."

"All rise!" the bailiff intoned, and all obeyed though O'Keefe lagged a motion behind everyone else, which the Judge noticed.

Bad timing. He had not finished with Malone. At risk, he continued, but in a whisper now, "What about our other matter?"

Malone obviously did not want to continue the conversation, not because he was reluctant to impart that particular information, but because Judge Montgomery was famous for calling out and issuing fines to those who "talked in class." Glancing back and forth at the Judge, then at O'Keefe, he said, "Yes, I'm working it. Stone wall so far."

"Who?" O'Keefe whispered.

Malone's face tightened, he did not want to continue out of fear of the Judge. He watched the Judge while whispering out the side of his mouth: "Calls into Jensen, the county liquor license people, the Cherry Pink, trying to find Bowman but that's a tough one…" Still looking nervously at the Judge, he brought his index finger to his lips in the traditional sealing gesture, like the well-behaved boy in the class being pestered by the jabbering, unruly one.

"Yes, Mr. Malone," the Judge said, "you understand correctly. Mr. O'Keefe, you know the rules, don't you?"

"Yes, Your Honor. I apologize."

"One more offense, no apologies or excuses accepted, and the fine will be $100, and, if I'm in the mood...expulsion. For those of you who do not know, only the lawyers within the bar may speak to each other while these proceedings are going on, and even then, not when I am speaking. Not out of respect for me personally but for justice. First offense, a fine, as I've said to Mr. O'Keefe there. Second offense, maybe a large fine, maybe expulsion, maybe both. Third offense, don't even think about it."

Turning his attention to the lawyers, he said, "Is there anything we need to take up before we call the first witness?"

Both Leclair and Lord stood up at the same time and told him "no."

"All right, Mr. Lord, call your next witness."

"That will be Mr. Forest Marler, Your Honor."

Max Trainer, serving as Lord's second chair, retrieved Marler from the hallway. Marler made his way slowly to the witness stand, shuffling a bit and seeming even more hunched over than before, like a man even older and more feeble than O'Keefe had seen him at home. O'Keefe took advantage of the transitional moment to move to Mary's side, attracting a quick glance, only of suspicion, not actual disapproval, from the Judge. Her eyes expressed welcome and relief, and she smiled a "you've been a bad boy, haven't you?" smile.

Standing in the witness box, Marler raised his right hand and intoned the oath uncomfortably loudly, startling many in the courtroom: "I swear that the evidence that I shall give shall be the truth, the whole truth, and nothing but the truth, so help me God!"

On the "so help me God," his voice croaked with emotion.

The Judge noticed and said, "Are you all right, Mr. Marler?"

"Yes, Your Honor."

"Let us know if you're having any problems."

"Thank you, sir," Marler said and sat down.

Lord took Marler on a travelogue through his life, which had been exemplary almost all the way. O'Keefe had seen so many in the business world who, like Marler, enjoyed a lifetime of success, or at least the avoidance of failure or disgrace, but then faltered and failed at the very end, the last act a tragic one. Lord directed Marler through that last act, detailing the roles of Morris Manning, Eddie Tremaine, and finally, Marler himself.

Lord asked, "Did you know this scheme was wrong?"

"I tried to convince myself that it was all right because Tremaine was going to use the proceeds to make a loan to the Manning/Marcus company, well-documented and even collateralized."

"But nothing in the bank records reflected that use of proceeds, correct?"

Leclair objected to the question. "He can't lead him that way, Your Honor."

"I'll rephrase," Lord said quickly, before Montgomery could, as was inevitable, sustain Leclair's objection.

"Did anything in the bank records reflect that use of loan proceeds?"

"No."

"What did the bank records say about that?"

"Only that they would be used for general business purposes of Mr. Tremaine's company."

"Could the bank have made the loan directly to the Manning/Marcus company?"

Leclair almost rose to make an objection but apparently decided against it and eased back into his chair. O'Keefe guessed the objection

("Calls for speculation, Your Honor" is what it would have been) was not worth the risk that the jury would become impatient with what might seem like pedantic overkill.

"No."

"Why not?"

"The Bank had already extended the maximum credit the bank regulations allowed to Morris and Mark and the companies they owned."

"So the making of this loan, given the re-routing of the loan funds as you've described, was a crime?"

"Yes."

"And you have pled guilty to that crime?"

"I have."

Lord then introduced the plea agreement into evidence. O'Keefe understood why: Better to bring it out on direct rather than wait for it to be revealed on cross and let Leclair create the impression that the government had tried to hide it.

"Mr. Marler, please state in your own words what benefits you receive under that plea agreement."

"The most serious charges, which come with lengthy prison sentences, are dropped, and I plead guilty to a lesser charge, and, assuming I fully cooperate with the government, I will not have to serve any prison time."

Marler seemed to be done. Leclair stood up again. "He left something out, Your Honor, and I shouldn't have to wait until cross to bring that out. He left out the part about Mr. Harrigan specifically."

Lord quickly said, "We'll fix that. We have nothing to hide. Mr. Marler, please continue."

Nothing to hide, yet Marler withheld it. What does that mean?

“Yes, sorry. The agreement specifically summarizes my testimony about Mr. Harrigan’s role and obligates me to specifically cooperate with the government in this trial consistent with my grand jury testimony and other sworn statements I have given in connection with the plea agreement.”

“And you have sworn today to tell the truth, the whole truth, and nothing but the truth, so help you God, correct?”

Leclair rose to object but Lord managed first to ask, “And you believe in God, don’t you Mr. Marler, you’re a Christian man?”

“Object!” Leclair shouted.

“Sustained,” the Judge said with a hostile look of warning at Lord.

Lord, in danger of distracting the jury from his moment of dramatic revelation concerning Harrigan’s culpability, tried to re-establish the climactic aura, taking a drink of water, letting the buzzing and rustling quiet down, and the Judge helped him by pounding his gavel.

“And what involvement did Mr. Harrigan have in this loan?”

“Mr. Harrigan’s firm represented Mr. Tremaine in the transaction...reviewing the loan documents, providing the bank a customary opinion that the documents themselves were duly authorized by the borrower, Mr. Tremaine’s company.”

Lord seemed impatient with his witness, as if Marler was deviating from the well-rehearsed script. “And he said, trying to lead his witness back to the scripted lines he had apparently forgotten, with respect to the use of the loan proceeds, the re-distribution of those proceeds to the Manning/Marcus company, did Mr. Harrigan know about that?”

“Not to my knowledge.”

A disturbance in the field. O’Keefe did not quite absorb what Marler had said, but he did notice that the more sensitive, knowledgeable players in the courtroom—Leclair, the Judge, Harrigan, and especially Lord—physically jolted, slightly but observably, as if a small electric shock had coursed through them.

"You may not have understood my question, Mr. Marler, so I'll rephrase it. To your knowledge, did Mr. Harrigan know that the loan proceeds would be routed through Mr. Tremaine's company and end up with the Manning/Marcus company?"

"Not to my knowledge."

"May I approach?" Lord said, flustered enough to forget the usual "Your Honor" salutation.

Leclair joined Lord at the bench, but Lord and the Judge did all the talking, at the conclusion of which the Judge announced, "We will stand in recess for thirty minutes." As the jury and the audience members, in varying degrees of understanding, confusion, surprise and outright shock, stood up, mingled, conversed, Lord could be seen holding onto Marler's elbow and guiding him from the courtroom, and Harrigan reported he heard Lord say, "What the fuck are you doing?"

So that's why Marler had failed to mention the section in the plea agreement about Harrigan.

The recess extended well beyond thirty minutes as the two sides huddled in separate rooms off the hallway. Harrigan said little, seeming like Saul struck down on the road to Tarsus, beneficiary of a miracle he hoped would not prove to be a mirage. Leclair, overjoyed, said, "Un-fucking believable. All these years and that's the first time I've seen that. A recantation right on the witness stand with no warning. So much for the cross-examination I worked half the night on. I need to get something else ready so give me some alone time here. Got to be careful not to overplay our hand and squander the gift."

They left Leclair to his chore. In the hallway, Mary said, "Didn't we just win?"

Harrigan impulsively hugged her. "Not yet, babe," he said. "They've probably still got enough to get to the jury with Tremaine."

O'Keefe noticed Marler sitting by himself on the same bench in the same corner where he had seen him earlier. Lord had originally taken him into the room with the prosecution group, but he had apparently been cast out and now seemed abandoned by everyone. All he had been required to do to evade the possibility of what would, as a practical matter, be a life sentence, is stick with that story. O'Keefe decided to take whatever risk might be involved in talking to the witness before he had finished his testimony.

"Forest, that was one of the most courageous acts I've ever witnessed in peacetime."

"Well, I hope that sustains me in prison. But you were right about my soul. I didn't decide until the last minute. It was that damned oath that sealed it. 'So help me God.' But He didn't help. I had to do my part first. Maybe now He'll help."

O'Keefe decided to take a further risk. "You're a good man, Forest. If there's anything I can do to help you, I'll do my best." He stood up and walked back to where the Harrigans stood. *If Lord wants to call that bribing a witness, fuck him.*

A sudden burst of activity erupted in the hallway as the word came forth from chambers that the Judge wanted to meet with the lawyers right away. Mary sat down while Harrigan and O'Keefe paced back and forth in separate trajectories. After almost half an hour, Leclair returned, and they could tell he was bearing news that wasn't bad.

"Lord first tried to get a mistrial. No way. Then they tried for a recess. Denied. We're going forward."

Lord had no choice but to put Marler back on the stand and try to reinforce the testimony Marler had given prior to this day. Then he asked, "And you are not testifying today, are you, Mr. Marler, that Mr. Harrigan did *not* know where those loan proceeds were ultimately going?"

Marler looked confused.

"You're only saying that you don't yourself know what Mr. Harrigan knew about that, correct? For example, if another witness testified here that he knew that Mr. Harrigan knew..."

"Stop," Leclair said, springing to his feet. "Objection, Your Honor, that's..."

"Say no more. The objection is sustained."

"And I request that the question be stricken and..."

Again the Judge interrupted. "Yes. Mr. Lord's question will be stricken from the record, and the jury is instructed to disregard it."

When Leclair's turn came, he took Marler through the same sequence with Lord that he had done with Tremaine—nothing about Harrigan on the first pass, then Lord's suggestion and the dangling of the leniency carrot.

"Yes," Marler said. "After that, I convinced myself that Mr. Harrigan knew, and that I knew he knew. I think I actually believed it."

Then Leclair asked a high-risk question because the cross-examiner was never supposed to ask a question that he did not know the answer to.

"What made you change your testimony today?"

Marler hesitated for an uncomfortably long time. O'Keefe wondered if the boomerang was heading back toward Leclair and Harrigan.

"It was either my body or my soul, and I decided my soul was more worth saving."

THE CASE WENT to the jury in the early afternoon. The Harrigan group hung around the courthouse, hoping the jury would return a quick verdict of acquittal. But by the end of the day they were still deliberating and were allowed to go home for the evening and resume deliberations the next day. Harrigan pulled O'Keefe aside. "I'm not telling Mary, but this is bad shit. This means at least some of them want to find me guilty. Even if it's just one of them, I might not get acquitted. Innocent or guilty, it has to be unanimous. One asshole can hold out. I don't know if I can take another trial."

THE NEXT DAY the jury deliberated all morning and into the afternoon. At 2 p.m. they sent a message to the Judge who assembled the parties in the courtroom. "They say they're hopelessly deadlocked, nine to three. Nine for acquittal, three for conviction. I don't see the point in keeping them here any longer. It's a tough case no matter how you look at it."

"We don't think it's tough, Your Honor," Leclair said. "Nine to three is awfully close to unanimous."

"All right, Mr. Leclair, I'll keep them another two or three hours, but no more."

Again, at the end of the day, no movement, same score. "I'm declaring a mistrial," the judge said. Which he promptly did, summoned the jury, thanked them for their service, and left the bench.

Lord turned to the Harrigan group and said, "There *will* be a retrial, gentlemen. Count on it." As he marched out, Max Trainer, lagging behind, looked at them and raised his head and eyes to the sky, the unspoken thought, *Heaven, help us. I can't control him*, evident on his face.

Leclair huddled with three of his associates who he had summoned to the courtroom to help interview the jurors. "I'll call you later, Mike. We've got to interview these jurors before they get away. I'll call you tomorrow. We'll get a motion for acquittal on file ASAP. It's got a good chance. It really does."

Harrigan looked defeated, depressed, and disgusted. "From your mouth to God's ears," he said to Leclair, and left without saying goodbye.

~

IT WAS AFTER 6 P.M. by the time O'Keefe left the courthouse. All he wanted to do was go home and fall into bed, his usual prescription for the deep, enervating kind of depression that the trial result had brought overwhelmingly on him. But his days spent at the trial had left a lot of work undone at the office, so he headed there, barely able to stay awake on the drive from the courthouse. When he opened the office door, on the floor in front of him lay a copy of that morning's *Herald* with Sara's block printing on it that said, "SEE P. 6!" On that page appeared Oswald Malone's article "County Strip Club Draws Scrutiny." The article discussed how the Cherry Pink would not have been allowed in the city itself but had managed to take advantage of sparse and sketchy county ordinances. There were rumors of illegal gambling, drug use, and even drug distribution associated with the club.

> Asked about such rumors, county liquor licensing and law enforcement authorities said there had been no such activities brought to their attention. The money behind the club is also unclear. The license is in the name of Elmer Popper,

> the uncle of one of the club's non-management employees. Mr. Popper is eighty-four years old and resides in a nursing home. Efforts to contact Mr. Popper were unsuccessful. Asked to comment for this article, Marty Lansing, the club's manager, did not respond. Peter O'Keefe, a local private investigator who has been looking into the situation, commented, "The ownership of that club is a real mystery. But we'll get to the bottom of it. Soon."

He was still tired, but the article furnished him a small jolt of energy and even hope. *Shake 'em up.*

CHAPTER ▶ 26

BECAUSE IT DISCUSSED the Lord-Harrigan-Davis triangle in detail, Leclair filed the motion for acquittal under seal. On the day that the government filed its reply, Judge Montgomery ordered the parties to appear in his chambers the following day for oral argument. The Judge, Leclair and his associate, Harrigan, O'Keefe, Lord, Trainer, a court reporter, and the Judge's courtroom deputy crammed into the Judge's office. All but Harrigan lined up in chairs in front of the desk. Harrigan sat alone on a couch behind the row of chairs. They asked Maura Davis to make herself available by phone if they needed her.

Leclair spoke first. "As Your Honor knows, the deadlock was nine to three for acquittal. I don't know exactly what to make of this, but all four women voted for acquittal. Personally, I didn't think Mr. Harrigan had that much sex appeal."

That was risky given the Maura Davis angle. But Leclair got away with it; they laughed, even the Judge and Max Trainer, though not Ken Lord.

"We interviewed extensively the three men who held out for conviction, and we have described those interviews in detail in our affidavits and motion. One of them thought we had probably bribed Marler to change his testimony. The second stated he believed all bankers and lawyers are crooks. And the third just said, 'I agreed with Mr. Lord that the taxpayers deserved justice.' Please note that all three of the hold-outs essentially ignored the evidence. Moreover, we strongly believe that if we had been allowed to present the Maura Davis situation in conjunction with Mr. Lord's manipulation—"

Lord sputtered, "Your Honor—"

But Leclair kept shoving forward. "—those jurors might have felt very differently, and that generalized 'plague on all your corrupt houses' attitude might have extended to the government as well—"

Lord interrupted again. "I object to the word 'manipulation.' Your Honor knows, and Mr. Leclair damn well knows, that what I did here is done all the time."

"That doesn't mean it's right," Leclair said. "At best it's dangerous, and this case damn well illustrates how dangerous it can be."

Now the Judge interrupted. "Did the government interview the jurors?"

"Max handled that," Lord said.

The Judge turned to Trainer. "Well, Mr. Trainer…?"

"I didn't hear those exact words."

"Well," the Judge said, his impatience about to boil over, "did you hear anything inconsistent with the gist, the import of Mr. Leclair's statements?"

Trainer, twisting uncomfortably in his chair, and glancing nervously at Lord, said, "I can't say that, Your Honor."

Lord glared at Trainer while Leclair continued, "I won't belabor all of us by repeating everything we have in our motion papers, but, Your Honor, once all is said and done, they have *no* evidence, not even any circumstantial evidence, except the evidence of Tremaine the crook, which has not one piece of paper or other evidence to support it. It's nothing but his "'lying eyes,' as the song goes."

On his turn, Lord said, "What happened to the government in this case…an ambush, a booby trap, whatever you might call it…a witness recanting his testimony right on the witness stand, not giving us even the courtesy of a warning, is more than extraordinary, it's unique in my experience and I've never heard of it happening anywhere else..."

"Actually," the Judge said, "I don't think he made up his mind until the moment you asked him the question."

O'Keefe nodded his head vigorously yes and said, "He told me exactly that—"

"Now," Lord said, his voice almost breaking under the stress, "we've got O'Keefe giving us hearsay and he's not even under oath and shouldn't even be in here."

The Judge said, "Let's move on. And, Mr. O'Keefe, it *is* unusual for you to be invited to this kind of meeting. I don't mean to patronize you, but, like children at a gathering of their elders, you probably should be 'seen but not heard.'"

"Be all that as it may," Lord continued, "we should be allowed to present our case next time without being sandbagged. Granting an acquittal and dismissal of the case at this juncture would be an extraordinary interference by the court with prosecutorial discretion. We would have to appeal."

"That seems like a threat, Mr. Lord."

"I didn't mean it that way, but there are important Justice Department prerogatives at stake here."

"Well, you say 'extraordinary interference,' but this *case* is extraordinary in any number of ways. If I deny this motion, I believe I will need to grant the defendant's request for an immediate appeal on the Maura Davis issue, and I'm not all that sure that my ruling on relevancy will be upheld. I had hoped the jury would solve the problem, but it just couldn't get there. Resolving the appeal could take a long time, while Mr. Harrigan would have to live both under a cloud *and* in limbo."

"Or he might resolve it by negotiating a plea agreement like the others. He's refused even to talk to us about it."

On that one Harrigan erupted, "That won't happen, Your Honor. This bastard is not gonna squeeze me."

"Move to strike," Lord said.

"Instead, Mr. Lord, let's just move *on*. I'm granting the motion..."

"Thank you, Your Honor," Leclair said.

"A 'thank you' is not appropriate. This is justice, not mercy. I did not grant your motion at the end of the trial because I wanted to give the jury a chance to simplify all of our lives by just acquitting him and ending it there. But that didn't happen, and so here we are. The government did not offer sufficient evidence, as a matter of law, to convict Mr. Harrigan of this alleged crime. I will write and file a more detailed opinion soon. Under seal of course. The gag order will remain in place. I still have some hope that we can avoid the government being exposed to embarrassment, disrepute, and shame..."

"Your Honor—" Lord started to protest.

"Save it, Mr. Lord. The motion is granted. And the gag order will remain in effect. And please don't any of you test me. Violation of that order will be severely punished."

The Judge gestured with his left hand in a "shut it down" motion to the court reporter who stopped transcribing. "And, Mr. Lord and Mr. Trainer, I do hope you'll go easy on Forest Marler."

Lord's head snapped backward. "He's now admitted to perjury in addition to his other crimes, to say nothing of causing havoc."

"As I said, Mr. Lord, I do hope you'll go easy on him. Ultimately, instead of perverting justice, he preserved it.

"Your Honor, I have to protest—"

"He'll lose his law license anyway. His wife is bedridden. Community service ought to be sufficient. Remember, I'll be the one doing the sentencing."

Lord rose to leave but stopped, looked toward the Harrigan group, and said, "We *will* appeal."

Trainer sheepishly followed him out. Leclair, O'Keefe, and Harrigan took a few minutes to gather up their things. In the hallway outside of chambers Trainer was waiting for them. He approached them and said, "That appeal might not happen. The Justice Department will have a say about that, and that will likely mean that I will have a say about that."

"Thanks, Max," Harrigan said. "I really am innocent."

"Ignoring the inescapable taint of Original Sin, I believe you, Mike. And, gentlemen, please keep to yourselves what I said to you here. You know, don't you, what Patrick Henry *really* said?"

None of them offered an answer, so he continued, "Give me liberty or give me death!"

He hesitated a moment, like a good joke teller knows how to do. "But don't quote me!"

As he walked away, you could have mistaken him for a man who had been on the winning side that day.

Leclair said, "That damned Montgomery, he's a wily one. I told you he's always steps ahead of everybody else. He did his best to have his cake and eat it too...keep the Maura Davis thing behind the gag until maybe you'd be acquitted without that evidence. But that didn't happen, and this was Plan B all along...to acquit you one way or the other and do his best to keep the Maura Davis thing from coming out in public."

"You think that gag'll really work?" O'Keefe said.

"No way. It's already leaking around the courthouse, and it'll be all over the street soon. I'll assure you of this: The words 'Senator Kenneth Lord' will never be heard together in sequence."

"Good for us and the world," Harrigan said.

"But another enemy," O'Keefe said.

~

HARRIGAN INSISTED that O'Keefe join him and Mary at their house for dinner that evening. "The kids are staying with their grandparents. Just us," Harrigan said. "Gentle, humble, and quiet."

He figured he could go by the office for a few minutes to handle some things. He said hello to the security guard who was quickly becoming an old friend. Sara was still there, pounding away at the computer, looking harried and tired.

"Rough times," O'Keefe said.

"It's a bitch," she said. "Following him around until it looks like he's turned in for the night and then getting back here to catch up. And not knowing what time he's gonna get up in the morning so I get up before the crack of dawn to make sure I don't miss him…"

"You need a couple days off. I'm ready for something other than sitting on a hard-on-my-ass wooden bench in a courtroom listening to lawyers savage each other. I'll take him on the weekend."

"I'm not even gonna fake like I want to talk you out of that."

The dinner went as Harrigan said it would, a mellow, pleasant time. After dinner, Mary drinking wine, and Harrigan and O'Keefe coffee, Harrigan said, "That was what some Civil War general, I forget his name, called one of his battles—'a close-run thing.'"

"Too close," Mary said.

"Thanks to Pete. He's the one that got to Marler."

He lifted his coffee cup in a toast. "To a true Knight of the Grail," he said.

"*Monty Python* version."

"Mary, our good friend here used to live in tragedy. Now he lives in irony."

"And, eventually, maybe even sincerity," O'Keefe said.

"We should join him, Mary."

Mary, who had drunk herself tipsy and merry, said, "I'm game… but what the hell are you two talking about?"

When O'Keefe left, Mary hugged him hard and long at the door, and he awkwardly reciprocated in his cast and sling. "Where's your coat?" she asked, "It's cold out there."

"Can't make it work with these things on my arm. It's hard enough to get a shirt on."

"Take care of yourself," she admonished. "You really do need to find a different line of work."

"Blame your husband for that."

"You're a pair of trouble finders and makers. Except that you, Peter, end up with the 'getting shot, burnt up, and blown up' part of the deal."

"I should've stayed in college. This is what happens to dropouts."

Harrigan, walking O'Keefe to his car, said, "You really ought to quit. You've only got so many lives to give. You might be all out."

"Hey Buddy, isn't it great to have a second chance? Think of all the people who never get a second chance."

Harrigan closed his eyes for longer than it takes to blink, absorbing and appreciating the point.

"In my case three or four," O'Keefe said.

Harrigan looked at him oddly, not understanding.

"Second chances," O'Keefe said.

"Oh…yeah," Harrigan said. "Sorry. I'm a little slow on the uptake."

They arrived at O'Keefe's vehicle. "You know," Harrigan said, "I discovered a whole bunch of things through this…It turned out I had more friends than I thought…and, no surprise, some who I thought were friends turned out not to be...and I found out that it's worth having a surplus...of money and friends and goodwill...and, most of all, that what's inside that house really does matter most...sappy shit like that..."

"No more pinball?"

Harrigan smiled a devil's smile. "Don't know about that. Those shiny lights and ringing bells and the wild bouncing around aren't all bad. But no more Eddie Tremaines or Double M&Ms...and maybe a little more of what Forest Marler vowed in high school...like most of us did...serving justice..."

"Don't get carried away."

"Little chance of that. Got to keep you in business...And speaking of that, I got you into this Jensen mess and haven't lifted a finger to help. What can I do?"

"Nothing. I've made my moves. The next one is theirs. I'm counting on them to make it. If they don't, I have no idea what to do next. They might just get away with it."

ON THE DRIVE home his phone rang. He was inclined not to answer it but did anyway, and was glad he did.

"I hear congratulations are in order." That sunbeam voice.

"Is this the scarlet lady?"

"The very one."

"You know, two courageous people made all the difference."

"You and who else?"

"Not at all. A man named Forest Marler...and a woman named Maura Davis."

"I'll try to remember that when they fire me."

He refused to try to deceive her with false comfort. It would get out, just as Leclair said it would, and it might go badly for her when it did.

"The people who know what you did will make a place for you."

They were both quiet until it became awkward, and she was not the kind who could allow such a silence to go on too long.

"So, good night to the good knight. Remember there's a certain lady who would take you in."

"I'm a danger to everyone right now."

"That won't last forever."

"Remember what I said about a heartache..."

"Oh you're another slippery one, aren't you?" she said with a merry laugh. "That won't last forever either."

The pause was even longer this time. He had no idea what to say next.

"Be careful," she said, her voice catching with choked emotion, "and don't be thinking you've heard the last from me."

He said goodbye to that voice that seemed made for joy, not tears.

PAUL WONDERED if he should be nervous. Such an out-of-the-way place for a meeting. A honkytonk bar out in the sticks. It immediately concerned him that this might be a setup, that he was being enticed into a trap. But that didn't seem possible for several reasons including that he had no current enemies and no indication of any punks who might be aiming to take over his sources of income. And he could not imagine that the person who had asked for the meeting would possibly try to do him harm, especially in such a public place. But of course he took precautions. He armed himself, that was a given. He also arrived an hour early and drove all around the place several times, back and front and on both sides. Then he parked a little way down the road so he could observe those going in and coming out. Sure enough, at five minutes before the appointment time, his "host" arrived.

"Nice to see you again," the host said. "Been a long time."

"It has."

"Different paths."

"No shit."

"I understand you're very close to Robert these days."

This seemed to be going in a dangerous direction. "I drive him around some if that's what you mean."

"He and Rose are still together, I assume."

Paul only nodded his head. He did not want, by any word or gesture, to disclose anything whatsoever.

"How's Rose?"

"All right, I guess."

"Still beautiful?"

"Maybe you'd better tell me why we're here."

"I've come across some information that I feel like someone other than me ought to know...for Rose's sake if nobody else's."

Paul waited, showing no emotion, no interest, did not even ask the obvious question, "Why me?" But of course whatever might involve Rose interested him.

"Robert has a lover...stashed away in a little house over in the Meadowbrook neighborhood."

A long pause, then Paul said, "So what. Doesn't everybody?"

"Everybody isn't married to Rose Jagoda."

"None of my business."

"It's a boy."

Was he talking about someone being pregnant? Had a baby? "What?"

"A boy. The lover is a boy."

It was hard not to show the shock he felt. "Can't be."

"But it is. I guarantee it."

Paul waited, not playing a game anymore. He really did not know what to do.

"I assume you want the address…so you can check it out for yourself."

He thought about saying "no," continuing to try to feign indifference, but this could not be ignored. He indicated a holder full of small paper napkins on the table and said, "Write it down."

"I'd prefer you write it. I don't want my handwriting floating around out of my control."

"No pen."

"Use mine."

Paul took the pen and a napkin out of the folder, wrote down the address Ross had given him, and said, "So what do *you* want from this?"

"I have a debt, you're aware of that. Robert's forcing me to repay that debt, let us say 'in kind'…with services. I want that debt to be forgiven."

"And those services would be?" Paul asked, though he already knew the answer.

"Killing Peter O'Keefe."

Paul was silent for an uncomfortably long time, then said, "Seems like a fair trade. But I can't make any commitment right now."

"Not asking for that now. But that's my request and my expectation when you check out my information and you do whatever you decide to do about it. I never want to be summoned again. Debt is paid, cleared, forgiven. Nevermore…quoth the raven."

"Is that all?"

"Poor Rose. I wonder if Robert and his boy wear protection."

He watched Paul rise and walk slowly, deliberately, even nonchalantly, out of the bar.

CHAPTER ▸ 27

O'KEEFE HAD REPLACED the ill-fated van with a Jeep Grand Wagoneer. Black with black-tinted windows, it also had wood paneling on the side, imparting what he vaguely hoped to be a deceptive "suburban mom" appearance to counteract the Batmobile black. He installed a specially souped-up engine and other custom features to make it easier do things like sleep and relieve oneself in it, plus a special door in the floor for weapons and other items that needed to be hidden away. Waiting all Saturday morning and into the afternoon for Jensen to leave his house, O'Keefe first listened to all six of the Brandenburg Concertos. That was just light refreshment, after which he resumed his project of listening to all of Bach's two hundred or so cantatas in numerical order. They seemed to average twenty-five to thirty minutes each, so he figured they would last him through fifty to sixty hours of tedious so-bored-I-want-to-blow-my-brains-out surveillance, and much longer if he mixed in occasional books on tape, Bob Dylan albums, and other miscellany. After finishing the two hundredth, he could start back at the first and march through them again. As far as he could tell, they would bear a lifetime of listening.

In the early afternoon Jensen left the house and O'Keefe followed him to his office. Within a couple of hours O'Keefe's head, heart, and soul brimmed with Bach while his disposable travel urinal brimmed with liquid, a somewhat blasphemous conjunction of the sacred and the profane that amused him. As he contemplated what he might do next in the way of waste management, Jensen mercifully exited the building, with a small bag that he had not carried in, and drove off.

Once Jensen climbed the on ramp to the freeway heading toward the county, Jensen's ultimate destination seemed obvious, and that knowledge, plus the absence of stop signs and street lights, and numerous corners to turn at, allowed him to keep a good distance behind with minimal risk of Jensen spotting him. He was glad this opportunity, and with it, extreme danger, had fallen to him instead of Sara. When Jensen took the expected exit, O'Keefe held back even a little more since the lightness of the traffic on the rural roads would make it easier for Jensen to spot him. He was sufficiently confident to linger far enough back so that Jensen could not possibly see him. As he approached Bowman's property, he noticed a few lingering streaks of white dust in the air, left over from Jensen's car churning up the gravel on Bowman's driveway.

He drove on down the road to the next turn-off, a driveway similar to Bowman's, leading to something hidden by trees. He pulled onto a flat patch of grass on the side of the driveway and parked, leaving enough room for another vehicle to pass. He would just take the chance that the property owner or someone else would drive by and wonder why this strange vehicle was parked there. Struggling out of the van and into the cold of the late afternoon, he wished he had figured out how to get a jacket or a sweater over the cast instead of just a shirt with the left sleeve unbuttoned. He jogged back up the road and up Bowman's driveway, stopping, out of breath and his arm hurting from the jouncing, when Bowman's house came into view with Jensen's car parked in front.

The open expanse between the tree line and the front of the house was just as George's map pictured it. The twilight was fading, it would soon be full dark, but he guessed he could still be seen from the house if anyone was looking in his direction. He unsnapped the strap and pulled his pistol from its holster. Guessing that no one was likely looking his way, he ran fast, despite the pain shooting through his arm with every step, straight for the house. He made it to the shield of Jensen's car, sat down with his back against the rear bumper, and panted until his full breath returned. A dim light, barely visible, shown from a window on the side of the house to his right. He crept toward it, stopping at the edge of the window. He could hear voices. It seemed like only two. He could not understand what they were saying. He peeked in. The light was so dim he could not actually recognize them, but he could identify two human shapes. He wanted desperately to hear what they were saying. He hurried around to the front door. Unlocked!

He had the pistol in his right hand. His left arm and hand were cinched up in the sling and cast, which he removed and tossed onto the porch. Awkwardly and painfully, and slowly, slowly, he turned the knob and eased the door open, so that any squeak would be virtually inaudible.

In front of him, the usual layout of most houses—first a living room, then beyond it some other room, probably a dining room, from which low light and low voices oozed. He moved slowly toward that other room.

A BOOM! Another bomb! He waited to be dead, then realized he remained alive and even unharmed except possibly for shattered eardrums. He managed to keep cool despite all his usual CPTSD sirens, flashes, and explosions firing, whirling, and zooming through his mind. He continued slowly into the next room, right hand and arm fully extending out in front of him, pistol at the end, wishing he was holding his M-16 instead.

Jensen stood sideways to O'Keefe, facing Bowman, or, rather, facing what appeared to be Bowman's corpse slumped in a chair. Sensing and then seeing O'Keefe, Jensen turned. Neither of them fired, and later O'Keefe cursed himself for hesitating, knowing his hesitation would have been his self-imposed death sentence if Jensen had been willing to execute it. Instead, Jensen said, "Stop, Pete. I'll put mine away if you will. I want him to be the last."

"You first," O'Keefe said.

Jensen brought his pistol to rest against his chest. After waiting long enough to determine that Jensen had indeed given O'Keefe the chance to shoot first, O'Keefe brought his own pistol into the same place against his chest as Jensen had done with his.

"I'd like to sit down," Jensen said. "You mind?"

Jensen sat down in the chair he had apparently been sitting in before O'Keefe arrived and gestured toward another chair for O'Keefe to sit in.

"You're a very inconvenient man," Jensen said.

O'Keefe did not respond, all his senses focused on the pistol against Jensen's chest to detect even the slightest movement.

"He was determined to kill you too. It had to stop. This was the only way."

"You were a little late."

"Bev?"

"Bev."

"I never wanted that. I just wanted him to scare her. But he did what he wanted. Always did."

"You let him in…unleashed him."

"Yes, I did. She came out of nowhere to ruin my life. I tried the gentler way with you and Mike. It didn't work. I panicked."

"What do you mean 'it didn't work'?"

"She was uncontrollable. Bitch from hell. Not just threatening me with what she called a rape. But, my God, the Mary Jane Donovan thing too. She was crazy. She would never have stopped. Blackmailers don't. I found that out the hard way. I would've paid her in the end. But I wanted to try at least to soften her up if not ward her off."

"David Fucking Bowman of all people. What rock did you find him under?"

"We grew up on the same block. He wasn't my friend, but we weren't enemies either. You heard about that trouble I had a few years back?"

O'Keefe shook his head. He had not been paying much attention in those days.

"It was in the press…couple properties in foreclosure…everything teetering…everything my father built and left for me…teetering. Bowman came to me with a proposition. Not for the first time. But this time I was desperate. He needed to finance a big load of cocaine. Easy in, easy out. Solved my problems. But he had me then. I couldn't get away."

"Cherry Pink? That you?"

"Yeah. And, by the way, it throws off more cash flow than any of my real estate projects." His smile was all pain.

"Did you rape her like she said?"

"I'm not sure."

"Not *sure*?"

"It was complicated."

"Did she resist…say 'no'?"

"Once…sort of…"

"Once wasn't enough?"

"I didn't think she meant it. They usually don't. She seemed to get to like it pretty quick."

Rocket flash across the sky. At the last possible moment, he pulled himself back from leaping out of the chair and onto Jensen, gun or not. *I guess he forgot about his hand gripping her throat.*

"And the other…Mary Jane?"

It burst from him. A shout: "NO! Bev was wrong, all wrong about that."

"What do we do now?"

In one quick move the pistol no longer rested against Jensen's chest but pointed at O'Keefe.

Idiot…letting this happen.

"If you drop your gun, I promise I won't shoot. If you do anything else, I will."

Idiot, he thought again. He dropped his pistol and waited for the blast.

"Good move, Pete. You see, I have my own plan to end this, and you've gotten in the way. Which seems to be a specialty of yours. As I said, you're an inconvenient man. But I'm gonna leave you with Mr. Bowman here, only one of you dead. I'm worth way more dead than alive. So much insurance. No suicide exclusion. A sale of my properties and business all set up and ready to go. Still lots of shame for my wife and kids, but not as much as the other way. Over quicker. Fade away from the headlines faster. Better than me clinging on like a cowardly piece of shit. It's not close to enough, but it's all that's left for me to do now. Him, then me. The end."

O'Keefe wasn't going to try to talk Jensen out of it, or try to scold him out of it either with the old "that's the coward's way" baloney. At the moment he felt nothing but relief that Jensen apparently didn't intend to kill him.

"How and when?"

"Not sure. A high-speed accident. Maybe even an explosion. A fireball maybe. Don't like that idea. But I intend to be dead before the fire."

Jensen rose from his chair, approached O'Keefe, kicked O'Keefe's pistol a few feet away, and picked it up.

"I assume you won't come stupidly chasing after me," Jensen said. "Wouldn't be good for either of us."

He sidled toward the living room, keeping O'Keefe in sight. At the archway leading to the living room, he turned, with the pistol aimed directly at O'Keefe now.

Shit. I have to rush him. Maybe he'll miss me.

"I ask myself how I got into this," Jensen said. "I was just a kid..."

No, he doesn't intend to shoot.

"Cupidity," O'Keefe said.

Jensen did not seem to understand. He turned and walked briskly toward his destiny.

"MORE THAN A HUNDRED miles an hour when he hit the bridge," Ross said when he told O'Keefe the news. The car did explode. It also burst into an incinerating fire. The coroner found a bullet in the blackened husk of Jensen's skull and speculated that he had put the gun in his mouth and fired the bullet just before he hit the bridge. "He must've wanted to make double sure to get the job done," Ross said.

And make sure to escape that fireball. I sure as hell can't blame him for that.

CHAPTER ▸ 28

NO HIGH-PITCHED, joy-tinged "Hey, Robert" to greet him. As he passed through the door from the garage into the kitchen, he tensed up without really knowing he was doing it, as if his body somehow sensed something wrong before it registered in his mind. When he opened the door from the kitchen into the dining room, still not fully perceiving danger, something clubbed him on the top of his head, and someone threw him to the ground. The blow knocked him into a confused stupor, leaving him conscious enough to know only how badly it hurt. He felt blood trickling down to his face. He understood that tape was wrapping around his mouth and eyes and head, his arms being jerked painfully in their sockets, brutally bent back, his hands being tied together behind him, excruciatingly tight, and his feet the same.

Someone grabbed his legs and was dragging him along the floor, his head bouncing along, across one threshold, then another, onto the concrete floor that must be the garage, then whoever was doing this to him grunted as they reached under his shoulders and propped him up into a sitting position and folded, lifted, and shoved him into the gasoline, motor oil, and tire smell of what must be the trunk of his car. He was terrified but grateful that he wasn't already dead. Might be hope still. Or it might be even worse than dead. They often tortured before they killed.

The car stopped several times on the way, he guessed for stop signs or traffic lights. Finally, he heard what he thought to be the electro-mechanical clank of a garage door folding up into a ceiling, then the car moving a few more yards, the trunk opening, them dragging him out by his feet, letting his head bang first on the car bumper and then on a hard floor, and dragging him again, his head bumping over another threshold. They pulled him up to his feet and then partly down again, sitting him in a chair. The tape over his mouth and eyes was then ripped off, wrenching off with it some of his hair and skin.

If he could have seen his face, he would have seen bands of raw flesh where the tape had been, one of his eyebrows mostly gone, a strip of skin hanging from his upper lip, the rest of his face smeared with dry, cracked, congealed blood. They had taken him to that place he had used as a cover story that time when Rose had discovered the remote in the glove box. He had been placed in a chair, in a small room, sitting at a table, facing a wall with, to his right, an opening in the wall, a doorless doorway.

He cried out in pain, then in horror when he realized what sat propped up in a chair across from him. He screamed, sobbed, and gagged all at once. He vomited onto the table. Then he was hyperventilating and choking on vomit. James, his lovely boy, tied to a chair, his head, sickeningly twisted to its left side, suspended just above his shoulder, his hair and face and the front of his shirt soaked with blood.

Someone moved around from behind him, walked around the table, sat down across from him next to his poor, mutilated lover, and laid down a pistol on the table. Paul. Robert's mind was now a jumbled mix: *Paul couldn't be doing this on his own. Good if it was just*

Paul. Not Tony Farina. Maybe his sole punishment would be the other's, James's…death…

"Who's," his voice croaked, dry in his throat, swallowing, trying to wet it enough to continue…"telling you to do this, Paul? I can do better for you than they can."

"Not in this case, Robert. But I will be a lot easier on you than the rest. They wanted to cut your dick off and watch you bleed out."

"Paul, don't do this. I've got a family."

"Not anymore," he heard a voice from somewhere say.

"Rose," he said as she came from the doorless doorway into the room. "Oh, Rose…"

She sat down next to Paul.

"Rose, please…"

"You were fucking *him*…and *me*…at the same time," a sob of rage exploding from her. "Do I have AIDS inside me now?"

"Rose, I'm—"

"And you intended to escape somewhere with him and all that money and leave me with who knows what festering in me?"

"Rose…"

She grabbed the pistol and pointed at him, her arm and hand quivering with the weight of the pistol and her rage.

When it became clear she would not pull the trigger, Paul took the gun from her and said, "You can go. I'll do the rest."

She pushed herself up from the chair. Robert tried to appeal to her, with his eyes, and then with, again, "Rose…please…"

She refused to look at him and left the room. Paul followed and left the door open, which allowed him to keep an eye on Robert.

"IS IT OVER FOR HIM?" she asked. "Any chance for him to save himself?"

"No chance. Just planning to steal all that money was enough all by itself...even if he wasn't a faggot...even if he didn't do what he's done to you. He really is lucky it's me that's handling this."

He couldn't read her expression, couldn't tell whether she was sad or satisfied.

"And we've agreed about what's next," she said.

"Yes."

"And the others?"

"They're in." He had covered it with those he needed to. Vince most importantly, the wisest of the wise guys, who had helped him bring the others around, some shocked and grumbling at first, but eventually either understanding the wisdom of the solution or at least grudgingly bowing to momentary necessity. They—Rose—and he, now the only consigliere in the history of the Jagoda organization—would need to be decisive, smart, firm—reward who they needed to, banish who they needed to, kill who they needed to.

Paul looked at her beautiful tear-stained face. Sad. Angry. And something else, something maybe he should be afraid of. He could see her father in her eyes.

She said, "I need to find a place to get an AIDS test. I need to find out if he's given it to me."

Paul wondered if he might end up with Rose after all. There was that saying, which he had always scoffed at: Good things come to those who wait.

After Rose left and Paul had extracted from Robert all the information about the hidden money that he could threaten, torture, and falsely promise out of him, Paul walked around the table, stood behind Robert, looped a thick rope around his neck, and strangled him to death. He called and summoned those he had selected to help with the clean-up. They did not finish until early morning. After they completed their work and departed, he checked the place thoroughly for anything that could tell what had happened there last night. Satisfied, he locked up and drove off. He was exhausted, afraid he would fall asleep at the wheel. He stopped at a convenience store for a cup of coffee. Outside the store he noticed a pay phone bolted to the store façade. When the other end of the line picked up, he said, "It's Paul. Your debt is paid. In full."

~

HE—THE ONE AT the other end of the line—did not shout for joy or make any noise at all, but a warm surge of relief infused his entire being. *Dodged the bullet. Not quite the right phrase. Dodged having to shoot the bullet.* He stood up, grabbed his suit coat, and left the office. Even though it was not yet noon, he thought he would go somewhere and have a drink. Maybe several drinks. He would go home early, make up a story to explain the surprise to his wife, why they were getting a babysitter, going somewhere special, getting drunk like college kids, and maybe fucking until dawn. He affixed the blue light to the top of his car and started it flashing, and, after a couple of blocks, could not help himself, he turned the siren on too. Lieutenant Ross was overjoyed not to have to kill O'Keefe. He had grown somewhat fond of the guy.

CHAPTER ▶ 29

HIS PLANE LANDED in the late morning. The bright sunshine, low humidity, and cool sea breeze tempted him to pop for a convertible, but he curbed his enthusiasm and rented a humbler vehicle, although he did make sure it included a CD player. He had brought the Brandenburgs, which seemed most fitting for a drive among the green California hills, as well as for the inspirational uplift he needed to say something useful today. Traveling down I-5 to Camp Pendleton produced more than a memory—more like time travel, back to that spring and summer he had spent in this part of the world: Boot Camp in San Diego—that first night they had shaved their heads and marched them, still in civilian clothes, around the parade ground all night in the pounding February monsoon rain; next, so called "Advanced" Infantry Training (the "Advanced" being mostly "advancing" the body's leg and lung strength through exhausting forced marches up and over the dusty hills of Camp Pendleton); finally, Staging—next stop Vietnam.

Sara had spent days wrestling with the military bureaucracy to persuade the martinets to allow the boy a pass to travel off base with O'Keefe on a weekday. They ended up allowing it but only for an afternoon. Dan must return to the base by 5:30 p.m. O'Keefe was just happy Private Dan Bronson still resided at Camp Pendleton, that he had not gone AWOL when he heard the staggering news from home. His mother murdered. His father not his father. Himself the child of a rape. His mother lying to both his father and to him for his entire life. He called, raging, to his grandmother, who had been lied to like everyone else, and she in turn called O'Keefe and asked for his help. At first, Dan refused to talk to O'Keefe at all because O'Keefe had not told him the facts he knew when they had met. O'Keefe did not defend himself, just kept saying "let me come out and see you," and Dan finally relented. And now here he had landed and had no good plan, idea, or clue how to try to make things better.

He had to wait in the visitor reception area for a long time. Finally, Dan arrived from somewhere in the building interior, walking fast and angry, wearing his standard-issue uniform: tan short-sleeve shirt with a single chevron stripe, indicating his "Private" rank; tan slacks and tan belt with Marine Corps insignia on its brass buckle; and just-out-of-the-box black shoes of a vaguely oxford style, but blunted and snubbed—cloddish, so that no one would mistake the wearer for anything but a soldier or a cop. In his hand he clutched the soft-peaked traditional informal military cap—something like soda jerks wore at old-fashioned drug stores—that most of the Marines especially disliked and called a "cunt cap."

"Those fuckers," he said in a low voice, "they found something wrong with the paperwork at the last minute, I thought for a while there they weren't gonna let me go."

Outside the building he looked around suspiciously and, apparently determining he could not risk the breach of compulsory military decorum by failing to wear the cap out of doors, shoved it onto his head, but, as soon as they reached the car, snatched it right off before climbing in.

"You probably remember what happens when you get caught out of doors without headgear," he said.

O'Keefe signaled affirmation to that and said, "What to eat?"

"Don't care."

"There's a place in Laguna, I remember. Long time ago, but good food and great ocean views."

Dan had no interest in small talk. "Why didn't you tell me?"

"Your mother warned me not to. She worried you'd do something... in her words, 'violent and stupid.' I thought I should honor that."

"What a lying bitch."

Brutal as it sounded, O'Keefe let that go. Considering everything, it would be hard not to feel that way, at least for now. They said almost nothing the rest of the way to the restaurant where they took a table on an outdoor patio overlooking Treasure Island Park and its beach. A boardwalk below them and above the beach wended through dark green vine-like vegetation. The beach was almost empty, a couple of women reclining on beach towels, a few boys body-surfing in the foamy waves. The Pacific seemed to go on to infinity beyond the jutting headlands. Dan ordered a steak. He tried to order a beer, but they asked for his ID and he was still underage in California, so he settled for a Coke. Their conversation remained sparse and exceedingly careful as if each of them was circling around a dangerous animal, searching for an opening to capture it.

"I heard about the car bomb," Dan said. Pointing to O'Keefe's left arm and hand, he said, "When does all that come off?" The arm was still sheathed in the tight compression garment meant to keep the new skin tight and in place and reduce the scarring. His hand was still covered by a removable cast, only the tips of his fingers protruding, to prevent the scar bands that constantly pulled at his fingers from curling the hand into a claw as they radiated from his fingers to the middle of his palm, creating small indentations, a kind of stigmata, where the surgeon had tied the bands together.

"Not sure," O'Keefe said.

"Does it hurt still?"

"Sometimes. It has to be changed every morning. Taking it off and on is a bitch...hurts like hell. Not that much the rest of the time. Just itches like hell and the scar bands are constantly pulling...trying to close up my hand."

"That was the same guys that killed her, right?"

"Same."

"At least they got them...*you* got them. Why'd you bother?"

"I thought she deserved it."

Dan said nothing, but his face flashed disgust, and he shook his head, resisting the idea that she deserved anything. "I guess I should say thank you," he said.

After lunch, they walked on the boardwalk, their conversation still pinched, desultory, not wanting to get to the heart of anything.

"Know where you're going after Pendleton?" O'Keefe said.

"No. Lots of rumors. Hope I go way overseas. Japan maybe."

It sounded like Dan had something to hope for. "Take advantage of it. It's a hard way to get there, but most people never have a chance to get to places like that."

They drove to a big box department store and Dan bought various items he needed that the commissary at the camp did not carry. O'Keefe offered to pay but Dan refused. "I can handle it," he said.

As they pulled up to the visitor center, Dan said, "They say that Jerry Jensen guy had money."

"True. I don't know how much, but some."

"I wonder if I oughtta try to get some of it."

"I can check with a lawyer on that, but I don't know that I'd go that way if I were you. Your choice, but I'd leave it all behind."

"Like she should've."

"Yeah, like she should've. She made some mistakes...Can I give you a gift?"

"Like what?"

"It's a gift in the form of a story. You don't have to accept the gift right now. Like a sweater your grandma might give you for Christmas that you think is ugly or doesn't fit, but you put it in a drawer and later you might dig it out, and who knows, it might fit or even look better to you then."

Dan said nothing but did not resist, waiting to hear.

"It's a story about a girl who was only seventeen years old, who was not only raped but got pregnant as a result. She lived in a world where an unwed mother was shamed, isolated, put away. They even wanted her to give up the baby to adoption. She wouldn't do that. Seventeen years old. Her rapist refused to take responsibility and threatened to cause her even more shame than she was already suffering. Desperate. Only seventeen years old. She then did something very wrong. Not to the baby she was carrying, who turned out to be Dan Bronson. But to Tim Bronson. She told him he was the father when he wasn't. Since he loved her, or thought he did...he was only seventeen himself...he married her. But as time went on, he did plenty of wrong things to her."

"Which she deserved."

"I don't think so. I don't think what he did to her had anything to do with what she did to him. They were separate wrongs. Unconnected. She shouldn't be blamed for everything. Actually, it might've been worse if she told him the truth *after* they were married and the son was born. She kept that secret as much for his sake as for hers. For your sake too, especially yours. There's a saying though...'that we're only as sick as the secrets we keep.' It was a mistake. It poisoned her whole life."

"And who knows" Dan said, "what would've happened to... Dad...shit, what do I call him now...if he hadn't got lied to and stuck in a shotgun marriage when he was still a kid?"

"He had sex with her without protection. He took the risk. That he wasn't the actual father was only by chance."

Dan folded his arms in a gesture of rejection and stared straight ahead.

"In any event, they ended up screwing up their lives and dealing a really lousy hand to their son. Eventually, it got so bad that Tim killed himself. So what good had it done Tim that she had kept that secret from him all that time? And she knew that they had given their son a raw deal, and he might be headed for a life that might be as tragic as his parents' lives had been. Once Tim was dead, and she managed to get clean and sober for a while, she decided to try to do something to help her son in life...to leave him a legacy better than what she'd given him so far...and it took some bravery to do that..."

"All I wanted was for her to get clean and sober and let me take care of her."

"I think she thought the only way to *stay* clean and sober was to out that secret and do what she could to make amends...repair what had been done to her and what she'd done to Tim, and you, and herself with that lie and that festering secret..."

"What a fucking disaster."

"You don't have to keep it going. Break the chain."

Dan sat thinking for a few moments. "Would you write all that down and send it to me? It might help me to take it out and read it once in a while."

"I will. Still want me to talk to that lawyer?"

"Ah...Fuck it."

"See you at home? After Japan?"

"Yeah. Maybe I'll come ask you for a job."

"Door'll be open." Lifting up his injured arm, he added, "At least if I'm still around."

Dan Bronson left the car, walked a few yards, realized he had not put on his cap, turned to O'Keefe and said loudly, "Fucking cap," stuffed it on his head and walked on.

A few miles up the highway O'Keefe pulled into a truck stop, bought a cup of coffee, and called his answering machine from a pay phone. There was only one message.

Kelly's voice came on, choked up. "Well, Dad, you blew it. She's getting married. You really blew it."

Sobs, then a click as she hung up.

He had intended to spend the night and some of the next day in Laguna, take a room at a small boutique hotel on the beach that he had stayed in one Saturday night on leave from Pendleton. Now he remembered it had a small bar outside, right on the beach. He could sit there drinking for hours in the soft ocean breeze, listening to the music and looking up at the stars. But he knew it would not end there. It would end somewhere else. In some very bad place. And he was very tired. And he had agreed to write up a story for Private Dan Bronson. There was an early morning flight home he could catch. He checked into a cheap motel near the airport and asked for an early wake-up call. He pulled some hotel stationery out of the desk drawer and took up his pen. *Chop Wood, Carry Water.*

ABOUT THE AUTHOR

DAN FLANIGAN HOLDS A PH.D. in History from Rice University and J.D. from the University of Houston. He taught at the University of Houston and the University of Virginia. His first book was his Ph.D. disseration, *The Criminal Law of Slavery and Freedom, 1800-1868.*

He moved on from academia to serve the civil rights cause as a school desegregation lawyer, followed by a long career as a finance attorney in private law practice.

Recently, he has been able to turn his attention to his lifelong ambition—creative writing. In 2019 he released a literary trifecta: *Mink Eyes*, the first in the Peter O'Keefe series (*The Big Tilt* is the second in the series); his heart-wrenching poetry collection *Tenebrae: A Memoir of Love and Death*, on the last illness and death of his wife; and *Dewdrops*, a collection of shorter fiction.

He has also written stage plays including *Secrets* (based on the life of Eleanor Marx) and *Moondog's Progress* (based on the life of Alan Freed). The stage play version of *Dewdrops* enjoyed a full-cast staged reading at the Theatre of the Open Eye in New York, directed by John Cappellatti who described the play as a "powerful" work about "addiction in America—addiction to drugs, alcohol, sex, danger, power, and to finding the Answer," with characters that are "well drawn, real, and actors love to portray them."

He has written a feature film screenplay of *Mink Eyes* and a pilot for a TV series called *O'Keefe.*

Over the years Dan has committed his time and energy to projects and organizations he is passionate about. He and his wife Candy established *Sierra Tucson*, a leading international addiction treatment center in Tucson, Arizona. Dan also serves on the Board of Directors of *Childhood USA*, a national nonprofit organization working to end child sexual abuse and exploitation.

He divides his time among Kansas City, New York City, and Los Angeles.

For more information about
Dan or to purchase one of his books,
please visit www.DanFlaniganBooks.com.